Georgetown Glen
Queermunity Living at Its Finest

Annette Mori

Georgetown Glen
Queermunity Living at Its Finest

ANNETTE MORI

Affinity
Rainbow Publications

2022

Georgetown Glen
© 2022 by Annette Mori

Affinity E-Book Press NZ LTD
Canterbury, New Zealand

1st Edition

ISBN: 978-1-99-004976-7 (paperback)
ISBN: 978-1-99-004973-6 (EPUB)
ISBN: 978-1-99-004974-3 (PDF)
ISBN: 978-1-99-004975-0 (KINDLE)

This is a work of fiction. Names, character, places, and incidents are the product of the author's imagination or are used fictitiously and any resemblance to actual persons living or dead, businesses, companies, events, or locales is entirely coincidental

Editor: Angela Koenig
Proof Editor: Alexis Smith
Cover Design: Irish Dragon Designs
Production Design: Affinity Publication Services

ACKNOWLEDGMENTS

A huge thank you to all of my beta readers who made brilliant suggestions to improve the initial draft: Emily Cubbage, Ali Spooner, Ameliah Faith, Carrie Camp, Dana Holmes, Dr. Valerie Moore, and Danna Micoletti. As always, I have to acknowledge Erin O'Reilly, who is a constant support and encouragement. I am honored to call her a friend and have her support me on my journey. I would also like to express my gratitude to Affinity Rainbow Publications and the wonderful trio—JM Dragon, Erin O'Reilly, and Nancy Kaufman—who continue to provide feedback to tighten up manuscripts that need help and publish my unconventional work. I am eternally grateful for the opportunities they give me to let my stories see the light of day. Thanks to Angie for her magic as the final editor to further tighten the story. She is a delight to work with. Inevitably, those pesky errors slip through, and I am thankful that Alexis Smith, the final proof editor, caught those before the book went to print. Thanks to Nancy Kaufman for the final cover. A huge thanking to all the other readers and fellow writers who have sent personal emails, written reviews, and posted nice things on Facebook (you know who you are). The Affinity authors are an incredibly supportive group and often share posts or send words of encouragement. Finally, my wife, Jody, continues her support even when it interferes with our time.

DEDICATION

To my older sister, who partially inspired this book after I spent time with her at the community she settled into with her husband after retirement. I want to settle somewhere like that, but with my sapphic sisters!

TABLE OF CONTENTS

PROLOGUE

Georgia crouched and hid behind the stairs as she listened to her parents talk about Horace Allen's desire to take Georgia for his wife. With his wife passing away so suddenly, Horace needed someone to care for his brood. Georgia knew if her father agreed, her life would be nothing but misery. Surely the rumors about Horace's viciousness would keep her from a fate Georgia felt would be worse than death. Horace had already worked two previous wives to death. Georgia did not wish to be the third.

"Georgia will not get many offers. She is my daughter, but her face is not fair and delicate like Mary's. Horace recognizes her value and believes she will make a good wife. Be reasonable, Clara. We cannot allow her to remain here. There is barely enough for us without another mouth to feed. At least Mary is already attracting suitors, unlike Georgia."

Every word out of her father's booming voice was like a knife to her heart.

"Samuel, please, Horace is cruel. He is no better than a slave owner in the manner in which he has treated his wives. Can we not wait another year? Then, perhaps she will attract the attention of another widower who will treat her more kindly," Clara answered. "Georgia is strong. She can help you in the fields."

"No, Clara, if I put Georgia to work in the fields, she will insist on wearing my breeches. I've already caught her prancing around like a dandy man. She isn't right. Best to marry her off and stop the rumors," Samuel insisted.

While Samuel was not an unkind man, he was pragmatic. Girls weren't useful on the farm. As soon as one of his daughters turned sixteen, her father actively sought a suitable husband. Despite her mother's objections, Georgia knew her father had already decided. If only she had been born a boy. Georgia quickly developed a plan. She would not burden her family, but marrying Horace was out of the question. Wagon trains were still leaving for the west, and Georgia would be on the next one. Young single men could easily find work. She slipped from her hiding place to find a razor or scissors. A bubble of excitement burst forth as she envisioned shearing off her long hair and donning a pair of her father's britches. Someday, she would buy herself a fine suit, but for now, her father's clothes would have to suffice. There were worse things than never marrying.

CHAPTER ONE

    Lucy Manetti bounded into her two-bedroom condo, bouncing like Tigger the tiger from Winnie the Pooh. Pushing back the bangs on her shoulder-length, mostly dark-brown hair, compliments of good genetics from her mother, the mirth in her warm brown eyes sparkled as she shared her good news. At least, it was good news for Lucy. Bea, her wife, would undoubtedly overreact at first, but then Lucy was sure she would be as enamored with the idea as Lucy was. Sometimes Bea needed to get used to change or new ideas.

    "You what?"

    "I bought a ghost town," Lucy exclaimed and grabbed her partner of thirty-five years, twirling her around.

    Bea scowled, disengaging herself, taking a disapproving posture. Then, with her hands on her hips, she asked, "Where did you get the money?"

Lucy grinned. "I used my forced retirement settlement. What a deal, right? I've always wanted to be the mayor, and now I am. Ooh, you can be the sheriff and keep out all the riffraff."

"Are you out of your fucking mind? What the hell are we going to do with a ghost town?" Bea shook her snow-white bob and narrowed her blue-green eyes that had first enamored Lucy over thirty-five years ago when they'd met at a potluck.

"I always wanted to live out my golden years in a lesbian commune. Now we can. All we need is to attract a few more lesbians to join us. The place isn't much right now, but there's this lovely young couple who own an alpaca farm in the adjacent unincorporated areas. Cute as two little bugs, those two. Great legs and ass, too."

Bea sat heavily on the couch. "Let me think for a minute. People have buyer's remorse all the time. I'm sure there is some period when we can back out of the deal. We might lose a few thousand, but at least we won't have thrown away the entire settlement. Who is the real estate agent you used?"

"Well, it was that cute alpaca farmer. She got her real estate license a few years ago. Apparently, it's difficult making ends meet as an alpaca farmer. She needed another occupation. Real estate sounded easy enough."

Bea's eyes narrowed into tiny slits again. "How could you let a pair of great legs con you? Wait until I get my hands on that swindling hussy."

"It wasn't like that. You have to see this town. Come on, with your carpentry skills, we can bring it back to its glory. A little loving care and the bedrooms above the saloon will be perfect for us." Lucy waggled her eyebrows. "I'll bet those bedrooms used to have ladies of the night in them. Isn't that a hoot? Not only do we own a saloon, but we also own the bordello attached to it. At least I think that's what those bedrooms above the saloon were for."

"We are not moving to some ghost town and into a place with rotting wood, no electricity, or plumbing."

Lucy waved her hand in the air. "Easy fixes. We can hire a few baby dykes to install electrical and plumbing in all the structures."

"How many buildings?"

Lucy shrugged. "Oh, I don't know. A dozen, maybe. Besides the saloon, there's the mercantile, several old houses, the hotel, and the church. But, of course, we don't need the church. We can turn that into a bingo hall or dance venue. Ooh, how about a theater for both movies and live performances? That would be awesome. I've always wanted to own a theater."

"I cannot talk to you when you're in this space. Your impulsivity is going to be the death of me." Bea leaned forward, putting her head in her hands while ruffling her hair in that adorably messy way that had Lucy panting with want over the years.

Joining Bea on the couch, Lucy rubbed her back. "It's all going to be okay, Bea, I promise. We need a little excitement in our golden years. Admit it, my adventurous nature is what you fell in love with all those years ago. I don't want to settle into some boring, sedentary retirement, gaining ten pounds a year until we're too wide to get through the door."

Bea turned her head and, with a tiny smile, said, "You'll never be too wide to get through the door. You better take me to this town that we now own so I can assess the damage. And, I'm still going to want to have a conversation with the real estate agent."

Lucy clapped her hands together. "That's the spirit. Wait until you meet Fi. She's absolutely adorable."

"Fi?"

"The all-around fix-it gal that Amelia and Darcy recommended. She has a fancy degree in restorations, so she'll be perfect for the job." Lucy held up her hand. "Before you get all judgy and jealous, she's practically young enough to be my granddaughter. Her full name is Fiona O'Reilly. We talked about all kinds of things, but mainly about how she wishes she could find someone to share her life with. I guess it's kind of lonely living in a town in the middle of nowhere. So we should help her find someone."

"Oh, no, no, no, no. You will not play matchmaker again. Your niece does not need any help to find available partners. She told you that the last time you tried to set her up with the firefighter that came to our place when the propane grill had a leak and flames nearly burned our house down. So promise me you'll stay out of her business. And who the hell are Amelia and Darcy?"

"The alpaca farmers. Fi is Amelia's best friend, and Amelia didn't think it was a horrible idea to introduce Fi to Chelsey."

"If Amelia is the real estate agent, I already question her ethics, selling a ghost town to an old lady."

"But..." Lucy began to protest.

"Chelsey will never forgive me if I don't stop you right now. Besides, you'll be too busy helping me whip into shape the dozen dilapidated buildings we now own."

"Fi can help us. So can Chelsey. I'm sure she'll want to lend a hand to her aunt." Lucy grinned at Bea, causing Bea to shake her head.

†

Climate change was alive and well in Washington state, and although the ghost town was closer to the wetter west side of the state, the dry heat had sucked all the moisture from the air. Washington, not unlike California, was experiencing a severe drought in the middle of the summer, with the heat climbing into the triple digits and staying there for weeks.

On cue, the dirt and dust swirled around, whipping small particles against Bea's face. All the scene needed was a tumbleweed, and her vision of the old Wild West would be complete. She scowled at Lucy, pointing her finger in the air as if to say, "See, I told you this was a bad idea."

Bea coughed and spit out what she presumed was a mouthful of dirt as she'd tried to suck in air with the stifling heat all around her. Lucy appeared unaffected by what was clearly irritating an already exasperated Bea.

"Where were we supposed to meet Amelia?" Bea asked.

Lucy grinned. "In the old saloon. It's one of the few buildings stable enough to trust at this point." She gestured to the large wooden structure, complete with swinging doors.

Bea shuddered, thinking about all the nasty critters that undoubtedly lived inside the saloon without proper doors to keep them out. That would have to be one of the first things to attend to.

7

Bea groaned. "How do we know the building won't fall down on our heads?"

"Amelia had it inspected before the town officially went on the market. She needed to show at least one structure to prospective buyers, and since the saloon had such charm, that was the one she ensured was stable enough to feature in her open house. Besides, it's one of the largest buildings in the town. We both suspect the hotel is stable enough to endure a walkthrough, but she didn't want to spend any more money than necessary to have that one inspected." Lucy nearly vibrated with excitement. The exact opposite reaction to Bea.

Lucy performed an exaggerated swagger as she approached the saloon and pushed the swinging doors open with an enormous smile on her face. Upon closer inspection, Bea was delighted to see that the second set of solid-wood doors lay flat against the outermost wall of the saloon.

A striking auburn-haired woman with deep-set, dark blue eyes sat on a stool in front of an ornamental, solid mahogany bar. When she smiled at Lucy, her face lit up in delight. Bea wondered if Lucy had also charmed this young woman as much as Lucy had captivated her when they'd met over thirty-five years ago. Lucy was still beautiful, and thanks to good genetics, looked at least fifteen years younger than her age. Dressed casually in cargo shorts and a tight-fitting tank top that accentuated her breasts and flat stomach, Lucy was a stunner, all right.

Putting out her hand to Bea, the young woman introduced herself. "Hi, you must be Bea. I'm Amelia. I can't think of a better couple to own this town and turn it into a retirement community for queer women. Maybe in another thirty years, there will be a place for my wife and me."

Reluctantly, Bea took her hand and shook it. The woman seemed genuine enough, but Bea was still adjusting to owning this albatross. "Doubtful either Lucy or I will be alive in thirty years, even if we can clean this place up. I'd check out Florida or Arizona if I were you. I hear those are the places to retire to." Getting right to the point, Bea asked, "There's an out clause to this purchase, right? Don't we have three days or something to change our minds?"

Amelia frowned but answered Bea's question. "That's correct. It was a typical contract. You'd be out the earnest money…" Her voice trailed off in quiet resignation.

"How much is that?" Bea asked.

"Thirty thousand."

Bea turned to Lucy. "Are you out of your fucking mind? Why in the world would you put that much earnest money down?"

Lucy shrugged. "I wanted to make sure they knew we were serious about the purchase."

"There is no we in this. You did this all on your own."

Amelia coughed. "Um, maybe I should let you talk on your own before I show Bea the rest of the town. If it's any consolation, my wife and I would have bought this town if we had the money. It really is a great deal. You'll see that when you look at the rest of the buildings." Amelia ran her hand over the beautiful bar. "Just look at this bar. With a bit of elbow grease, this place will be spectacular. They don't make anything like this anymore." Amelia slipped out of the saloon to let the two women talk.

Lucy pouted. "You promised you would keep an open mind. You haven't even seen the rest of the town."

Bea softened her stance and held her hands in supplication. "Okay, okay." Looking around the saloon, she had to admit the inside was nicer than she expected if a person imagined the bar without all the dirt and grime. Polishing the bar and the brass lighting fixtures would undoubtedly bring the old saloon to life. The floor didn't seem salvageable, but replacing a floor wouldn't be too difficult. Plumbing and electrical would be the highest costs.

Bea began calculating everything silently and wondered if they had enough in their retirement accounts to bring this town to life. The banister on the staircase that led upstairs was just as decorative as the bar. Bea had to admit that she'd always wanted a house with a curving staircase. She wondered if the steps that led to the upper level were solid enough to check out what Lucy envisioned as their living quarters. She let the wheels turn in her head and wondered how much they could get for their condo on the lake. Fortunately, it was a booming housing market, but could they sell before the contractors completed a remodel of the old saloon? Would the bare minimum be possible to make the upstairs livable while they worked on the rest of the structures?

When Lucy wrapped her arms around Bea's middle and then laid her head against Bea's chest, that was the final undoing. Bea always put up a fuss when confronting one of Lucy's harebrained ideas out of the gate, but then she capitulated and gave into Lucy's whims. Because, when all things were said and done, Lucy was the love of Bea's life, and she'd do anything to see that glorious smile of hers.

Bea wrapped her arms around Lucy, squeezing her in a hug before pulling away and stroking her cheek. "Go on, get that cute little lesbian to show me the rest of the buildings and the upstairs if it's safe."

Lucy's dimple was on full display when she responded. "It's safe. We went up there the other day when I was checking out the town before making an offer. You just want to follow her up the stairs so you can check out her ass." Lucy winked. "Totally worth the view."

Bea laughed. "What a little letch you've turned into in your old age." Walking closer to the winding staircase, she noticed the wood on the steps was not nearly as weathered as the floor, and she made a mental note to ask Amelia about that.

"Hey, who you calling old? I seem to remember showing my considerable flexibility in bed two nights ago. I've still got it. Don't put me out to pasture just yet."

Bea smiled. "Never."

†

Amelia paced outside the saloon, waiting for the older couple to decide. Her nervous energy was almost palpable. She wondered if the famed ghost could feel the energy waves emanating from her, although she wasn't sure that she actually believed the rumors. Lucy was such a sweet woman. It wasn't precisely that Amelia had lied to her. She just hadn't provided all the information. Amelia needed this commission. Their entire farm was at risk if she couldn't pay the property taxes that were due in less than a month. Darcy, her wife, would break down and cry if they lost the farm, and Amelia could never watch while her wife let her emotions overcome her. The farm had been in Darcy's family for nearly a century. Amelia had promised Darcy she'd earn enough to make it through another year with her new job as a real estate agent. But Amelia's sense of right and wrong was eating its way into her soul. She decided to come clean, and if she lost the sale, so be it. They would find another way to save the farm. As she lifted her head, she saw the couple exiting the saloon. Lucy had a broad smile on her face. That was a good sign, but Amelia would probably wipe that smile from her face as soon as she confessed.

"I'm ready to see the rest of the buildings that are safe enough to inspect, but first, I'd like to see the upstairs portion of the saloon. I want to get a sense of how much work it will take to make that space livable before we sell our condo," Bea declared.

Lucy jumped up and down, clapping her hands. "Oh, Bea, I knew you'd come around. Really, we can sell the condo so we have enough money to bring this town back to its glory days?"

Bea nodded once, adopting a serious expression. "I'd rather not tap into our retirement accounts in case we need those to live on. I know you have visions that this retirement community we're about to establish will bring in income, but that's not a guarantee. By the way, the wood on the staircase looks a lot newer than the rest of the structure. I was happy to see that because I wasn't looking forward to tumbling ass over teakettle when we climbed those stairs."

Amelia sucked in a mouthful of air. It was now or never. Bea had just provided the perfect opportunity for her to come clean. Nervously, she explained, "Um, I know I should have mentioned this before Lucy made an offer on the town…"

Bea scowled at Amelia. "I knew it, you little con artist with your tight ass and long legs—"

Lucy grabbed Bea's arm. "Now, Bea, remember what the doctor said. Let her finish before you give yourself a heart attack going into a tizzy."

Bea huffed once but acquiesced by gesturing for Amelia to continue.

"A real estate developer owned this property and had started with a remodel to the saloon. He thought this might make a unique tourist destination. Unfortunately, he didn't get very far before George ran the workers off."

"Who the hell is George?" Bea asked.

"Legend has it that George used to be the sheriff of this town until a gambler who was passing through discovered George was actually Georgia. He'd been living as a man. When the townsfolk turned against George and hanged him and his ladylove, the saloon owner, for treacherous behavior against God's nature, he swore to seek revenge. If the story is true, he had to watch the love of his life die first."

"Oh, that is so sad. I'd want to kick ass too if some bible-thumping asshole hanged my wife," Lucy said.

Bea shook her head. "Yeah, right. All 110 pounds of you."

"I'm a lot tougher than I look. Besides, being a ghost gives you more tools in your toolbox to deal with narrow-minded asswipes."

"You actually believe this nonsense? At least the little con artist didn't leave something major out of her sales pitch, like they've condemned this whole place, and we aren't allowed to rebuild." Bea crossed her arms and continued to shake her head.

"Stop being an old stick in the mud. I want to hear the rest of the story. It'll make a great narrative for when we market the place." Lucy looked expectantly at Amelia.

Amelia smiled. Maybe she wouldn't lose this commission after all. "Well, a slew of accidents occurred after the hanging, causing the remaining residents to abandon the town, seeking a place that wasn't haunted by vengeful ghosts. So, I guess the story gives new meaning to the term ghost town. Honestly, I don't believe in ghosts, but even if I did, somehow I think George and his lover would appreciate that the new owners are lesbians, about to create a retirement community for mature queer women."

"I agree. Your revelation about this town has not dissuaded me one bit. In fact, this makes me want to follow through with the sale even more." Lucy fluttered her eyes at Bea. "Oh, Bea, can't you just see it? This is so perfect. I don't care how much it costs. We're going to bring this place back to its glory and make George and his ladylove proud. What was the saloon owner's name?"

Amelia frowned. In all her research, she hadn't learned that piece of information. "You know, I don't really know. I wonder if there are historical archives that give more of the story? I could check if it's important to you."

Lucy waved her hand in the air. "Nah, it'll be fun doing the research on our own. Besides, we're retired with nothing else better to do than research the history of this town and gawk at the young, fit lesbians we plan to hire to help us remodel this place. Any other friends we should consider hiring? Bonus points if they are young, hot, and lesbian."

Amelia chuckled. She liked Lucy. Bea was a lot harder to warm to, but if Lucy married her, Amelia decided

Bea must have redeeming qualities. She racked her brain for another suggestion to give to Lucy for a female contractor. Unfortunately, there were slim pickings in the area.

"We'll need a licensed electrician," Bea noted as Lucy beamed in her direction. "If we're going to make a go of this retirement community, I don't want anything impeding the required inspections."

Amelia was desperate and hoped that suggesting Saville wouldn't result in too much angst for her best friend. Indeed, by now, the two of them had worked through their issues. So maybe Fi would not think she'd thrown her under the bus to seal the deal.

"Saville moved back to town a few years ago, and I think she's between jobs right now," Amelia proposed. "She's an electrician, which should work well since Fi doesn't have a license to do electrical work. Fi is an all-around fix-it person and could have done almost anything needed, but not being licensed has been a barrier to Fi getting more work. Besides, Fi specializes in restorations of old Victorian buildings, and there isn't a lot of work in that specialty."

Yes, it looked as though this sale wasn't going south anymore. Amelia had to refrain from a visible sigh of relief.

She wrinkled her nose. "Um, there's a little history with Saville and Fi…"

"Ooh, that sounds like a juicy story." Lucy's eager expression encouraged Amelia to provide an explanation without violating Fi's privacy.

"Don't worry. Saville and Fi are both ultimate professionals. I'm sure it will all work out. It will be nice for them to work together on future projects, maybe establish a lucrative partnership. I could send them business from my real estate sales. Yours will be their first project together. Saville is Darcy's best friend, and the four of us used to get together when Saville first moved back home. Too bad Saville is quite the ladies' magnet, or the partnership with Fi could go further than just a business arrangement. We had hoped that would happen, but unfortunately, it went a little sideways. I don't believe anyone has tamed Saville yet. We keep hoping she'll settle down, but I suppose she enjoys being single. And, she doesn't mind one bit when other women, of any age, ogle her."

"Perfect. We'll call Saville and Fi soon to start work on Georgetown."

"Georgetown?" Bea raised one eyebrow.

"Yup. I think it's appropriate to have a West Coast Georgetown in honor of the prior sheriff. Maybe naming the town after him will help us get on the right foot with our ghost." Lucy linked her arm in Bea's. "Ready to see the rest of the buildings?"

Bea nodded. "Sure, why not. Maybe George will make an appearance, and you can introduce yourself," she added with a touch of sarcasm.

"Don't be such a fuddy-duddy. Stop making fun of me. When George appears, I'm going to tell him all about your skeptical nature. Perhaps a harmless prank or two will make a believer out of you."

"Whatever," Bea answered.

†

Lucy wasn't paying attention as a plethora of ideas began floating around about how to take advantage of the news that the town had an actual ghost. In her mind, she was already calling this place Georgetown, and it felt right. She was eager to drive to the nearest library and discover any archives about Georgetown. They'd been to nearly every building in the town, and Bea had asked so many questions, Lucy feared the library trip might have to happen on another day. Amelia had patiently answered all of Bea's questions. Bea was nothing if not thorough, but Lucy had already shown signs of boredom with the minutia.

Startled by Bea touching her shoulder, Lucy said, "Sorry, what did you just say?" She hadn't been paying attention, losing interest at least an hour ago.

"I asked if you were ready to go home and talk about all of this? I think I've seen enough and gotten all the relevant information I need for us to decide."

Lucy noticed how Amelia's face fell at Bea's declaration. Lucy was as Zen as a person could get most of the time, but occasionally she dug in, and no amount of argument would change her mind. Should she have consulted with Bea before making an offer? Sure. They were married, after all. Her money was Bea's, but Lucy had fallen in love with the place and had to have it.

Lucy took a step back and glared at Bea. Her stubborn side emerged. "I have already decided. We're not backing out of this." She noticed the tiny smile flare on Amelia's face.

"We haven't even talked to a real estate agent about putting our condo up for sale. I'd like a ballpark figure on that. And then we can contact Fi and Saville to get an idea about how much it would cost, even if we plan to do some of the work ourselves. Don't you think we ought to slow this train down a bit and thoroughly consider all options?"

Lucy crossed her arms in front. "No. I. Do. Not. You should never have mentioned selling the condo and getting my hopes up if you weren't going to follow through."

"I'd be happy to help you sell your condo. Give me the address, and I'll work up comps this afternoon," Amelia offered. "If it's any consolation, I feel confident that Saville and Fi will be very reasonable with their estimate, with you being 'family' and all. It's the queer women discount. Of course, most contractors won't let anyone work alongside them, but I know both Fi and Saville won't have any problem with you helping."

"I'm so excited to learn some new skills. I always wanted to get more knowledge about electrical systems and plumbing."

Bea sighed. "Fine, but I'm not climbing any ladders, no matter what."

With that declaration, she knew it was a done deal. Lucy grinned at her wife. "I'll climb all the ladders. You can do all the detail work that you're so good at." Offering that small amount of flattery would hopefully get Bea excited about their new adventure. Lucy was over the moon at the possibilities. She wanted the love of her life to share in the joy.

CHAPTER TWO

Fiona O'Reilly was about ready to grab a cold microbrew from the refrigerator in her 1920s historical home when her cell phone buzzed in the back pocket of her loose-fitting overalls. She'd lovingly brought the old house back to glory with her own two hands. She was hot, sweaty, and ready for a nice cool shower after the demolition job she'd agreed to because the money was good. Fi didn't have the luxury of turning any job down, no matter how soul-sucking it was. She preferred to restore old buildings, not tear them down, but work was work. Small-town living was killing her in more ways than one, but she'd agreed to give the move at least one more year.

Fleeing to the rural Pacific Northwest after her epic break-up had been the only option for her sanity. Amelia was her best friend, and Fi needed her shoulder to cry on. Bonus that Amelia had found the 1920s home less than two miles

from her farm. Fi was happy to be the first client after
Amelia had gotten her real estate license. It wasn't much of a
commission for Amelia because the place was in poor shape
and needed a lot of work, but at least she'd given her friend
the sale. Fi knew how critical the supplemental income was
to maintaining the alpaca farm. Lately, the number of
properties had diminished, and Fi worried that Amelia and
Darcy wouldn't make it. If they left, she'd have nothing to tie
her to this wasteland.

After less than a month, Fi realized what a backwater
town she'd moved to. Most everyone in town had very
specific views of who was qualified to fix or build their
homes. And that qualification included an ugly dangly organ
between the legs. Women did not gravitate to the
construction trade in these parts. The only other person was
that full-of-herself electrician, Saville. The few jobs Fi had
secured were thanks to Amelia. Don't even get her started on
the lack of available women. If things did not change soon,
she'd have no choice but to search for greener pastures.

"Fi's Fix-It Shop," she answered.

"Hello, cutie."

Fi scrunched her face as she pulled the phone from
her ear and looked at the screen, hoping to discover who was
calling her a cutie. She didn't recognize the voice. Not being
a one-night stand kind of gal, she knew this wasn't someone
she'd made mad passionate love to and then promptly forgot
about the next day. No, that was Saville's modus operandi,
not hers.

"Um, I'm sorry. I don't know who this is."

"We bought the town, and now we need your help.
Can you meet us at the saloon tomorrow at ten? I'll call
Saville and see if she can make it at that time. We'll let you

know if we need to change the time, but hopefully, Saville is free tomorrow. Bea thought it would be best to get quotes from both of you at the same time. You can do the plumbing and everything else, right? Bea insisted on a licensed electrician. I didn't think it was that big of a deal, but I had to throw her a bone, or she might have continued her hissy fit about the purchase. And, I could not let her ruin this dream that I have for a lesbian retirement community."

"Lucy?" Fi remembered the spunky older woman that Amelia had introduced her to. Lucy was a hard woman to forget.

"Yes, hon."

Fi laughed. "It's been a long time since someone called me a cutie, or any other pet name. Are you sure you're happily married?" she joked.

"Now you know I am way too old for you. But I have a niece I could introduce you to. Or maybe the love bug will bite while you're working with Saville. I haven't met her yet, but Amelia assures me she's a hottie and single, too."

"I know Saville, and she is definitely not a love match." Changing the subject, Fi continued, "Sure, I can make it tomorrow. I'm excited for you and your wife. I have so many ideas to modernize the buildings without losing the whole feel of the place. Are you sure you want to hire Saville?"

"Why? Is Saville not a good electrician?"

"No, no, nothing like that. She's just…"

"You two have history," Lucy stated.

"Sort of." Fi thought back to her moment of weakness. Feeling bad about herself, she had consumed one too many microbrews, and Saville had been there for her. One thing led to another, and that's when things got complicated. They both had agreed it was a mistake, never to be repeated. Saville had shown a different version of herself that night, one that Fi desperately wanted to see again, but then Saville promptly returned to the arrogant woman she'd first met at Amelia and Darcy's house. She imagined the happy couple thought she and Saville would fall madly in love at first sight. Total bullshit. Sure, there was a kind of chemistry she felt when she first met Saville, but that faded fast once Fi learned what Saville was really about.

"You still there?" Lucy asked.

"Oh, yeah, yeah. I was just thinking. I wish it didn't take so long to get an electrician's license. You wouldn't want to wait four years, would you?" Fi laughed to show she wasn't serious.

"Listen, Fi, I have many years on the planet, and trust me when I say that the playgirl lifestyle gets old. Eventually, Saville will be where you're at. Have a little patience."

"Oh, I don't want to have anything to do with that arrogant little—"

"There is a minuscule line between love and hate. Just saying…" Lucy chuckled. "Isn't that what you young folks say?"

"You just interrupted a perfect swear word."

"Oh, really? I'm always looking for something to replace *fuck*. It's gotten so bourgeois."

Lucy's delivery sounded so deadpan it pulled Fi from her dark mood, and she held her stomach as she laughed with abandon. "Twatwaffle," she offered.

"Good one. So we'll see you tomorrow at ten?"

"Absolutely. I'm so excited to share my ideas for restoring the town to its former glory with a few modern upgrades for good measure. I'm not letting that twatwaffle ruin my fun. I promise to give you and Bea the absolute best price imaginable."

"Well, I don't expect you to give your talents away. So don't quote us a price too low for you to make sufficient money on the job. I'm sure having two old women who insist on helping will be enough of a hassle that you need to charge prime dollars for the aggravation. I am so looking forward to learning all about construction. I totally rock a tool belt, and it gets Bea's motor going like nothing you can conceive of."

Fi sighed. "I hope someday to find a woman who appreciates my tool belt as much as Bea seems to admire yours. See you tomorrow, Lucy. Stay out of trouble now."

"Oh, you're no fun. Will it be sexist if I drool over you and Saville while you work? I always say there is nothing wrong with looking, as long as I don't touch. An old woman has to have her extracurricular activities. Bird-watching didn't do it for me, but babe watching does." Lucy cackled at her own joke.

Fi chuckled. "Have at it. It'll boost my confidence that I might still have it, at least enough to attract a new girlfriend if there's any to be found in this tiny corner of the world. And you are not an old woman. If you weren't married, I'd definitely ask you out. Bye, Lucy."

"Oh, swoon. Bye, cutie."

†

Saville rolled over and meant to poke the snooze button on her phone alarm, irritated that somehow she'd set the thing in her drunken state last night and hadn't remembered.

"Shit." Saville's bloodshot eyes landed on her phone as she realized someone was calling at an ungodly hour. Well, ungodly for someone who'd been out late last night and had accepted a ride home from an attractive stranger who she hoped wasn't still in her bed.

With the phone in her hand, she croaked, "Hello." Then she rolled back over and found a very naked woman in her bed. "Double shit."

"Saville? Did I call at a bad time?"

"Who is this?"

"Lucy Manetti. I got your name from Amelia."

"My name for what? I don't do blind dates."

Lucy chuckled. "Neither do I because I'm married. But, no, we want you to meet us at the saloon in the ghost town we purchased. We plan on restoring the entire place to its former glory, and we need a licensed electrician to update the electrical systems in all the buildings. Fi will help us with everything else, but she doesn't have her electrician's license. My wife insists on hiring someone with a license. Plus, we prefer to work with queer women."

Saville sat up, suddenly awake, and glanced at the woman whose auburn hair fanned across the pillow. She'd begun to stir, and all Saville wanted was for this woman to get dressed and leave her alone. Instead, the woman's bleary eyes opened. Saville struggled to remember her name. Bethie, Barbie, Brenda? She was sure it was a B name. She'd try a simple nickname. Moving the phone away from her mouth and attempting to cover the phone speaker, she said, "Mornin', B." Pointing to her phone, she added, "Sorry, work. Um, you're welcome to take a shower before you leave. I don't have any food to offer."

Saville mentally slapped her head for bringing the woman back to her place, but she had been too drunk to drive herself home. Damn, she'd left her Harley at the bar. She would have to con Amelia or Darcy into coming to get her so she could drive herself to the meeting. Unless this woman in her bed would take her to the bar. Her heartbeat increased with the prospect of seeing Fiona again. The last time she'd seen Fi had not gone well. No, not well at all.

"Saville, are you still there? We haven't interrupted you, have we? Oh, to be young again."

"No, uh, you haven't interrupted anything." She winced, not venturing a look at the woman who'd thrown the covers aside and huffed. It wouldn't be the first time she'd pissed off a woman by encouraging them to leave first thing in the morning. She thought for sure she'd laid out her rules, but the last drink may have impacted her ability to make her intentions clear. "What time do you want me there? Is Fi meeting us there?"

Saville's heart started beating double-time again at the thought of seeing Fiona O'Reilly. The fiery redhead with the blazing green eyes had captured her attention from the very first moment she'd met her. They were becoming friends until she'd fucked everything up. A single, attractive woman was far too tempting, and she'd taken advantage when Fi was in a vulnerable place one night. But, in her defense, that had not been her intention. She had wanted to only comfort her. Then one thing led to another, and they'd traveled the road to sexapolis.

Ever since that fateful night when everything went to shit, Amelia and Darcy had gone to great lengths to keep the two of them apart. Saville wondered why Amelia had recommended her for this job. Maybe Fi had mellowed, realizing that Saville was no good at relationships. It wasn't personal. Or maybe it was too personal, and Fi deserved better than Saville. She needed to stop drinking so much. That always got her in trouble.

"Yes, I called her last night. I tried you, but it went to voice mail, so I thought you might be out, and I didn't want to disturb your evening. She's meeting us at ten. How does that sound? Will that give you enough time?"

Saville scratched her head, quickly doing the math. "Um, yeah, as long as I can get a ride to the bar where I left my motorcycle." Saville glanced at the woman emerging from her bed. The woman simply shook her head and glared at Saville, promptly stalking into the bathroom and slamming the door. She'd have to call Amelia and Darcy after all.

"Ooh, dykes on bikes, my favorite kind of lesbian. Sexy."

Saville chuckled. "I thought you were married."

"Oh, I am. Been with Bea for thirty-five glorious years, but I'm not dead yet. I can appreciate a fine-looking woman. See you soon. I'm looking forward to meeting you."

"Uh, yeah, okay." Saville set her phone on the side dresser, pushed the covers away, and placed her feet on the ground. She stood and stretched her long, lean body, listening while the shower turned on. Joining her in the shower was out of the question based on the reaction from the woman earlier. Saville guessed that calling her B was not the right thing to do. She should have just said a generic good morning and eased her into leaving quietly after making her a to-go cup of coffee. Sniffing her armpits, Saville scrunched her nose. Maybe Amelia and Darcy would let her take a quick shower at their place. It was worth a shot.

Grabbing a fresh pair of shorts and a T-shirt, she quickly dressed and then retrieved her phone. Navigating to her contacts, she called Darcy's phone. "Hey bestie, what are you doing this morning?"

An audible sigh traveled through the tiny speaker. "You need a ride to your Harley, right?"

"How did you know?"

"Educated guess. I don't suppose you can con the woman you slept with into taking you back to the bar. I presume she took you home last night."

"Um, no. I get the sense I offended her this morning."

"Ya think. How is it you manage to find the only lesbians within a hundred-mile radius nearly every time you go to the bar?"

"Wit and charm. It isn't hard. I think I'm safe with this one, though. She was just passing through on business. Hey, congrats to Amelia for unloading that white elephant. Please tell her thanks for the recommendation. If my memory serves correctly, there are at least a dozen buildings. This will be an enormous job for me. The woman who called sounds like quite the character. Lacy, Lorrie, Libby?"

"Lucy. God, you are so bad. My guess is that you pissed off the woman you slept with last night by forgetting her name."

"I'm pretty sure it starts with a B, so I said, 'Mornin' B.' Smart of me, huh?"

"No, you dumb shit. Any woman with half a brain would have seen through that ruse."

"Whatever. Can you come and get me? And, can I take a shower at your place before you take me to my baby?"

"What's wrong with your shower?"

"B's in it, and I would kind of like to sneak out while she's still getting ready, so can you please hurry?"

"Fine. I'll be there in thirty."

"Make it three, or things could get very awkward fast," Saville joked. "Thanks, Darc, you're the best."

†

Fiona had toured the ghost town with Amelia, but that was in the spring when the dirt road didn't contain as much dust. Climbing from her work truck, she coughed as the unwelcome particles made their way into her lungs. One other car had parked in front of the saloon, but Saville's Harley was nowhere in the bar's vicinity. Ironic, since Saville seemed to spend all her free time at bars. *Figures she'd be late for this meeting.*

Someone had already pinned back the outer doors to the saloon, so Fi pushed her way into the place using the swinging doors, which appeared to be in perfect working order. At least she wouldn't have to replace them. It would be a shame to not have the original doors. She would need to give them a little loving attention, but nothing a bit of sandpaper and high-quality varnish wouldn't fix.

"Hey, cutie," Lucy greeted.

She waved her hand in the air. "Hey, Lucy." Glancing at the woman with the short silver bob, Fi held out her hand. "You must be Bea. I'm Fi. It's nice to meet you."

Bea shook her hand and nodded, her expression all business.

Lucy held up a box of donuts and handed Fi a paper cup with coffee. "I got coffee and donuts for everyone." She pointed to the packets of sugar and creamer. "In case you don't drink your coffee black."

The roar of the Harley momentarily distracted Fi as she automatically turned her head toward the swinging doors before refocusing on her new clients. She couldn't afford to screw this up. The job would provide months of work for her, and this was a project she had a passion for.

Fi accepted the coffee and reached into the box, grabbing a cinnamon twist—her favorite when she was younger. "Thanks. Gosh, I haven't had a donut in eons. I suppose a splurge now and again won't kill me. Most of the time, I try to eat right. Gotta stay in shape to do the work I do."

"Yeah, living a good life does not mean you have to abstain from every damn thing you think is bad for you." Saville had entered, and her eyes roamed over Fi's body in that irritating way that seemed to send goose bumps up and down her arms, no matter how much Fi hated reacting. "Looking good, Fi. I doubt you've had anything remotely forbidden touch those lips in a long time."

Fi glared at Saville, who looked casually sexy in her tight T-shirt and shorts. Damn her. How was it possible that her helmet hadn't even smashed her glossy, wheat-blonde hair, pulled haphazardly into an untidy ponytail? Bloodshot, light-amber eyes revealed what was probably a late night at the bar. Even so, her eyes were as compelling as the first time Fi had met Saville.   "Shut it, Saville. I don't need your approval."

Lucy jumped from the stool and linked arms with both Saville and Fi. "Come on, girls, we need you to look at all the buildings and give us an estimate of what it's going to cost to turn this town into a sapphic retirement community.

We'd like to keep the mercantile and sell goods from it. Of course, we want to restore the saloon and plan on living in the upper portion of the building. We haven't quite decided what to do with the hotel. Do you girls have any ideas? Maybe we could make it a small, assisted-living facility for down the road when the residents need a little extra help. Or we could turn it into a clubhouse. Do you think we could have a pool installed? I know that's a little modern for a ghost town, but it gets hot in the summer, and a pool would be a huge draw, don't you think, honey?"

Bea frowned. "A pool requires a lot of upkeep, and it's costly to install. I think we better put that on the back burner for now."

"Right. Phase two." Lucy clapped her hands together. "I feel like a big-time developer. Ooh, this is so exciting. Don't you think?" Looping her arms again with Fi and Saville, she tugged on the women, bringing them closer to her.

Saville laughed. "I like her. Why are all the good ones taken or too constipated to have any fun?"

Fi bit her tongue so she wouldn't be tempted to respond to the barb that she knew Saville had intended for her. "I know a little about pools and could maintain it for you. There are even some DIY kits available. I promise to charge a very nominal fee to install and maintain your pool, but Bea is right. It will still be expensive if you want anything of quality. Although, that would undoubtedly be a draw to potential residents. I'd recommend monthly dues to everyone who plans to live here. That would enable you to cover the costs of any upkeep to a pool, landscaping, or other community buildings."

"This damn project is going to bankrupt us," Bea mumbled, barely loud enough for the trio to hear.

Lucy turned to face her wife. "What was that you said, hon?"

"Never mind. I'm making that hearing test appointment for Monday. By the way, in your grand vision of us living above the saloon, surely you aren't planning on keeping it open until all hours of the night. There's nothing wrong with *my* hearing, and you know my bedtime is early," Bea groused.

"Well, it's not like we're going to have hundreds of women living here. We should open the saloon on select nights, like Friday and Saturday only. It can be a community gathering place. I wonder if we need a liquor or cannabis license? If it's more like a casual place for socializing, how would the authorities know? It'd be like inviting people into our home for a potluck. BYOB or BYOP."

"What the hell are you rambling about? BYOP?" Bea asked.

"Potluck. Get it: bring your own pot. Things have evolved since we first met at that potluck all those years ago. Surely potlucks today have that double entendre," Lucy said, appearing to look toward Fi and Saville for confirmation.

"We are not selling cannabis," Bea stated.

"I suppose that would get more complicated than we want. Potluck sounds like the perfect answer. Then we won't have to mess with the government and all the regulations around licensing. I'll bet those are a total pain in the ass." Turning her attention to the two young women, Lucy gently pushed them. "Go, time's a-wastin'. Don't you two need to do some measuring and inspecting, or whatever, to give us a quote on everything? Plus, we'll want you to add a few more buildings, maybe ten new tiny houses."

"Ten! No, no way. There are already enough homes for all the couples we know who might buy into this crazy idea. I don't want to live with a bunch of cranky old dykes that I don't personally know." Bea shook her head while gulping her coffee.

"We'll screen everyone. How about if we make that phase three?" Lucy walked back to Bea and slung her arm around Bea's shoulder. "What do you think, girls?"

"I think this is going to be an incredible place. If I hadn't restored my home, I'd want to live here." Fi smiled at the couple.

Fi could see the love between them despite the half-hearted grumbling from Bea. She suspected that when all was said and done, Lucy always got her way. She wanted what they had, but finding that was proving nearly impossible. She hadn't enjoyed living in Seattle, but at least there were eligible women to date.

Amelia had moved for love to where Darcy had grown up, taking to the alpaca farm and country living like she was born into it. Fi had followed her best friend to the small town because living close to her best friend and getting to spend some of her time on projects she had a passion for almost made the move worthwhile. Almost.

At least with the way Lucy had talked about the project with its three phases, she'd have plenty of work for a long time. Besides restoring old homes, she had built a few tiny houses before and loved designing the space for optimal efficiency. She had tons of ideas for Lucy's phase three.

Saville stared at the bar, licked her lips, and pointed to the donut box. "Hey, are those donuts up for grabs? I didn't have time for breakfast this morning."

Lucy grinned and handed Saville a cup of coffee. "Oh, yes. I'm so sorry I forgot to offer you coffee and donuts, but I was just so excited to get started."

Saville walked to the bar, grabbed a powdered donut, and took a large bite. The powdered sugar left remnants all over her lips, and Fi had the insane desire to kiss and lick her clean. Just as she was about to turn her head, Saville brought the bottom of her T-shirt to her mouth and wiped, showing off her tanned abdomen, which was as flat and solid as Fi remembered.

"Gross." Fi set her cup of coffee on the bar, grabbed a napkin from the stack next to the box of donuts, and handed it to Saville. "You didn't need to use your shirt. There are napkins, you know."

"A second ago, you didn't seem to mind the view." Saville winked.

After a hard pivot away from Saville, Fi pulled her measuring tape from her belt and announced, "Just give me a few minutes to measure down here and then take a peek upstairs." Fi measured the room's length, then pulled a small notebook from her back pocket and the pencil from behind her right ear. After documenting the first measurement, she progressed to the next, methodically noting the dimensions as she moved around the room.

Saville continued to eat her donut and then grabbed another. When Fi took a moment to glance at Saville, the obnoxious woman had winked at her and followed the flirtation with that self-satisfied smirk that had both irritated and aroused Fi when she'd first met Saville.

"Aren't you going to take any measurements, or are you expecting me to share this with you?" Fi pointed to her small notebook. She tried to keep the irritation from her tone but realized that sounded bitchy when the slight frown appeared on Saville's face.

After popping the last bite of her donut into her mouth, she answered. "How about I measure the upstairs while you finish down here, and we can share our results." Fi opened her mouth to protest, and Saville held up her hand. "Whatever else you might think of me, I am a professional. The measurements will be precise."

"I, uh, wasn't about to suggest you aren't a good electrician. I know you are. You wired my house, remember?" Fi's face flushed.

Saville smiled. "How could I ever forget? This will go a lot quicker if we split up the buildings. I'll still need to look at the old wiring, and I'm sure you need to inspect the buildings as well, but at least the measurements won't take as long."

"Uh, sure, that works for me."

"See, we can work well together without spilling blood." Turning to Lucy, Saville said, "Thanks for breakfast. You're a peach. I noticed those stairs look pretty solid. Is there anything else I need to know about the upstairs?"

"Can you add those USB plugs to the rooms? Oh, and we'll want to convert a few bedrooms into a small kitchen and bathroom. So I guess we'll need some of those GFI plugs that you can reset by pushing the red button."

"I'll come with you. We may need to knock out a few walls to open the space for a central living area and kitchen. First, I need to see the basic structure to determine how solid the frame is," Fi interjected.

"We?" Saville raised her eyebrow. "I'm just the electrician. I don't do general contractor work, especially nothing related to demolitions. Too dirty."

Lucy jumped up and down, raising her hand in the air. "Oh, oh, oh, I love to get dirty. I can help."

"The 'we' wasn't meant to include you. God, you are such an arrogant—"

Saville wagged her finger. "Uh, uh, uh. And to think a mere minute ago, we were getting along so well. Look, if it makes you happy, I can lend my muscle to this project and help with more than rewiring and upgrading the electrical systems. All you have to do is ask nicely." Saville grinned.

"I don't need or want your muscle." Fi sent daggers at Saville.

Holding her hands up, Saville responded, "Fine, but the offer will still be on the table if you change your mind. I take orders well. Sometimes I like to switch things up. I don't always have to be the top." Saville grinned.

Fi gritted her teeth. "Why must you always make everything sexual?"

"I did no such thing. It's your dirty mind that went there, not mine." Saville smirked again.

†

Saville hadn't the foggiest idea why she had to goad Fi. Working on this project alongside Fi was the opportunity she'd hoped for. She didn't like how their friendship had turned sour after she fucked up and slept with Fi. The woman was like a beautiful roaring fire, and if Saville wasn't careful, Fi would fry her to a crisp. Yep, she'd be a crispy critter, no good to anyone else. And Saville did not roll that way.

Unattached was how she liked things, no matter how alluring Fiona O'Reilly was.

When it was just the two of them, Saville had touched Fi's arm and apologized. "Hey, I'm sorry. I don't want us to be enemies, and my offer to help was genuine. Before everything went sideways, we were friends. I miss that."

Fi squinted and wrinkled her nose. "You're being serious?"

"Yes, I am. Is that so hard to believe? Just because I'm not marriage material does not mean I can't be a good friend. Ask Darcy. She and I have been friends for twenty years."

"Did you sleep with her too?"

"God, no. That would be like sleeping with my sister. But, I am still capable of friendship after, you know. It's the lesbian way. Come on, be a good lesbian, and let's bury the hatchet. Besides, we both agreed that it was a mistake. I don't know why you're all pissed off about it."

"Because you took advantage of me in my weakened state."

"We were both drunk, and I sure didn't hear any complaints while my face was between your legs."

"Do you have to be so crass?"

"Do you have to be so uptight? It was just sex. People have sex every day. You ought to try it more than once a decade, and then maybe you wouldn't have jumped my bones that night."

"Me? I did not make the first move. You did."

"And you kissed me back, tugging on my shirt. What was I supposed to do? Push away a gorgeous woman? Unfortunately, I don't have that kind of self-control."

"No, you certainly don't. Let's just forget about that night like we promised. If you're serious about helping, I could use some assistance. I'm afraid to give Lucy or Bea a task that would be too hard on their bodies. I know they want to help, but I think I can keep them occupied with the easier tasks. The two-person jobs will be too physically taxing on either of them."

"I don't know. Lucy looks pretty spry for a woman in her sixties. But you're probably right. I wouldn't want her to wreck her back. So, truce?" Saville held out her hand.

Hesitantly, Fi offered her hand and shook. Saville knew she shouldn't have caressed the back of Fi's hand with her thumb when they shook, but the compulsion was too strong to resist. She was so close, and she smelled so good.

Fi frowned when she removed her hand. "Are you ready to inspect the other buildings?"

"I was born ready." Saville grinned, extended her hand with a flourish, and bowed her head. "Lead the way, my fair lady."

CHAPTER THREE

Bea sat nervously on the old worn stool, noting the need to replace the leather at a minimum. Surprisingly, the wood inside the old saloon was solid. With a bit of elbow grease, a fair amount of sanding, and a natural finish to bring out the wood grain, she could see the end result in her mind's eye. And it wasn't half bad.

The problem wasn't how well the saloon or other buildings would look after Fi and Saville restored them. Bea had seen the gleam in Fiona's eye, and that spelled passion, which usually translated into stellar work. But no, Bea was worried about having enough money in their retirement accounts to justify the expenditure required to restore the town. She'd convinced Lucy to remain in the saloon while Saville and Fi measured and inspected all the other buildings. Bea knew it would go faster without Lucy pestering them.

Lucy's intentions were always pure, but Bea knew she'd just be in the way.

Swishing her hand back and forth on her thigh was her nervous tell. Lucy grabbed her hand and entwined their fingers. After thirty-five years, she'd learned how to ground Bea.

"Honey, rubbing your thigh until it's raw will not make the process go any faster. The estimate will be what the estimate will be, and then we can decide how much we can do in phase one. I honestly don't believe it will be hard to recoup our initial costs once we sell a few houses. Fi's idea to charge monthly dues for upkeep is a good one. Maybe we can hire someone to run the mercantile and saloon for a little extra income."

"I don't want to live above a rowdy bar," Bea exclaimed, pouting like a two-year-old. "Maybe we should reconsider where we choose to live, or, even better, reassess this whole crazy idea of yours. I like our condo. It has a pool already."

"How rowdy can it get with a bunch of retired lesbians? This is your resistance to change talking. Besides, you enjoy our gatherings on the weekends. It'll be just like that, only we'll be inviting a few more people because our place will be a lot bigger than a 1,000-foot condo."

"We have friends over maybe once a month, and that's being generous. I don't want a big party every single weekend."

Lucy laughed. "A big party? Since when in the last ten years have we hosted or attended a big party? The saloon won't be like that. You won't have to go downstairs unless you want to. We'll add soundproofing to our living area. That way, you won't hear the music from the granny gala you're envisioning will happen every weekend. I'd say that's highly doubtful."

"Don't make fun of me, or I'll pull the plug on this ridiculous venture."

"No, you won't," Lucy insisted.

"Oh, yes, I will. Don't tempt me."

"No, you won't because you love me, and I haven't wanted anything so bad since I first laid eyes on you."

"Sweet talker." Bea leaned in and kissed Lucy on the lips.

"You know it. Hey, did you notice the sparks flying between Saville and Fi? Those two are destined to become a couple." The twinkle in Lucy's eyes foretold her impending meddle.

"I saw sparks all right. Separately, I get the sense those two are quite capable, but I have my doubts about their ability to work together."

"Because they'll want to rip each other's clothes off every chance they get?"

"No, because they'll want to rip each other's throats out. You need to stay out of it, Lucy. I mean it. Your matchmaking skills aren't as good as you think they are."

"Stop being mean."

"I'm not being mean. I'm merely stating a fact. Your niece is a perfect example. Chelsey doesn't need or want you to meddle in her love life. Unfortunately, you seem to keep forgetting the firefighter debacle."

"How was I to know she was straight? I'd have bet my left tit that hottie was family. She's more butch than any of our friends. I still think she's a repressed lesbian. Mark my words, in less than ten years, I'll bet she's divorced and in a relationship with a woman."

"Maybe, but Chelsey won't forget what you did in this century. The whole ugly situation mortified her."

"All I did was ask that nice woman to go to Chelsey's school and talk to the kids about fire safety. They do that, you know. Community service or something." Lucy plucked some invisible lint off her T-shirt.

"That is not all you did, and you know it. Chelsey spit nails. She was so angry. First, she didn't know a thing about the woman showing up, and then you had to make things worse by plopping in like you owned the place and leaving not-so-subtle cues about your true purpose for arranging the presentation. I think she might have murdered you had I not been there to intercede on your behalf."

Lucy shook her head. "God, who is being dramatic now? Total exaggeration. She would have eventually forgiven me. I think I'm going to touch base with the cute firefighter. I know I saw chemistry between the two. Maybe the divorce has already happened."

Bea grabbed Lucy by the arm. "You'll be too busy with Georgetown Glen. Don't make me have to save your ass again. Come on, let's go see if Saville and Fi are almost done. The waiting is killing me. I'd rather hear the shocking sticker cost before I change my mind."

"Georgetown Glen. I like it. Queermunity living at its finest."

Bea squinted one eye. "We'll keep brainstorming on the tagline."

"But I like queermunity living. Or, how about Georgetown Glen: where you'll find your pot at the end of the rainbow? Then we really could look into selling cannabis."

"We are not going into the cannabis business, no matter what. The saloon can be open for weekends, but no pot brownies. That is my last and final offer."

"I'll take it. That doesn't mean I can't still bake pot brownies or cookies, does it?" Lucy asked.

"Oh, heavens no. It just means we aren't selling them." Bea winked. She had to admit that after the state made pot legal and she'd retired, nothing had stopped her from enjoying Lucy's excellent baked goods. It always made Lucy frisky, and that was a very good thing at their age.

The saloon doors swung open, and Saville swaggered in with a smile on her face. Fi was less jovial as she flipped through the pages in her small notebook. She ripped out a page and handed it to Bea.

Bea coughed as she looked at the amount written on the piece of paper. Although she expected the sizeable number, it was still an enormous amount of money. If she were honest, she thought it might be double the figure noted.

"Does this include everything? Or do you have a separate estimate for the electrical work?"

Fi frowned. "Um, this is only for the work I'll be doing. Although Saville might help with some of the two-person jobs. I'll pay her from my pocket. If it helps, that figure includes the ten tiny houses. Cut that by roughly a third without the tiny houses."

"Okay, wow, this is a very fair price for the work required. I was just getting clarification. Saville, do you have an estimate for your part?"

"With the friends and families discount, let's say a nice round eighty k should do it. By the way, that quote includes the tiny houses."

"Would we need to give you all the money upfront, or could we do a big down payment and then provide the rest after we sell our condo?"

"I'd just need enough to purchase the materials to get started. I could work out a payment plan for the rest if that works better for you. That would give me stable income to live on and might work out better for everyone," Fi offered.

"I'd be willing to do that as well," Saville added.

Lucy bobbed her head excitedly. "I know this means we'll have to dip into our retirement accounts, but it will be worth it. Aren't you glad I insisted on putting half of our money into a Roth IRA? Ooh, we should buy an RV to live in while Fi and Saville make the saloon livable. By the way, will it cost a lot more to soundproof the upstairs?"

"Less than ten thousand, I suspect. We can add that to the contract. In fact, I'll put in a clause to accommodate any additional change orders."

Lucy looked at Bea with such hope in her eyes that Bea didn't have the heart to put the brakes on Georgetown Glen. "Will a hundred-thousand-dollar down payment be enough?" Bea asked.

"More than enough." Fi looked at Saville. "How much will you need to get started?"

Saville winced. "Unfortunately, for me, most of the cost of the bid is materials, so I'll probably need close to half."

"That'll work. I can easily make do with sixty thousand. Do you want me to write up the contract? It probably would be more efficient to have one document. If you give me your standard language, I can incorporate that into the agreement. Will that work for you, Saville?"

"Yeah, yeah, of course. Since this is the biggest job I've ever done, I don't have formal contract language. Mostly, I've just written an estimate for people."

Fi shifted uncomfortably from one foot to the other. "Okay," she said hesitantly. "Um, I'll write it up tonight."

†

Fuckity, fuck, fuck. Why did I offer to write up the contract? Then Saville had to confess and be honest about the fact that this was her biggest job. It was also Fi's biggest job, and she'd never had to create a legal document before. She hoped her nonchalant offer would impress Saville. For whatever reason, Fi wanted Saville to view her as a competent professional, which meant a formal contract. She figured that she'd simply steal whatever language Saville typically put in her arrangements and maybe search online for standard construction agreements. Now Fi was stuck. She wondered if she should come clean about the fact that she had no blinkin' idea what she was doing. But, if she did that, she'd see that self-satisfied smirk from Saville, who would probably offer to help.

As Fi walked to her truck alongside Saville, Saville turned and narrowed her eyes. "What's got your knickers in a twist?"

"What? Um, nothing."

"You're a terrible liar. Wait. You don't know anything about construction contracts, do you?"

"How did you figure that in your little pea brain?"

"I pay attention to the tiny details. That's what makes me so great in bed." Saville grinned. "You have several tells. Shuffling your feet is just one of them. I could share them all if you don't believe me. I can even reveal what Lucy and Bea's tells are."

Fi scoffed, "Right, like you're always so observant of other people's emotions."

"Bea swishes her hand against her thigh when she's nervous. Lucy covers her nervousness with excitement and flirtations bordering on inappropriate. But who am I to talk?" Saville laughed. "Lucy probably believes if she's overly optimistic, she can bend anything to her will. And honestly, I believe that's exactly what occurs. That little spitfire has Bea wrapped around her pinky."

A warm feeling flooded Fi. "Yeah, on that front, you're right. They are adorable, aren't they?"

"Sure, I suppose if you're predisposed for marital bliss after thirty-five years together. They're something special, all right." Saville sighed.

"And you really don't want that someday?"

Saville shrugged. "Who'd want to put up with my shit for thirty-five years? Hey, don't change the subject. If you need help to put together the contract, I could spare a few hours tonight. How about we grab some dinner and work on it together?" She held her hands in the air, palms out. "No alcohol, and I promise to keep my hands to myself. I'm just offering my big brain."

Fi sighed. "Fine, but if you try any funny business, I won't hesitate to smack you."

"You know that's not a very good threat to make. A little spanking here and there can be quite fun. Just like love and hate, pain and pleasure share a fine line."

"I've never been into that. Maybe a little light bondage, but never pain. Oh, why am I telling you this? God, you're impossible. We need to stick to business talk from now on. Nothing personal and nothing sexual."

"Hey, I wasn't the one to take us down lover's lane. You started it with the question about what I envision for my future love life."

"Well, I respectfully withdraw that question from the record. May God strike me dead if I ever ask you another intimate question."

Saville wiggled her eyebrows. "Intimate, huh? Please don't stop on my account. You can ask me any intimate question you want, and I will be one hundred percent honest with my answer."

"Just meet me at my house at five, and you're buying dinner. Do you remember how to get there?"

"Of course. How could I ever forget?" Saville winked.

That Fi couldn't forget that night either made her more irritated because she was sure the reason she couldn't forget was utterly different from Saville's.

†

Fi smoothed her hair in front of the mirror when she heard the telltale sound Saville had arrived. It was hard to miss a Harley roaring up her drive. *Damn, why do I even care what that arrogant twatwaffle thinks?* But she did, and that was about the saddest thing. God, she needed to get laid by anyone but Saville. Her face scrunched in confusion as she tried to work out how in the world Saville would bring dinner on her motorcycle. Fi pushed aside the blinds, registering how Saville balanced two pizza boxes and a couple of four-packs in her hands.

46

Fi smiled. Only Saville would have the talent to carry all of that on her Harley. Opening the door before Saville knocked, she asked, "Okay, I give up. Please tell me how in the world you were able to carry pizza and beer on your motorcycle? And, I thought I said no alcohol."

"Bungee cords and insulated saddlebags." Saville held up one four-pack while balancing the rest of her bounty in her left hand. "I got your favorite. Organic IPA from that brewery you wouldn't shut up about. I'm relatively confident there's a rule somewhere that says you can't eat pizza without beer. However, I won't drink that piss water that parades as a real beer and got myself some nut-brown ale."

"Whatever. Come on in. I've got my laptop fired up and have already started searching for a generic contract we can use. I printed two different versions for us to look over."

"Of course you did." Saville smirked.

After Saville set the pizza boxes on the antique dining room table, Fi couldn't help herself and lifted the lid. "Is that arugula?"

"Yep, arugula, goat cheese, and sun-dried tomatoes on a pesto base." Clearly, Saville was proud of herself, and Fi had to admit, the thoughtful gesture had duly impressed her.

"You remembered," Fi said, with a considerable amount of awe in her voice.

"It wasn't that hard. Literally, no one I know orders those toppings on their pizza."

"Well, what did you get for yourself?"

"I debated on the meat lovers special, but I thought that might offend your delicate never beef or pork standards. So, I decided on ham and pineapple. Sure, the ham might bring out 'the face,' but it's a lot better than the meat lovers special. Besides, I was in the mood for something sweet and salty. Kind of like you."

"And there it is. That little dig that you just can't resist."

"It wasn't a dig. I like sweet and salty in both my women and my pizza."

Fi didn't know what to think. Saville had remembered what she liked on her pizza and had undoubtedly gone out of her way to find the organic beer she preferred. Fi knew the small town they lived in did not carry that beer. Saville would have had to drive at least an hour away to find it. She'd attempted to please Fi. The least Fi could do was be gracious about it.

"Thank you. When I said you should bring dinner, I didn't expect you to go to so much trouble."

Saville shrugged. "You're worth it. Besides, I wanted to start things off on the right foot. Considering we'll be spending an awful lot of time with one another completing this project, I didn't want us fighting the entire time. That would be a total buzz kill."

"Why do you have to be so sweet sometimes," Fi mumbled, too low for Saville to hear. Saville was definitely an enigma that Fi did not understand, but she was damned if she'd let Saville suck her into the vortex again.

"What'd you say?"

"Nothing important. I'll grab some paper plates and forks. We can eat while you look over the two different blank contracts I pulled from the Internet." Fi wrinkled her nose. "Both forms include a clause for insurance, but I don't carry general liability insurance." She grabbed the plates, napkins, and forks, setting them on the table next to the pizza. "After hearing a horror story about another independent contractor who fell from a ladder and screwed her leg for life, I went out and got worker's compensation insurance for myself. Do you think we could delete that liability section? Or maybe just include the part about worker's compensation insurance?"

Saville pulled a beer from each four-pack, set them on the table, and then walked to the refrigerator to place the remaining cans inside. Fi noted how comfortable Saville appeared, moving around in her kitchen like she lived there full time. If only they'd remained friends.

"Just like old times, huh? Don't worry about the general liability. I can put you under my policy. But that will mean you would technically be my employee, and that gives me the right to boss you around." Saville rubbed her hands together. "Ooh, this could be fun."

"Forget it. I'd rather get my own general liability insurance than have to answer to you. It should be the other way around. You offered to help me. I think I'll pass if there are strings attached to your offer."

Saville held her hands in supplication. "Sorry, it was a joke. General liability insurance isn't a big deal. However, if you plan to take on other big jobs like the one for these ladies, I recommend you look into it. You could get a policy for around five hundred a year. Construction is higher than other industries, but I found a really inexpensive policy that should suffice. I'll give you the name of the guy I used."

"Okay, thanks. That settles that. I'll call tomorrow. Just text me his name."

Saville pulled her phone from her pocket. Her thumbs flew over the tiny keyboard, and she declared, "Done."

"We should eat before the pizza gets cold."

Saville pulled out a chair and sat, helping herself to a slice of pizza. After taking a big bite and setting the piece on her plate, she picked up one contract and scanned the document. Fi watched while her eyes moved quickly across the pages. She set down the first set of papers and, with a slight nod, picked up the other pile, repeating the process. Lifting a document in her hands, she said, "I like this one better. It's cleaner and simpler than the other one but has all the same elements."

"Agreed."

"Wow, that was simple. I thought I'd get more of an argument from you. Look at us, getting along so well." Saville smirked as she set the sheaf of papers back on the table.

"Don't push your luck. Just because I agreed about the contract doesn't mean I'm always going to agree with how to proceed. We obviously have differing opinions on many things."

"No, we don't. We only have differing opinions on relationships and, more specifically, sex. I seem to remember that on everything else, we agreed more than disagreed. Come on, don't you miss our friendship?"

"You miss spending time with me?" Fi's voice came out in something like a squeaky whisper.

"I'm not afraid to admit that I miss hanging out with you. I love Darc and Amelia, but they're a cozy, married couple, and playing the third wheel is not a lot of fun. I was so excited to have another single person to hang with. I never would have moved back if I'd known how things would go down. You were the deciding factor in my return to my hometown."

"I was? You never told me that."

"And give you a gigantic head?" Saville laughed. "Not a chance. You're lucky I even gambled on a confession now."

Deciding that things were getting too real, Fi popped up and began rummaging in a drawer. "I'll grab a pen, and we can fill in the blanks. Then I'll transfer our answers onto the computer, so we have a professional-looking contract."

"I don't think the ladies care about that, but why not just type in the answers? Your other tell is showing, you know. So why don't you sit down and relax? Drink your beer. Filling in the blanks will not take all night."

Fi returned to the table and sat down heavily. Popping the top of her beer, she took a big swig. "Thanks again for the beer and pizza."

Saville popped the top to her own can and lifted it in the air. Grinning, she said, "To a successful partnership, may we have many more."

Fi clicked her own can to Saville's and nodded before both women tipped the cans and gulped the golden liquid into their mouths.

CHAPTER FOUR

Lucy had gone to the local farm and feed store that stocked the old durable work pants with nifty pockets. She bought herself two pairs to prepare for the first day on their worksite. Adjusting her tool belt, Lucy looked at herself in the mirror. She felt like a real laborer.

"Stop preening in front of the mirror. Yeah, you look good. We're going to be late. You know how I hate to be late," Bea said.

Lucy grinned. "Admit it. You are just as excited as I am to be working on the town. I wish you would have let me buy you these Carhartt pants. They are surprisingly comfortable."

"I don't like tan."

"Well, don't come crying to me when you rip your shorts or skin your knees. You don't have any protection for your legs. Fi's too nice to say anything, but maybe Saville will tell you the truth. That young woman's got sass and a nice ass." Lucy chuckled.

"Don't forget, Amelia arranged for a showing of our condo this afternoon. I told her we'd be available by phone in case we get an offer. We might need to find temporary housing while we wait for Saville and Fi to finish the upstairs remodel of the saloon. The sooner we decide on the bathroom and kitchen, the faster they can make the space livable."

"I know, I know. Don't rush me. Fi sent so many wonderful choices, it's hard to decide."

Bea groaned. "Is this a premonition of how painful this is all going to be? If we can't even agree on a toilet, how are we going to make all the decisions necessary to finish this before I die?"

"Don't be so morbid. We're just going to have to learn to compromise a little."

"You mean you're going to need to compromise. I believe I've already done my fair share. We bought the damn town, didn't we?"

"Let's independently select our first, second, and third choices, then we can compare notes. Hopefully, we'll agree on a few things, and then we can look to see if any of the top three choices overlap."

Bea squinted at Lucy. "That's far too logical for you. What's the catch?"

"If our choices don't overlap at all, either I get the final say, or we ask Fi to give us more options."

"We're going to be homeless," Bea grumbled.

"Come on, we're going to be late." Lucy looped her arm inside Bea's and pulled her to their car.

†

"What do you think?"

Fi stood in front of the wall separating the two largest rooms above the saloon. She'd tried convincing Lucy and Bea that it would be too dangerous to help with the demolition and promised, once they knocked the walls out and they'd inspected and reinforced all the beams, she would put them to work sanding and refinishing the old bar. But the two women wanted to be a part of everything, so she'd told them to come later in the morning, hoping to get far enough into the job that it wouldn't be dangerous for them to work below.

Saville had agreed to help her with her least favorite part of the job, and they'd started at an ungodly hour. Fi wasn't sure that Saville would show up at six in the morning, but she had. *Maybe we can become friends again.* Just because Fi had wanted more than friendship, but was too embarrassed to admit it to Saville, didn't mean Saville was the evil ogre Fi made her out to be. Saville didn't have to agree to help with the hardest and dirtiest part of the job.

"Might be a little tight, but this wall could certainly come down without affecting the structural integrity," Saville answered. "It's just two people, so if you arrange the appliances for maximum space efficiency, it should work." She pointed to the left. "There's plenty of room for a table with four chairs over there." Saville nodded. "Yes, this is a good place for the kitchen and dining area."

"I need to decide on which other wall is better to take out for the living area."

"I'd recommend across the hall. You may be able to make this an open living space that seems preferable to people these days."

"Yup, that's what I thought, too. I'm just not sure about removing the doors and the wall into those rooms. I wish I had blueprints of this place. Will you grab that ladder? I want to inspect the wall joist." Fi squinted at the ceiling before glancing at Saville and noticing her bulging biceps as she easily carried the wooden ladder.

Saville quickly set up the ladder, and Fi scrambled to the top as Saville almost casually held the bottom.

When the ladder shook, Fi yelled, "What the fuck, Saville? Are you trying to kill me?"

Saville's muscles strained as she held on, veins popping in her neck with the amount of exertion. "It's not me. I'm trying to stabilize the damn thing."

Fi lost her battle to hang on and tumbled ungracefully from the top of the ladder while Saville looked on in horror, only shifting enough to catch Fi as the two of them tumbled to the dusty wood floor. As Fi lay on top of a wide-eyed Saville, she inwardly cursed her out-of-control emotions when her lips remained mere inches from Saville's. Damn, if she didn't want to close the gap and kiss the arrogant woman.

"Um, sorry." Fi blushed. "Are you okay?"

Saville tightened her grip on Fi's waist. "More than okay. You know you didn't have to fake an earthquake just so you could land on top of me."

Fi quickly rolled off of Saville. "What the hell was that? Earthquake?"

Saville sat up and shook her head. "I don't think so. It certainly didn't feel like one. It was more like…" Her eyes widened again. "Don't put me in the loony bin, but it felt like someone deliberately shook that ladder."

"Yeah, right. The invisible man has nothing better to do than fuck with us."

"First, that's sexist. Maybe it was an invisible woman. And second, I think it's George."

"Don't tell me you buy into that ghost town crap." Fi pursed her lips.

"I was at the bar when the previous contractors came in after walking off the job. The way they relayed the stories…" Saville let her words dangle in the air. "Let's just say they were pretty convincing. I thought George might give us a break, ya know. Us being family and all." Saville stood and looked at the ceiling. "Hey, George, come on, can't you give a sister a break? Don't you think that having lesbians turn this town into a retirement community for queer sisters is enough poetic justice? That'll be the perfect revenge."

A gust of wind blew open the cracked window, and Fi and Saville shared a look. Fi decided she wasn't about to let some angry ghost ruin the biggest job she'd ever secured in her life. Not to mention the job would be a labor of love. Restoring old buildings was what she was good at. With precision, she scrambled to her feet and stalked to retrieve the sledgehammer she had lugged upstairs in case it was safe to tear down the walls. Her first swing felt so good. Every ounce of energy went into the initial hole she put into the old divider. Splinters flew everywhere as the wall exploded on impact. "I'm. Not. Leaving. Take that, George."

A loud wailing noise emanated from one of the other rooms, and it was hard not to feel the pain in that sound. Fi and Saville both turned their heads toward the wailing.

"Maybe we shouldn't piss him off. He did try to kill you. I prefer using charm. It usually works a lot better than anger. He sounds like he's in pain. Maybe a bit of empathy? I mean, I'd be a total wreck if I had to see my wife die."

"You'd never be in that position because you'll never have a wife."

"That's a mean thing to say."

"Why? It's the truth. You pretty much said so, you know after we, uh..."

"Did I? I don't remember saying anything about marriage. Just because I don't think someone like you deserves to be saddled with someone like me for the rest of their life doesn't mean that I'll never find a woman more in my league to settle with."

"What the hell is that supposed to mean?"

Before Saville had a chance to answer, the loud crash in the other room startled both women as they stared at one another.

"That's it. George and I are going to have a serious chat. Woman to woman, or maybe I should say, woman to man." Saville stalked off toward the origin of the crash.

Fi quickly followed, letting her curiosity get the best of her.

†

Saville stood inside the room from where the noise had emanated, her eyes blinking rapidly at the semi-transparent figure holding a piece of the floorboard. Before the ghost could toss the board at the wall, Saville yelled, "George, you put that down. We decide what needs to be replaced and demolished. We don't need your help."

The ethereal creature let the wood drop to the floor. Dressed in trousers, a button-up vest, and a loose bow tie, the figure tilted his head and laid his right hand on the gun holstered on his hip. It seemed more of a familiar gesture than a threat. Saville hadn't interacted with a ghost before, and she wondered if her observational skills would figure out George's tells. *Was this something he did to rustle up enough bravado against outlaws that might disturb the peace in his town?* Saville wondered how the gambler had bested George, who stood nearly six feet in height. *Did ghosts grow tall in the afterlife? Or was George always this intimidating?*

Without a word whispered or spoken, George vanished.

"Hey, you come back. We haven't finished with you. We need to establish some ground rules around here if we're all going to get along peacefully," Saville yelled into thin air before sensing Fi's approach.

"How's that charm going?" Fi snickered.

"He isn't still throwing shit around, is he?"

Fi frowned as she looked at the hole in the floor. "I hadn't decided whether I needed to replace the floor or try to refinish it, salvaging the wood. Looks like George decided for us."

Saville crouched down to inspect the hole. "Oh, I don't know. We can probably fix this." When she pushed aside the other floorboard that was slightly off-kilter, she glimpsed a metal box.

"Hey, come and take a look. There's something tucked beneath the boards."

"Really?"

"Yeah." Saville tugged at the large metal box. "Wow! It's super cumbersome. Give me a hand, will you?"

"Sure." Fi pushed aside the other loose board and pulled while Saville pushed. Finally, they lifted the heavy metal box.

"Maybe there's gold in here. What a find, huh?"

"We should wait to open it until Lucy and Bea arrive," Fi said.

"Are you crazy? We won't finish the demolition for days. I can't wait that long. Come on. Aren't you just a little curious? Besides, it's not like I'm suggesting we keep whatever is in the box, but maybe they'll give us a bonus for finding it."

"It has a lock on it," Fi answered weakly.

"Seriously, this flimsy thing. I can pop this off in a matter of seconds."

"We shouldn't."

"Oh, no, we really should." Saville grinned and then abruptly stood and walked out of the room.

†

Fi nearly had to run to catch up to Saville as she jogged down the stairs. "Where are you going?"

"I'm going to get something from my saddlebags to open the box. Where do you think I'm going?" Saville frowned. "I'm not sure that any of my meager tools will work. I really need to get a work truck. It's damn hard lugging around what I need for a job site on my Harley."

"I probably have something in my truck. You can put what you need for this job in the back."

"Thanks. So, you're down with opening the box?" Saville grinned.

Fi sighed. "Yeah, I guess I'm kind of curious, too. But only because we're handing over whatever we find to Lucy and Bea. We should try to open the lock without breaking it. The box itself might be worth something. I've never tried picking a lock before, but I have a paper clip in my pocket. I'm not sure if those work."

"Why do you have a paper clip in your pocket? Never mind. I think that could work. My cousin taught me a few tricks. I was just going to bust the thing open. Good idea to approach this with a bit more finesse. We're a good pair. See how well our individual talents mesh to get the job done right?" Saville winked.

"I don't even want to know about how your cousin taught you the art of lock picking."

"I was a kid. My parents expected me to get in trouble. Don't worry. I've tempered my wild side since then."

Fi quirked her eyebrow.

"Okay, okay, so not every part of my wild side has been tamed." Saville held out her hand. "Give me that secret lock picking tool."

Fi shook her head, but then she dug into her pocket and offered Saville the paper clip. "Here. Have at it."

The women returned to the upstairs bedroom where they had left the locked metal box, only to discover it was no longer there.

"What the fuck? Where did it go?" Saville asked.

"I don't know. You're asking me. I was with you the whole time on your scavenger hunt for a tool to break open the lock."

"Do you think George tried to get to it before we found it? Maybe that's why he's haunting this place. He doesn't want anyone to find his treasure. I didn't hear him moving anything around, and that thing weighed a ton. Do you think his lover helped him? Can a ghost move big objects? I thought it took incredible energy to move a penny."

Fi scrunched her face. "Are you serious? Like you're some expert on ghosts. Where did you get that information?"

"The movies. *Ghost* was a classic. Patrick Swayze had a heck of a time learning how to move an object. Demi Moore was hot in that movie."

"Come on, we need to finish the demolition after I secure the corner joists. I probably shouldn't have used that sledgehammer yet."

"Yeah, I was going to say something, but you needed to send a message or, I don't know, declare your dominance." Saville smirked again. "Don't you want to go looking for the box?"

"No. We've already wasted valuable time. I hate falling behind on a job. Let me grab my drill and the hardware to add a bit more insurance. Thankfully, the wood is in good shape. I guess that's thanks to the use of old-growth trees, which are structurally stronger and more rot-resistant than the crap lumber used today. That's why I love restoring historic buildings."

Fi watched as a slow smile appeared on Saville's face.

"You're passionate about this, aren't you? You should have seen your eyes light up when you were explaining about the old wood. Your infatuation is infectious."

Saville's penetrating gaze, along with an almost fond expression, was too much, and Fi looked away. "I need you to use those muscles of yours to hold that ladder in place."

Saville mock saluted Fi. "Aye, aye, Captain. Anything you need. So, you've noticed my muscles, huh?" Saville flexed her bicep and grinned.

"Are you done preening yet?" Fi turned away from Saville and made a beeline for the rooms where she'd begun knocking down the wall. Fi didn't need to see Saville to know she swaggered as she followed Fi into the rooms across the way.

"After we finish the demolition and whatever else you have planned for today, do you want to join me for dinner and a little exploration?"

Fi turned her head to see an almost hopeful expression with a touch of insecurity. *Well, that's new.* "Exploration?"

"Yeah. I think these old structures have a story to tell, starting with that box we found. Maybe there's more to discover, like a journal or a stack of love letters. Wouldn't that be cool? Come on, for someone who gets their rocks off restoring old buildings, you gotta love the prospect of finding the real deal on the history of this old town. Sure, I believe the story about George because we saw him with our own eyes, but there's more to it. I can feel it in my bones."

"Get their rocks off? What are you, twelve? What you're feeling in your bones is probably old age and arthritis. Our chosen occupation isn't exactly healthy for the body, you know, having to crawl around tight spaces and smashing down walls."

"Speak for yourself. I'm in top shape. Dinner and adventure?" Saville asked again.

"Sure, why not. Take out?"

"Yeah, we can get something from that Vietnamese place you like. I'll buy."

"No, I'll buy. You brought the pizza and beer the other night. It's my turn to pay."

Saville wiggled her eyebrows. "This is getting to be an almost regular deal with us. Some might even think we're dating now."

"That'd be highly unlikely since you don't date, and you would be the last person I would want to date."

"I date."

"Picking up women in bars is not dating."

"Okay, I used to date before I saw the error of my ways. Unfortunately, anyone worth dating clarified that isn't what they wanted from me." Saville shrugged. "It works for me now."

"Aren't you afraid of getting some disease?"

"No. Should I be?"

"Yeah. Lesbians are not immune from sexually transmitted diseases, you know."

"The odds are in our favor, though. Isn't it a lot harder to catch an STD?"

"Harder, but not impossible. I got tested right after, uh, our mistake. I wanted to be sure I didn't catch anything from you."

"You did? Man, that's cold." Saville crossed her arms.

"Why is that cold?" The comment genuinely perplexed Fi. She thought that was the only responsible thing to do, knowing that Saville had sex with a lot of different women.

"Because you thought you were going to catch something from me. Like I'm some piece of garbage. A skank you made the mistake of sleeping with."

"That's not what I said. So quit twisting my words."

"But that's what you think. I know you don't believe I'm worth much. Just some arrogant womanizer who would sleep with anyone with a pussy. Isn't that your opinion?"

"Can we just drop it? I thought we had a truce going."

"Just admit it. You have a meager opinion of me. That's why it was a mistake to you because you would never see me as partner potential." Saville's eyes glistened with emotion.

Fi felt bad. She hadn't expected to touch whatever nerve she'd hit. She rushed to Saville's side and touched her arm.

"Hey, I said it was a mistake because you said it first. Why would I want to explore something with you when you were obviously so dead set against it? I've always been upfront about wanting to find someone special to share my life with, and that is not what you want. It was a mistake because we're not on the same page about what we want. I'm even thinking about downloading one of those online dating apps because, so far, the more organic approach is not working for me."

"Oh. Have you signed up yet?" The frown on Saville's face was comical. If Fi didn't know any better, she'd think Saville was jealous or somehow invested in her relationship status.

"Not yet. I guess I'm still holding out for 'the one' to cross my path."

"Good. You shouldn't rush into it. I've heard there are a lot of weirdos that use those dating sites. Or people looking for hook-ups."

"How do you know? Personal experience?"

"Hell no. I don't need a dating app." Saville's shoulders lifted again. "Just something I heard."

"Well, I'm not getting any younger, so I think I'll give it a try."

"It's your funeral." The frown returned to Saville's beautiful face, and Fi couldn't understand why she was so negative. That was so unlike carefree and fun-loving Saville.

"Why are you being such a Debbie Downer? Why do you care about my dating challenges?"

"I don't. Just telling it like it is. I wouldn't be a good friend if I didn't warn you about those predatory sites." Abruptly changing the direction of the conversation, Saville said, "Hey, I thought we were going to secure the joists." She turned away from Fi and carried the ladder, placing it below the corner joist.

Scratching her head, Fi watched Saville's jerky movements. If she had a hundred years, she'd never figure out Saville. She didn't want a serious relationship with Fi, and yet she also didn't seem to want Fi to date anyone else. At least that was the way it appeared to Fi. She'd have to worry about that later. Right now, they were behind schedule, so she grabbed her drill and the hardware intended to secure the frame.

†

"Yoo-hoo, anyone up there?" Lucy called.

65

"Yeah, but don't come up. It's dangerous in the middle of a demolition job. Stay there. We'll come down," Fi answered.

Saville followed Fi down the winding staircase with her hands deep in her pockets. Lucy sensed something was wrong. There was a bit of tension between the two women, and she wondered what had happened. Never one to keep her thoughts to herself, she asked, "What's up with you two? I thought you both buried the hatchet? You seemed to get along the other day."

"George showed up," Saville blurted.

Lucy clapped her hands together. "Really? Oh, how exciting. I hope he makes another appearance."

"Um, I don't think his first appearance was amiable. He shook the ladder so hard, it caused me to fall." Fi nervously shuffled her feet.

"Oh, dear. Are you okay?"

"She's fine. I caught her. Well, sort of, and then we tumbled to the floor together. If you'd walked in after that happened, you might have had a different impression of what was happening." Saville chuckled. "But, after George's little temper tantrum, we found a locked box."

"Really? What was in it?" Lucy asked.

"If we're lucky, maybe someone stashed a bunch of gold in the box. Then we won't lose every cent of our retirement trying to maintain this albatross," Bea mumbled.

"What was that, hon?"

"Nothing. So, what was in the box?" Bea repeated the question.

"What makes you think we opened the box?" Fi asked, a slight wobble to her voice.

Lucy laughed. "Oh, you don't have to feign innocence with me. If I'd found a box, that sucker would be open right now."

"We lost it. George must have hidden it somewhere. We went to get some tools to crack the lock open, and when we returned, the box had disappeared."

"And you didn't look for it? Pity. We should go search for it now."

"I wanted to make sure the upstairs demolition was at a point where it wouldn't be dangerous for the two of you, so we left the mystery alone for now. I still recommend waiting to search for the box. Give us a few more hours."

Lucy pouted. "But Amelia arranged for some showings this afternoon, so we only have a few hours to work or explore." The twinkle returned to her eyes. "Are you sure we can't take a few minutes to search for the box? I'm dying to know what's in it. Besides, I want George to come out of his hiding place. Then I can reassure him about our intentions for his town. We've decided to call it Georgetown Glen: Queermunity living at its finest."

"I love it," Saville exclaimed.

"We could call it the G-spot for short and add the tagline, 'If you can't find it, you can't come.'" Lucy laughed at her own joke.

"Damn, makes me wish I was over fifty-five and retired so I could live here too. Sounds like heaven." Saville smiled. "Where's your condo? Maybe I should go to one of those showings. I need a better place to live. My neighbors are assholes. I don't mind them mumbling 'dyke' under their breath every time our paths cross, but they leave their dog chained outside, no matter what the weather is like. So I sneak her fresh water and food every chance I get. She's such a sweet dog, too."

Lucy wasn't a dog person, but she approved of the horrified look on Fi's face and how Saville took it upon herself to make sure the poor thing had water and food.

"We should rescue that unfortunate animal," Fi stated.

One corner of Saville's lip turned up. "Are you suggesting we steal the dog? Why Fi, I didn't know you were such a rebel."

"I'm serious. Either we call the Humane Society or give her a proper home. I don't live anywhere near you, so I could take her in. Sassy loves dogs."

"Sassy?" Saville asked.

"My cat."

"I'm not sure what surprises me more. That you got a cat, or that you named him Sassy."

"Her, and you'd have to meet Sassy to know it's the perfect name. She keeps me company at night."

"Now that I can believe. You definitely need to go out a lot more. How come I didn't see Sassy when I came over the other night?"

"She was outside, probably stalking a bird. She's quite the hunter. Of course, I disapprove of her catching and killing birds, but I suppose that's her nature."

"Hmm." Saville smirked. "You give a pass to your cat, but look down your nose at me when I pursue my nightly activities."

Lucy followed the back and forth between Saville and Fi and noted the interaction with interest. They would make an adorable couple. However, when she chanced a glance at Bea, her wife shook her head. Bea had developed a knack for reading her mind, and Lucy knew she would disapprove of any attempts to bring the two young women together.

"I say you two take a break, and we look for the box. Then we can have a nice picnic lunch together before we have to head back. I don't think you would like the condo, Saville. It's too far away from here. Maybe you can move in with Fi? Your neighbors sound awful. It's probably dangerous for you. We live in crazy times. You never know. I'm sure Fi would never forgive herself if something happened to you."

Fi coughed. "Um, Saville is allergic to cats."

"No, I'm not."

"You're not? Oh, sorry, I guess that's commitment you're allergic to. Wrong C-word." Fi had apparently recovered from Lucy's suggestion and had stuck her tongue out at Saville.

"Funny, another C-word just came to mind that I am definitely not allergic to. Cunnilingus. Your tongue reminded me of that." Saville threw her head back and laughed. "Let's return to the mysterious box. Not your mysterious box, the other one. I've already unlocked yours." Saville whispered the last remark close to Fi's ear, but Lucy still heard it.

Fi glared at Saville. "I'd rather get back to work and finish the demolition in this century."

"Let's take a vote. All those in favor of searching for the box, raise your hands," Saville said.

Saville and Lucy's hands shot in the air. Bea crossed her arms, and Fi remained glued to the spot, still glaring at Saville.

"Ooh, it's a tie." Saville dug into her pocket and produced a quarter. "Heads, we search for the treasure, and tails, we continue pounding on the walls."

Fi held out her hand. "Let me see that quarter. It's awfully suspicious you happen to have a quarter in your pocket. It's probably a two-headed trick quarter."

Saville smacked her hand against her chest. "I'm wounded. For the record, I have never once cheated in my life. Just because I don't have a metal rod up my ass does not mean I am a cheater." She handed the quarter to Fi. "My mom always taught me to have spare change in my pocket. She had a soft spot for homeless kids. It's a habit I never broke."

Fi looked at Saville as if she were discovering a brand new species. Without inspecting the quarter, she handed it back. "Fine, toss it in the air, but I'm calling it." Saville flipped the quarter in the air as Fi called, "Tails, we look for the box, and heads, we continue working." She stuck out her tongue again.

Saville laughed as she caught the quarter in her palm, effortlessly slapping it onto her other hand. "There's that tongue again. You better watch it, or I might do something rash with it. And tails it is. Treasure hunt time."

"Figures," Fi grumbled. "You are the luckiest damn woman. You always seem to get your way."

"Not always." Saville's expression faded, and her usual mirth slipped from view.

Heavy steps above interrupted the women's debate over the box, and all four women lifted their heads and looked to the stairs leading to the bedrooms above.

CHAPTER FIVE

"Right on cue. I reckon that's George," Saville said. "Let's go check it out. Maybe we'll catch him trying to hide the box."

Fi noticed the smile had returned to Saville's face. She was almost worried about the melancholy expression that occasionally appeared but was so out of character for the ordinarily flippant and playful woman she'd come to know.

"Reckon?" Fi shook her head.

"You can say the spirit moved me to adopt a colloquialism especially appropriate for the occasion," Saville called over her shoulder as she jogged up the winding staircase, closely followed by Lucy.

It amazed Fi how quick Lucy followed Saville up the stairs. Bea shrugged and began a slow climb, carefully navigating the area at the top of the stairs. She was adept at avoiding the piles of debris from the partially demolished wall.

"Lucy, please be careful," Fi called.

Saville methodically checked each room and then waved the group over to the farthest bedroom, placing her finger against her lips and pointing inside.

Although Fi had already seen George with her own eyes earlier that day, it surprised her to find the crouching figure in the corner of the small bedroom. Fi silently approached Saville and whispered into her ear, "What's he doing?"

"Hiya, George," Saville called. "Fi wants to know what you're doing? You wouldn't be trying to hide that box we found, now would you? Sorry, bud, but this place belongs to Lucy and Bea now. I hate to break this bad news to you, but you're dead and won't be needing it anymore."

George stood, reaching his menacing height, and hissed, "Leave. Now."

"Not gonna happen. Look, I know you aren't going to hurt a fellow sister. We're only curious about the box. You can't blame us for wanting to know what's so special inside," Saville answered.

George slumped against the wall and slid down, bowing as his head fell into his hands. Fi's compassion overtook her as she squatted before the broken ghost. She wanted to reach out and touch him. Comfort him. Instead, she quietly assured him, "I promise. We don't intend to add to your suffering. Lucy and Bea are good people." Fi glanced over her shoulder at Bea and Lucy, who remained frozen as they huddled close together. Bea's mouth hung open, while Lucy had a kind of serene expression on her face.

The ghost lifted his head and stared at Lucy, almost as if he recognized her. Then he stood and approached warily. Gliding around her body, he took in every detail. His hand extended as if he were about to stroke Lucy's cheek until Bea grabbed her wife and pulled her back.

"Stay away from my wife," Bea ordered.

A quizzical expression formed on George's weathered face, and Fi noted how much older George appeared than when she'd seen him from afar earlier. Maybe people aged more rapidly in the Old West, but George looked at least fifty to Fi.

"Ooh, I love it when you get all butch and protective," Lucy crooned.

Before returning to a standing position, Fi noted the piece of wood on the floor that was slightly ajar. She continued to watch as George let his arm fall back to his side but lingered to stare at Lucy.

"Would you like it if I got all butch and protective with you?" Saville whispered in Fi's ear. She turned to George and clapped her hands. "Okay, clearly, you're enamored with Lucy. What I'd like to know is how we break apart this little logjam? Any chance you'll give a pass on haunting us while we restore this old saloon? In exchange, you can ogle Lucy all you want, but no touching. She's married," Saville added as an explanation.

"Saville! How the hell did you make it past the age of twenty? That's Bea's wife you're offering as some prize heifer. That's beyond rude."

"I said no touching," Saville defended.

"I don't mind being ogled. At my age, I'll take anything I can get." Lucy turned to her wife. "Not that you don't do it for me, honey, or that we don't get enough sex. No complaints there."

Bea's face flushed red. "Can you please not announce our private business to every Thomasina, Vic, and Harriet?"

"What? These youngins should know that just because we're old, that doesn't mean we can't have great sex. Never let that pussy of yours dry up. Keep having sex, and it won't. I've heard a dry vagina is no fun at all. Use it or lose it, girls."

"I know, right? That's my motto, too," Saville chimed in.

"Of course it is," Fi added.

With all the sex talk, Fi hadn't noticed that George had disappeared again. She thought the other women hadn't spotted his absence either. She didn't know if that was a good or bad sign. Would George leave them alone now? She didn't know, but she thought it might be a good time to change the subject and tell the rest of the women about the board she'd spied that was off-kilter, suggesting another hiding spot under the floorboards.

"Um, I think George has left the building. At least for now. Do you think we got through to him?" Fi asked.

"No clue. But we should take advantage of the reprieve George is giving us. Let's check out that corner over there." Saville pointed at the floor. "I saw another loose board on the floor near where George was crouching."

"Where do you think he went?" Fi asked.

"Don't know. Wherever ghosts go when they're not haunting people. I suppose there could be a special waiting room or something and every ghost gets their turn for like ten minutes, then they have to come back."

Fi blew out her breath. "That's the most ridiculous thing I've ever heard."

"So now you're an expert on ghosts? Okay, what's your theory? I'm all ears." Saville pulled her ears out and smirked at Fi.

"Forget I said anything. Come on. Let's find the box, get it open, and then we can return to work. I really hate lagging on a job."

"Awesome." Saville didn't waste any time and found the loose board. Pulling it and another from the floor, she announced, "I found the metal box. And guess what else?"

Curiosity got the better of her, and Fi asked, "What?"

"There's a stack of letters here," Saville answered.

"I can't decide which I want to check out first. The letters or the box. Isn't this exciting, Bea? Maybe we won't have to do a bunch of research after all. The letters could answer all our questions about what happened to George and his family." Lucy did a little dance.

"What makes you think George had a family?" Bea asked.

"I don't know. It sort of popped into my head. Maybe he adopted, or his partner had a child before they got together. If he was living as a man, what better way to hide his identity than having a family?" Lucy suggested. "I don't suppose birth control was very effective. I'll bet the ladies of the evening had babies all the time. It'd be easy to pass one off as your own to help one of the painted ladies out."

Saville held out the letters, and Lucy quickly snatched them from her hand. "Fi, can you give me a hand with the box again?"

Fi grinned and started clapping her hands.

"Hardy, har, har. I didn't take you for a comedian."

"I have my moments." Fi squatted in front of the hole that Saville had created after removing several of the floorboards. They lifted the large box and set it to the side, well away from the hiding spot.

"Hey, there's something beneath the box," Saville exclaimed. "It's wrapped in some old silk." Saville pulled the small swatch of fabric from the hole. "The cloth seems to be wrapped around something small and solid. Ooh, it's a key, I think." Unraveling the silk, Saville held up the small key. "Ta-da!"

"Do you think that key fits the box?" Fi asked.

"Pretty sure it does. Unless there's another locked treasure to find." Saville closed one eye and squinted at the rest of the group. "Argh, I feel like a pirate, uncovering the buried treasure. A land pirate."

Fi laughed. "God, you're such a child. I don't remember reading about land pirates. Ever."

"Come on. Where's your imagination?"

"Screw imagination," Lucy declared. "I'm dying to find out what's in the box. Hurry and open it."

"All right. Calm your britches," Saville answered.

"Not wearing any." Lucy snickered.

Saville stuck the key into the lock and wiggled it a bit until she heard the click. Gently pushing the lid up, four sets of eyes peered into the metal box, and three out of the four exclaimed, "Holy shit."

†

"Do you think that's actual gold?" Lucy asked.

"If I had to make an educated guess, I'd say yes. Why would someone hide fool's gold in a locked box under floorboards?" Saville picked up one of the larger nuggets and held it out for inspection. "It sure is pretty. I wonder if it's worth more in this format before someone melts it down. You know, kind of like an antique. This is the real deal. I'm sure of it."

A genuine smile appeared on Bea's face. A rare sight since Lucy and Bea had finalized their purchase of the ghost town. Lucy knew Bea would do anything to make her happy, but it was no secret that Bea had lost a bit of sleep lately worrying about the cost of bringing the town back to its glory days and finding enough like-minded individuals to share their little corner of the world.

"Maybe the gold will pay for the entire reconstruction project. How about you take the gold, and we'll call it even?" Bea suggested. There was a teasing quality to her voice, but Lucy wondered if a part of her was serious. Not having to pull from their retirement funds and maybe not even sell the condo would undoubtedly take a huge load off.

"Really? I'm certainly willing to gamble on that proposition. I don't exactly know about the value of gold these days, but I'd be willing to bet this is far more than what we quoted," Saville said.

Lucy frowned. "Sounds fair to me. After all, the girls found the box and should get a finders' fee or something. So if it's worth a lot more, that should take care of the fact that they discovered the treasure. Quite proficient land pirates, if you ask me."

"Absolutely not. Saville and I would be happy to find out how much this is worth, but we aren't about to take advantage of you. A finders' fee isn't necessary. If you like the job we've done for you, you can add a bonus to the fee." Fi glared at Saville as if to dare her to object.

Saville held her hands in supplication. "Hey, don't set your death laser on me. I wasn't the one who suggested the deal. I just said it was a good one." Saville pulled her phone from her pocket. "I'm going to do a quick Internet search, just to get a ballpark figure. How much do you think the box weighs? It was pretty heavy. I'd say twenty pounds, minimum."

Fi nodded. "Probably a little more."

Saville started scrolling and typing quickly into her phone. "Okay, so it says here that twenty troy pounds are worth over four hundred thousand. And gold nuggets are worth about thirty percent more."

"What's a troy pound?" Lucy asked.

Saville shrugged. "No clue, but it says it's lighter than a regular pound." Saville kept typing into her phone. "Oh, here it is. A troy pound is about eighty-two percent of a customary pound."

Lucy jumped up and down and hugged Bea, spinning her around. "We're rich."

"Well, rich is a bit of hyperbole, but this certainly increases my comfort level with this project. Would you mind if I had a private word with Lucy?" Bea took Lucy's hand and pulled her into one of the other rooms that didn't have a partial wall from the earlier demolition.

†

Never in her wildest dreams had Bea imagined owning an entire town. A dilapidated one, but still. And now, they had found enough gold to pay for the restoration, and then some. Bea had an inner sense of fairness about her. Even in her limited knowledge of construction costs, she knew that Saville and Fi had seriously underbid the project. That hadn't sat right with her, but Bea wasn't sure they could afford a lot more. However, now she knew they had more than enough and wanted to compensate the young women starting out in their prospective businesses.

"I think we should share the gold. Give Saville and Fi at least twenty percent. Ten percent for each one. Do you think that seems fair, or should we offer more? Maybe we should wait until we know exactly how much the gold is worth. If it's worth a lot more than what we're going to pay them for the job, we can reconsider giving them more."

Lucy grabbed Bea by the shirt collar and pulled Bea in for a steamy kiss.

After catching her breath, Bea asked, "What was that for?"

"I love your practical side because it balances me out, but what I love most about you is your sense of fairness and generosity. I think it would thrill the girls to receive twenty percent. You old softy."

"I get the sense that both of them are struggling a bit. It can't be easy to compete with men in the construction industry, especially in this redneck part of the state. Sexism is definitely alive and well here. Don't you remember what it was like for us when we were younger? We should pay it forward."

"I love you." Lucy smiled adoringly at Bea. "Now, with that settled, we should talk about how to get those two together. They're obviously hot for one another. Maybe if I introduce Fi to my niece, the jealousy bug will hit Saville." Lucy held up her hand. "I'll tell Chelsey that I'm not trying to set her up. I'm sure she'll help once she meets both of them and sees what I see."

"Nothing I say is going to convince you not to go forward with this harebrained plan, is it?"

Lucy shook her head. "Come on, don't you want to see those lovely young women happy? I feel like we could all be friends, and it wouldn't hurt to surround ourselves with their youthful energy."

"Your youthful energy has been quite enough for me, but I suppose they are nice young women. Hard workers, too. Did you catch a glimpse of the other room? They got a lot further on the demolition than I thought they would. I'll bet they started at first light. I thought the younger generation was supposed to be slackers."

"That's Millennials, but I always hated those stereotypes and would argue every time some expert did a talk about dealing with the different generations in the workplace. Besides, Saville and Fi are Generation Z. Generation Z is known for their ambition and entrepreneurial spirit. I think that fits," Lucy answered. "We should rejoin them. They might worry about what we needed time to discuss. Besides, I'm eager to get a peek at those letters."

"You think they're love letters?"

"Don't you?"

"Such a romantic, you are."

"You're not fooling me one bit. I know you're just as curious and a true romantic at heart." Lucy kissed Bea on the cheek while tugging her arm and leading her back into the other room.

†

"What do you think they're talking about?" Fi shuffled her feet and began picking at her cuticles.

Saville laid her hand over Fi's. "Stop stressing out. I'm sure it isn't anything to do with us or this job. Why would they terminate the restoration? It makes little sense now that they have more than enough money to have us complete the job."

"I need this job. The restoration on my house cost a lot more than I thought it would, and I'm a little behind on the construction loan I took out to complete the remodel," Fi confessed as she bit the bottom of her lip.

"Did you underbid this job?" Saville asked.

"Not exactly, but I won't be making a ton of money, either. I hoped I could use this job as a springboard for other jobs. If I do quality work, then there's a chance I'll get more restoration work, which is what I have a passion for."

"You're good at what you do. Remember, I've seen your work."

"No, you haven't."

"Uh, duh, yes I have. I've had an intimate perusal of your brilliance."

"What the hell are you talking about?"

"Your house. I've seen every single corner of your place, including your gorgeous master bedroom. If I decide to stay here and buy an old house, I'm hiring you to do the work."

"You're thinking about moving?" Fi brought her hand to her mouth and bit the hangnail that had bothered her all morning.

"Aw, you care about whether I stay or go. That's sweet." Saville leaned casually against the wall.

"I didn't say that. I'm just curious why you want to move. I thought you were happy to be back in your hometown."

"It's what I know, but the work has also been sporadic for me. And don't even get me started on the limited number of lesbians in the area. I'd miss Darcy like crazy, but now that Darcy and Amelia are all domestic and trying to have a baby, I feel like a third wheel. Time for me to spread my wings. Besides, I'm barely getting by. I would like to purchase my own home someday. Even you have your own place."

"What's that supposed to mean? Even you."

"I did not mean it to be derogatory. I just meant that we're the same age, and you already have this awesome house. I haven't anything like that."

"Yeah, and I just confessed to the mountain of debt that goes with the house." Hearing Bea and Lucy re-enter the room, Fi turned her attention to the mature couple, eager to learn her fate. She'd have to follow up on her conversation with Saville at a later time. It disturbed Fi more than she wanted to admit that Saville would no longer be a mere thirty minutes away. Even though they hadn't seen one another for several months after the "mistake," she had missed spending time with Saville. Secretly, she had hoped they would resolve their issues, even if it killed her to be around Saville when she knew Saville didn't feel the same about her as she did about Saville.

"So, Lucy and I have come to a decision," Bea announced.

Fi sucked in air and held her breath for the bad news she knew was about to come her way.

"We're giving the two of you twenty percent of whatever we get for that gold. Ten percent for each of you," Lucy added.

Fi blinked her eyes. "What? You aren't canceling the project?"

"Of course not. We signed a contract," Bea stated. "Why would you think that? It makes no sense that we wouldn't continue to restore the town now that we have ample funds to pay for the job. Initially, it might not have exactly been my vision, but now we can turn this into a reputable retirement community, complete with a pool, fitness center, and clubhouse. This is going to rival any of those boring places in California, Arizona, or Florida. You should probably work up an estimate on adding those features."

"I'm not sure we can accept your generosity with the gold. You own this town and everything in it, which includes this gold. But I'd be happy to work up an amendment for the change orders. Saville might have to update her estimate as well for the additional electrical work."

Lucy bounced on her feet. "Can we add a hot tub next to the pool?"

Wide-eyed, Fi answered, "That would be easy to add, and probably more cost-effective to do it now, versus add it later." She couldn't believe her luck. Not only did the women still want to go forward, but they had also added several new projects.

"Speaking of cost-effective, we really must insist on sharing the gold. It didn't exactly sit right with me that your bid was so low. I knew the margin was so slim that I worried you wouldn't make much money at all on this project. Sharing the gold seems fair to me," Bea declared as Lucy nodded vigorously.

"We'll accept that generous offer. Because although my bid was slightly under what a contractor would normally quote, Fi's was ridiculously low." Saville gently squeezed Fi's arm. "Don't argue with your elders. We know best."

"You're not my elder," Fi responded with a slight smile on her face.

"Yes, I am. I'm six months older than you. Pisces have always drawn me in." Saville winked. "Actually, Leos and Pisces are quite compatible. At least that's what I read somewhere."

"You know my birthday and my sign," Fi answered incredulously.

Saville shrugged. "Yeah, I pay attention sometimes."

Fi realized they were getting off track and veering into a personal conversation that wasn't appropriate in front of Bea and Lucy. She felt uncomfortable with Lucy staring at her and smiling like she knew how Fi really felt about Saville.

It had cut her to the bone when Saville expressed regret over what was the most passionate night Fi had ever shared with another woman. Not that she had a lot of experience. To save face, Fi had quickly agreed that, yes, it was a mistake. She'd swallowed her confession about having feelings that went beyond friendship. She'd been angry about her inability to be truthful with Saville and had taken it out on her. Sure, Saville had hurt her, but could she blame Saville for not sharing those same feelings? It wasn't fair, but sometimes that was how raw emotion worked. People struck out in anger when someone they cared about hurt them.

Fi pushed back a lock of hair that had fallen out of her loose ponytail. "Um, okay, well, we really need to get back to work. I'll draw up the amendments tonight with the new numbers. Think about how big you want the pool, fitness room, and clubhouse. I might recommend creating something that will have all three. Perhaps an option for both an indoor and outdoor pool. Swimming is a popular exercise for mature women."

Lucy laughed. "Mature women. How politically correct. You mean for us old farts. I like the idea of having both. I don't know that we have the foggiest idea on size. Whatever you recommend."

"In the meantime, I don't want you two working on the saloon until we complete the demolition upstairs and make sure the subfloor is secure. I suppose you could work on restoring the old bar stools if you take them outside. These stools aren't as old as the structure, so someone must have purchased them later on. I don't believe the original Old West saloons had bar stools. The wood is solid but needs to be sanded, and then we'll put a protective coat on it to keep it looking good for years. Don't worry about the leather. I'll take care of that later."

"Oh, goody. I can't wait to get my hands dirty." Lucy pulled the bundle against her body in a protective hold. "I need to put these letters in the car. I don't want anything to happen to them."

Fi was curious about the stack of letters. She wanted to know more about the ghost and wished Saville hadn't already handed them to Lucy. She'd ask Lucy about them later, but they were falling behind and needed to make up time. "Right, then. Let me get my hand sander and sanding blocks." Fi began her descent and gasped as she ran into George at the bottom of the stairs. Or rather, ran through George before realizing what was happening. "Um, guys, George is back."

†

Saville rushed down the stairs, with Lucy following close behind. Although Saville could understand how George might have spooked the previous contractors, she got the sense that George would harm none of them, especially after his strange reaction to Lucy. George was an imposing figure, but that haunted expression in his eyes told a different story of loss and love that was hard to miss. Saville wished she'd held back the letters, but they weren't hers to keep. Technically, they weren't Lucy and Bea's either. She wondered if finding the letters had upset George, and he would try to keep Lucy from taking them out of the saloon.

George tilted his head and kept his gaze on Lucy. His eyes traveled to the stack of letters in Lucy's hand. "My letters," he whispered.

Fi stood rigid at the bottom of the stairs, while George floated closer to Lucy. Saville was hesitant to move as she watched the interaction between Lucy and George play out. Bea quickly came from behind to join Lucy.

"My letters?" Lucy repeated. "Are you upset that we removed your letters from their hiding place? We don't want to upset you, but we're curious."

"Pearl…" George lifted his luminous hand, attempting to caress Lucy's cheek, but like smoke, the outline of his hand dissolved on contact. Lucy shivered in response, and Bea placed a protective arm around her wife.

"She's not Pearl, whoever that is. She's Lucy, my wife, so keep your ghostly hands off of her," Bea stated.

Although it really wasn't funny, Saville put her hand over her mouth to keep from giggling. Saville had to hand it to Bea. Clearly, Bea wasn't about to take any shit from a hundred-plus-year-old ghost.

George narrowed his eyes at Bea, placing his hand on his gun. "You, leave. Pearl can stay."

"Oh, hell no…"

"Now, George. I'll be the first to admit that having two people fight over me is quite exhilarating, but Bea is my wife. If she goes, so do I. I also want you to leave our friends alone. Saville and Fi have done nothing to you, so stop being a bully. There's no excuse for your behavior," Lucy admonished. "I hope you had better manners when you were alive."

At the last comment, Saville could not keep her laughter at bay. Lucy lecturing a ghost as if he was a small child was too much for Saville to hold back her mirth. "Sorry, sorry. I'm not laughing at you. Either of you," Saville amended right before George's form faded again.

Fi sighed. "This is going to get old. I wish he would either stay, say his piece, and be done with it, or leave us the hell alone. This popping in and out is going to drive me crazy. Do you think it would be rude if we ignored him while we're working?"

"Well, Lucy seems to know how to handle him. I'm not sure that we can ignore him if he rattles the ladder again. You could have gotten hurt. Did you hear that, George? I'm talking to you. Not cool. So not cool. You'll piss Lucy off if you cause her contractor to take a spill, and it delays completion of this project." Saville looked around, wondering if George would respond. "He is like a child. I can almost hear him muttering, 'whatever.' I agree that his disappearing and appearing act is getting old."

"Maybe after we read the letters, we'll have a better idea of what we're dealing with." Lucy lifted the stack of letters in the air. "He looked sad, not scary to me. Do you girls want to come over tonight for dinner, and we can check them out?"

Fi glanced at Saville, who shrugged. "We'll probably be here late tonight. So we were going to get some Vietnamese takeout and do a little more exploring. Do you want to join us?"

"Sounds like a plan. I think I'll call Chelsey and have her join the party. She only lives thirty minutes from here." Lucy grinned at Bea who was shaking her head.

Saville wondered about the unspoken words between Bea and Lucy. Lucy was up to something. She could tell. "Chelsey? Who's that?"

"My niece. Cute as a button, single, and a lesbian. She's a teacher. A damn fine one, too. She loves her kids, and they love her right back. The parents are always raving about Chelsey, telling her she's their child's favorite teacher. You two would be perfect for each other, Fi."

Saville frowned. The prospect of Fi dating Lucy's niece did not sit well with her. "How come you're trying to set her up with Fi? What about me? I'm single and a lesbian."

Lucy flicked her hand. "She isn't interested in meeting players. She's had enough of that. Her words, not mine. That's not to say she or I have any judgment at all. I was a bit of a player myself until I met Bea."

Fi held her belly while she laughed. "Pegged you right off. I'd love to meet your niece, Lucy. She sounds lovely." Fi smirked at Saville, who was sure her sudden foul mood was showing.

"Maybe I should pass on this little love fest. I wouldn't want to be in the way." Saville knew she was pouting now, but it was hard not to react. She'd wanted to have a nice dinner with Fi while they explored the rest of the buildings, and now, not only had Fi invited Lucy and Bea, but the adorable Chelsey was coming.

Fi grinned while smacking Saville's arm lightly. "Don't be like that. Come on, don't you want to read those letters? Is seven too late for you? Hopefully, we'll have most of the demolition work complete by then."

"Sounds like a plan," Lucy answered. "Since we'll be out and about because we have to meet Amelia at our condo, we can pick up the food and bring it here. Just tell us what you want and where to go. We aren't very familiar with this area."

CHAPTER SIX

Lucy and Bea had left several hours ago, and Saville had been uncharacteristically quiet while they worked. Thankfully, George had left them alone while Fi and Saville secured the joists and removed both walls, opening the space a considerable amount. After Saville helped her remove the walls, a large open area remained that seemed perfect. Fi flipped her wrist to look at the time.

Saville had returned to the room after carrying another large load and tossing it into the dumpster Fi had arranged for the duration of the job. Wordlessly, she began picking up the final oversized pieces yet to be removed.

Fi grabbed the large broom and broke the silence. "Well, what do you think?" She pointed the edge of the broom at the inside of the newly opened space.

"It's larger than I thought. I'm sure it will be beautiful."

"I'm going to finish sweeping and then run home for a shower." Fi began sweeping.

"A shower? What? Primping for your big date?" Saville scowled. "Personally, I think you look sexy enough right now. That disheveled look really works on you." She reached over and plucked a small piece of wood from Fi's hair, then brushed at something on Fi's cheek. "Just a speck of dirt marring those impossibly high cheekbones of yours."

Fi felt her cheeks flush. She knew how to handle arrogant Saville. She didn't know what to make of the compliments or of this quiet, almost introspective side. Saville was upset, and Fi didn't enjoy seeing her this way. "Since we're done early, I'll meet you back here, okay?"

"I think I'll just go home. I'm exhausted. I rarely do demolition work, and it's kicked my ass. I think I found muscles I never knew about, and they are screaming at me."

"If I agree to give you a shoulder massage to help those wimpy muscles, will you come back and join us? It won't be the same without you. Besides, you were the one to suggest we get takeout and have an adventure."

"Yeah, an adventure with only the two of us, not with Chelsey, the wonder lesbian."

Fi chuckled. "I'm impressed you remembered her name. You don't even manage to do that with your dates."

"If you're just going to give me more shit, why would I come back for that?"

Fi stopped sweeping and rested on the broom. "Aw, come on. I'm sorry. I was teasing. Please. It won't be the same without you. Aren't you curious about those letters?"

"All right, but I'm going to spruce up as well. I can't have you showing me up. I'll pick up that cider you like."

"That's sweet, but you don't have to. Isn't it a hassle to carry on your motorcycle?"

"Nope. I've adapted well to carrying things on my bike."

†

"I still think you're playing with dynamite. What if Chelsey hits it off with Fi? Your big plan to get Fi and Saville together is going to backfire." Bea turned her head to catch Lucy's eyes while she drove them back to Georgetown Glen.

Lucy pursed her lips. "Shit, I didn't consider that as a possibility. Fi really is a lovely young woman. I guess I can see Chelsey hitting it off with her." Lucy shrugged. "Well, I suppose if that happens, then fate will have taken over, and I'll be happy for them."

"What about that chemistry you seem to insist is off the charts between Fi and Saville? I'll admit, it was pretty evident from Saville's reaction to Chelsey coming."

Lucy snickered. "Oh, yeah, did you see her face? It looked like she'd just sucked on a lemon. But I guess I would feel awful if Saville got hurt because of my scheming," Lucy amended.

"And that is why you should stay out of it. I'm not even going to say, 'I told you so' when this all blows up." Bea pulled her car next to Fi's truck, noting that Saville's motorcycle wasn't still there. She wondered if Saville might decide not to show, and Bea didn't know if that was a good or bad thing.

"Yes, you will. And I'll probably deserve it. But if two people find their soul mate, even if this leaves one out in

the cold, it'll be worth it. I'll find someone for the third
wheel once it all shakes out."

After undoing her seatbelt, Bea reached for one bag
while Lucy grabbed the other, along with a bottle of wine.
"Are we early?"

"I don't know, but it looks like Fi is the only one
here. Do you think Saville is going to blow us off? I figured
Chelsey wouldn't be here yet. She usually runs late."

Bea turned her head when she heard the loud rumble
of Saville's motorcycle. "There's your answer." She gestured
with her head toward the Harley, rolling in next to Fi's truck.
Chelsey's Prius followed close behind the bike.

"Perfect."

Saville dismounted, took off her helmet, and shook
her hair. Bea couldn't hear the conversation, but it looked
like Saville and Chelsey were introducing themselves as
Chelsey emerged from her car with several bottles of local
hard cider in her hands. Saville had a strained smile on her
face as she pulled her own six-pack of cider from her
saddlebag and lifted it for Chelsey to inspect.

"Let the games begin," Bea murmured. "I'm not sure
how friendly this little competition you've set up is going to
remain."

Fi emerged from the saloon and met the group as they
converged in front of the swinging doors. She waved at Lucy
and Bea and then turned her attention to Chelsey and Saville.
"Hi, you must be Chelsey. I can see the family resemblance."
Fi held out her hand as Chelsey shifted her cider to the crook
of her left arm.

Chelsey shook Fi's hand. "I just met Saville, so you
must be Fi. My aunt speaks highly of you. I'm glad you took
on this project. When Aunt Lucy told me about it, I was

excited for her and Aunt Bea. I'll get to see my aunts more now that they are closer to where I live. Although, I'm not so sure about this ghost business." Chelsey smiled.

"George was quiet as a church mouse this afternoon. He left us alone, which I'm thankful for. I'm looking forward to unraveling a little more of the mystery. He has to be hanging around for a reason. Maybe the letters will reveal what that is."

Chelsey scrunched her face. "There really is a ghost named George haunting this place that you've actually seen? I thought Aunt Lucy was pulling my leg."

"Nope. And to say that our first encounter was a bit unsettling would be an understatement. George rattled the ladder I was on hard enough for me to fall."

"Oh, my God. Are you okay? You didn't get hurt or anything, did you?"

"No, Saville was there and sort of caught me on my way down."

"Right place, right time," Saville added. "I don't think George wanted to hurt Fi. He only wanted to make his presence known. I see you brought pineapple cider. You know what they say about pineapples?"

"Don't you dare," Fi warned.

"What?" Saville held her hands out and grinned. "Aw, come on. I thought it was common knowledge among lesbians. But I don't think it applies to cider. You have to eat the real thing for your pussy to taste like pineapple."

Lucy laughed. "I did not know that. Bea, did you know that?"

Bea blushed. "Um, yes, I did read that somewhere. The article also mentioned other fruits and spices."

"Ooh, really." Saville pulled out her phone, balancing it in her right hand while still holding onto the cider. She began typing with one thumb. "I need to find that article."

Fi grabbed Saville and pulled her toward the swinging doors, interrupting her Internet search. "Come on, you need to behave, and I'm starved."

The corner of Saville's mouth turned up as she looked back at Chelsey, who followed the two young women into the saloon. "I didn't offend you, did I, Chelsey? We're all women here. By the way, the blackberry cider I brought is her favorite." Saville returned her phone to her back pocket.

"Good to know. I'll be sure to bring that the next time I come around," Chelsey answered.

"That brand of pineapple cider is excellent. Thanks for bringing it," Fi said.

Bea looked around the bar, and although they had not refinished the wood yet, it looked like someone had tidied the place. She could envision how magnificent the saloon would be once they restored it to its original splendor. Five camping chairs sat in the middle of the mostly empty bar, along with a small card table. Bea set her bag of takeout and the bottle of wine on the table.

"Shit on a cracker," Lucy exclaimed. "You know what we forgot?" Lucy set the bag of food on the table but continued to hold on to the other bottle of wine.

"No, what?" Bea asked.

"Wine glasses and a corkscrew."

"I have my Swiss Army knife in my car. I'll get it, Aunt Lucy. But, I can't help you out with the glasses." Chelsey set her pineapple cider on the crowded table next to the food.

Saville found a spot on the table for her cider, then whipped out her Swiss Army knife. "I've got it. Never know when I might need to rescue a beautiful woman, so I always carry mine in my pocket." She took the bottle from Lucy and efficiently pulled the cork from the bottle. "We can drink the cider. That way, the two of you can drink straight from the bottle. It isn't like you haven't swapped spit with one another. I assume you brought the cider for yourself, Chelsey."

"I'm happy to drink cider, but I brought it to share. Aunt Lucy mentioned y'all drank beer and cider. I thought the cider would go better with Vietnamese food."

"So, Chelsey, you're a teacher, huh? I'll bet you have to be careful. Kids are like little Petri dishes, smearing their germs all over you. Hopefully, you showered after work. You probably can't stay out late, either, with it being a school night and all," Saville said.

Chelsey wrinkled her nose. "Uh, it's summer. School is out. I do some private tutoring in the summer, but I'm good."

"Oh, right, yeah. I forgot that teachers only work nine months out of the year. Must be nice."

"Actually, most teachers work other jobs in the summer to make ends meet, but it is wonderful to have free time when the weather is pleasant. Plus, having the summer off gives me time to help Aunt Lucy and Aunt Bea with their new venture. I thought I might start coming here to help. I'm relatively handy with a hammer. I'm taking on fewer students this summer so I can assist my favorite aunts."

"It's probably not a good idea to add more people to the mix. You never know how George will react or if the subfloor collapses. I wouldn't want you to ruin your nails or get those lily-white hands dirty." Saville crossed her arms.

†

Fi had about had enough of Saville's antics. "Excuse us for a minute, please." Fi dragged Saville to the far corner of the room and hissed, "Stop being an a-hole."

Chelsey seemed like a delightful woman. Lucy was spot on about that. It didn't escape Fi that Chelsey was adorable. Besides, Fi was a sucker for dimples and freckles. Chelsey had both, along with wavy dark hair that barely touched her shoulders. Rare emerald green eyes, a heart-shaped face, and full pink lips came together in perfect symmetry. By most people's standards, Chelsey was a beautiful woman. But the sad truth was Fi was still more drawn to Saville than Chelsey, even after Saville's complete assholery act the minute she met Chelsey. It honestly surprised Fi that Saville hadn't tried to hit on Chelsey. She imagined Chelsey was her type.

"Don't tell me you're interested in her?"

"If I am, it's none of your business who I choose to date."

"It is if she's going to come to the worksite and mess up our mojo. I'm not going to sit around and watch you two make goo-goo eyes at one another while I'm busting my ass."

"What the hell are you talking about? We probably won't even be in the same rooms. I'll give her the same tasks that I give Lucy and Bea. They'll be far from the danger areas where you and I will be working."

"Fine, but don't come crying to me when that Jezebel breaks your heart. With looks like that, no way is she not a player."

"So, I'm not a player because I'm plain. Because surely, I don't have the looks to screw everything with a pulse and a pussy. Is that what you're saying?"

"No. You're the exception to the rule. Hot and nice."

Fi shook her head. "Thanks, I think. Just be polite, okay? I know that deep down, you have the capacity for kindness, so show a little of it, will you?"

Saville bowed. "Anything for you. Blackberry is still your favorite, right?"

"Yes, but it's not a competition. I like the pineapple, too."

"But you like what I brought better."

"God, you're such a child. Yes, the blackberry is still my preference."

Saville pumped her fist in the air. "Yes! Round one to me."

Fi smacked her hand against her forehead. "This is going to be a very long night."

CHAPTER SEVEN

After putting away the leftover food, Lucy ran back to their car and retrieved the letters. It had taken all her willpower not to undo the silk ribbon and begin reading them. Pulling on the ribbon that tied the stack of letters together, Lucy began inspecting them. After opening the letter on top, she noted, "This one has a date at the top. Let me see if the others have dates on them. We should probably read them in chronological order." She gently set the letter aside and opened the next one in the stack.

The rest of the women sat back in their chairs, sipping their adult beverages. On a whim, Saville had checked behind the bar and found two glasses, but since there wasn't any running water to clean them out, Lucy and Bea had opted to drink from the bottle, giggling like schoolgirls. Lucy loved bringing out Bea's lighter side.

After opening each letter and noting the date at the top, Lucy announced, "They are already in order. I'll start with this bottom letter. Anyone opposed to me reading it out loud?"

"Go for it, Aunt Lucy," Chelsey exclaimed.

"'September 20th, 1908,'" Lucy began. "'Dear Papa. I wish you were here with us on this grand adventure. Mama and I found comfort in the Pullman Berth, and thank your foresight, as the trip is long and tiring. I wish you could have joined us. You would have loved the dining car. The elegance compares with The Gold Nugget. Mama sends her love. She misses you terribly. As do I. By the time you receive this letter, we will be in Boston. I shall write more about our adventure when we arrive at Wellesley. Your loving daughter, Pearl.'"

"Wow, Lucy! You were right. George had a daughter. Do you think she married her lover and passed Pearl off as their own?" Saville asked.

Lucy set the letter aside and picked up the next one. "Maybe the rest of the letters will fill in the blanks."

Bea twirled her hand in a gesture for Lucy to continue. "Well, go on, read the next one."

"You old softie. I knew you would love this. Okay." Lucy continued, "'September 25th, 1908. Dear Papa. Mama helped me settle into College Hall, and I met my roommate today. Clara is from Chicago. I feel so common compared to her. The West is nothing like Boston. I pray Clara does not consider me uncouth and provincial. She has assured me we will become close, and I already feel affection toward her. She is so beautiful and sophisticated. I am thankful for the new dresses you commissioned for us. Without those, I would certainly feel like a fish out of water. Your letter was waiting for us upon our arrival. I felt such gratitude to learn all is well back home. I understand the importance of your job but must admit to secretly wishing you had accompanied us on this journey. Perhaps you will find a temporary replacement and can visit Boston in the future. It is such a great city. Your loving daughter, Pearl.'"

"Poor George. This must have been such a hard time for him. To be apart from both his daughter and lover. I can't imagine how lonely he felt with both of them gone. I never went across the country to college, but I doubt either of my parents would have gone with me to settle into the dorms if I had. Do you think that's what people did back then? Accompany their children across the US to help them settle into college?" Fi asked.

"Considering all the gold we found, I'm betting George wanted her to have the best of everything, including a solid education." Saville picked up the letter on top of the stack. "I say we cut to the chase and read the last letter."

"Ugh, you're one of those," Fi remarked.

"What's that supposed to mean?"

"You go to the end of a book and read the ending, don't you?" Fi plucked the letter from Saville's hands.

"Hey, what's wrong with that? I prefer not to waste my time if the ending sucks. Only happily ever after for me." Saville held out her hand. "Now, give it back. I wasn't going to read it out loud."

Fi scrunched her face. "Don't tell me you read romance novels."

"Yeah, what's wrong with that? Most seem to have steamy sex scenes. What's not to like about that?"

Fi chuckled. "Nothing. Not a single thing. I'm not giving you this letter back. Just because you read the endings prematurely doesn't mean the rest of us are inclined to travel that same heinous road. That's blasphemy if you ask me. Authors put their heart and soul into a book. You should read from start to finish, not cheat along the way."

"I read the last few pages once I'm familiar with the characters. I'm with Saville on this. Life is too short to waste my time on a shitty ending." Lucy grinned. "I also agree with those sex scenes in romance novels, but might I recommend erotica. Twice as steamy." Lucy pointed to the letter in Fi's hand. "Go for it, Saville. I'm a bit curious myself."

"We should take a vote," Bea offered. "Read them in chronological order or skip to the end. All those who want to keep reading them in order, raise your hand."

Chelsey and Fi raised their hands.

"Figures that Chelsey, the wonder lesbian would vote with Fi," Saville mumbled, barely audible to Fi and Lucy.

"I assume you and Saville want to read the last letter. Well, I guess we have a tie," Bea announced.

"You need to be the tiebreaker, my love."

"Oh, I don't think so," Bea answered.

"Aw, come on, if you don't break the tie, I know Saville will barrel on as if she's won the vote." Fi clutched the letter to her chest.

A sheepish expression crossed Bea's face. "I will occasionally read the last page of a book, so I guess I'm okay with reading the last letter."

"Fine, here you go, but I'm going to take a walk because I don't want to skip to the end. Chelsey, do you want a tour of the other buildings while they read ahead?" Fi handed the letter to Lucy, then stood and stretched her body, revealing a toned abdomen that both Chelsey and Saville openly stared at.

"Sure," Chelsey answered amiably.

Saville scowled. "Sore loser."

"I am no such thing. Have fun, ladies. We'll be back." Fi offered her hand to Chelsey, who accepted it, and pulled her to her feet.

†

"I'm sorry about Saville. It isn't like her to be so surly."

"Jealous," Chelsey offered.

Fi frowned. "I doubt that's why she's acting like she is. Normally, if there's an attractive woman within a ten-mile radius, she turns on the charm, especially if that woman is a lesbian."

"Look, you seem like a nice person, so I'm going to be honest with you. I love my Aunt Lucy. She's definitely quite the character, but sometimes she can stick her nose where it doesn't belong. She's always trying to play matchmaker. She had this harebrained notion I should show up tonight to make Saville jealous. I didn't want any part of her misguided plan. I told her that, but I wanted to see this ghost town she bought. So here I am." Chelsey tilted her head and held out her arms.

"I know. This place is incredible, and I can't believe I get to be the one to restore it to its former grandeur. Winning this bid was insanely awesome in more ways than one." When they reached the old hotel, Fi lovingly stroked the outside wall. "The wood from years ago was so much sturdier than the crap they sell today. I scrounge around junkyards and recycle places, looking for materials that will fit whatever restoration project I'm working on. When I restored my house, I got almost everything I needed by being patient enough to find the right wood."

"Aunt Lucy told me you were the perfect choice for the job. She's right. I can see the passion in your eyes. I'm a historical romance fanatic with a specific passion for certain time periods. The history of the Old West has always fascinated me. Hollywood gets it all wrong, you know?"

"How do they get things wrong?" Fi asked.

"First, there were two types of 'bad'"—Chelsey made air quotes with her hands—"girls. Saloon and dance hall women and painted ladies. The dance hall girls were not typically prostitutes. They would sing and dance for the men, encouraging the men to buy whiskey." Chelsey followed Fi into the hotel, carefully navigating the well-worn steps.

Chelsey continued her mini-history lesson. "Sometimes, they would keep them company by talking with the lonely men who outnumbered the women in the Old West by at least three to one. The more whiskey the men drank, the more the saloon girls made. While the proper women of the time looked down on the saloon girls, the men considered these women reputable and would often lavish them with gifts. The painted ladies were the prostitutes of the time and hung around the shabbier saloons. The one here would probably not have had painted ladies. Even though the bar is old, there is an elegance to the carving that surely suggests this was not a shabby saloon in its heyday."

"Hmm, what about all the bedrooms upstairs? I just assumed they were for the prostitutes."

"Doubtful. Although, I'm certain there were 'painted ladies' in this town. Most Old West towns had them. In fact, they usually outnumbered the 'proper' ladies by as much as twenty-five to one. I'm not sure which of these buildings was the bordello, but that's where they would have entertained customers, not in the saloon. The other misnomer is that the Wild West wasn't that wild. It was far more civilized and peaceful than we're led to believe."

"How do you know all this? Are you some kind of history buff?"

"Kind of goes with the territory. I'd have to love history to teach it. Fortunately for me, social studies teachers were in high demand, and then I found my calling with history and politics." Chelsey turned her focus on Fi. "It's probably none of my business, but what I saw tonight kind of gives credence to Aunt Lucy's theory. I still don't like being part of any game playing, though. Have you told Saville how you feel about her?"

"What?" Fi sputtered.

"It's obvious that you two are into each other. Which is honestly too bad because this is one matchmaking scheme I would have embraced if Aunt Lucy had tried to get us together."

"It's complicated with Saville and me. We were friends before. Good friends. And then one night, we crossed a line and haven't been able to return to our friendship. It was a big mistake that both of us agreed should never happen again. It's been awkward and tense ever since."

"I see. Maybe it wasn't such a mistake, at least not from where I'm looking. Sometimes a person needs to take a step back to gain perspective. Perhaps that's what you both are trying to do," Chelsey suggested.

"Doubtful. Saville is a total commitmentphobe. We don't want the same things. She made that abundantly clear." Fi looked at the ceiling. "God, isn't that chandelier stunning? I can't believe it's still here and in good shape. With a little elbow grease, it should give the purest diamond a run for its money."

"Have you ever considered there might be a reason for Saville's apparent allergy to commitment? I know this is cliché to say, but maybe she's had some bad relationship experiences."

"Allergy to commitment. That's funny. It's probably why Saville seems to sneeze pickup lines as easy as breathing. And she's not even thirty yet. How much can a person have had their heart broken at that young age?"

"Isn't that what Saville did to you? Aren't you the same age? I'm just saying that different people react differently to rejection. If Saville was trying to hide her feelings, she wasn't doing a very good job of it. Neither were you. I doubt either of you really believes that when you crossed that line, it was a mistake. You should talk to her. And, if it doesn't work out, maybe you'll call me." Chelsey smiled, prominently displaying her dimples.

Dammit, why can't I fall for someone like Chelsey? As that thought crossed her mind, Fi wondered if she would ever have the nerve to be honest with Saville. She barely knew Chelsey and had already mostly spilled her guts.

"I suppose working on this town will give me ample opportunity if I ever gather the courage to show my vulnerability with Saville. In the meantime, if your offer is sincere, I'd love to get your digits. Sometimes it's hard to hang out with my best friend, Amelia. She's found domestic bliss with her wife, Darcy. I'm always the third wheel when I go to their farm for dinner."

Chelsey held out her hand. "Sounds good to me. Friends without benefits. At least until you figure things out with Saville. I'm willing to leave the door open for more if the Goddess of fate so decries."

Fi shook Chelsey's hand and was glad to have made another lesbian friend. "We better get back before the pout on Saville's face calcifies."

Chelsey giggled. "She does like to get her way, doesn't she?"

†

Saville watched as Fi and Chelsey ambled into the saloon. She looked for any clue that Chelsey had made her move. Although Fi and Chelsey appeared friendly with one another, Saville didn't see any sparks flying between the two of them. She would need to have a long, hard talk with herself to uncover why she'd acted the way she had. Lucy had politely taken her to task earlier. She had been rude.

"So? Did you figure out the mystery yet by reading the last letter?" Chelsey asked.

"Saville felt bad, so she suggested we wait until the two of you returned," Lucy answered.

"And if you really want to continue reading the letters in chronological order, we'll do that," Saville added.

Fi raised her eyebrow. "So what have y'all been up to while we were touring the hotel?"

"Drinking adult beverages." Saville lifted her bottle of cider and took a swig. "We're way ahead of you two now." Setting her bottle on the ground, she grabbed two bottles, expertly removing the caps and handing one each to Chelsey and Fi. "Um, I realized with Lucy's help that I've been a little surly. Sorry about that. I'll try to behave myself."

"It's getting late, so if you have to read the last letter, fine by me. It's not that important for me to win the argument," Fi offered.

"Okay with me, too, but I will want to read every letter to get a better feel for what happened. I'm a little disappointed that George has not made an appearance." Chelsey returned to one of the camp chairs and lifted the bottle to her lips.

Lucy retrieved the last letter and was about to begin reading, when all five pairs of eyes turned toward a squeak on the winding staircase.

"My letters," George wailed.

"Oh, shit. George doesn't seem thrilled about us reading his letters," Saville noted.

Lucy gathered the letters into a small pile. "We meant no harm. We're just curious about what happened."

"My sweet Pearl." A tear fell from George's eye. "You've grown old, and we weren't there for you." George glided to Lucy and stared down at her.

Bea grabbed Lucy's hand in a protective gesture.

"George, we're trying to unravel the mystery by reading these letters, but your wife and daughter have been dead for many years. You have to realize that, right?" Saville stated as calmly as she could. She figured if she didn't flinch in front of George, things would go much better for the entire group. She hoped George respected someone who stood their ground.

George's attention pivoted to Saville. But then, as if dismissing a lowly peasant, he returned his attention back to Lucy, leaning in for a closer look. "Why did you stay away so long?" With his final plea, George once again dissipated.

Chelsey's eyes widened. "Oh. Holy. Hell. I thought Aunt Lucy was exaggerating. This town really does have a ghost. So, that was George. Does he do that often?"

"Do what often?" Fi asked.

"Pop in, say a few cryptic words, then pop out," Chelsey answered.

"Yeah, that's kind of his thing. Other than the first time we met when he rattled the ladder or when he ordered us to leave, he's been a relatively tame ghost." Saville shrugged.

"Why was he looking at you like that, Aunt Lucy?" Chelsey leaned in and propped her arms on her legs.

Lucy shrugged. "I don't know. Maybe I look like his dead wife."

"Hey, didn't your mother's family live in Boston?" Chelsey inquired. "Do you think you're related? Wouldn't that be something if you're a descendant? Good thing you bought this town."

"I never met my great-grandmother. My mother told stories about her. Apparently, I look just like her. I saw a picture once of her when she was young. She had her arm around another young woman. They looked very cozy. They were standing in front of this enormous brick building with these pointed dome-like steeples."

"Is the picture with those albums you took for safe-keeping after Grandmom died? I remember flipping through them as a kid, and Grandmom told us stories about her aunts and uncles. I don't remember that picture. I think I would have remembered if it looked like my favorite aunt." Chelsey leaned back in her chair.

"I do still have the family albums, but a few are a bit mangled. Unfortunately, I had them in a box in my truck when my car and I took a swim in the river," Lucy answered.

Chelsey giggled. "Yeah, I remember that story. It was icy or something, and instead of calling 911, you called Aunt Bea."

"I didn't know what to do. The ass of my car had submerged in the river while the rest dangled on the rocks. I had high heels on," Lucy declared, as if that was the reason for calling her partner instead of the police. "How was I supposed to climb over those slippery rocks?" she added. "I was only a few minutes late for work, but I called anyway. My staff thought it was hilarious to save the voice message. I suppose I was a bit rattled by the whole ordeal. I can't swim, you know."

"So, the photo. Do you still have it?" Chelsey asked.

"I think so. Many of the photos were marked with dates. Some had names, some didn't. I never knew my great-grandmother's name because Mom just called her Nona. I think that means grandmother in Italian. I guess my grandfather was a wealthy Italian financier. We joked about having roots in the Italian mafia, but those jokes always offended Mom. She said the family money came from owning large olive groves and wineries in Italy, and her ancestors were not thugs."

"You should definitely dig out those old photo albums. I'd love to see them again. Maybe I could take over being the keeper of those pictures since I'm the historian in the family."

"That sounds like the best idea all evening. We had to rent a storage unit for all our crap when we moved from the house. Lucy is a secret hoarder. I'm signing her up for the TV show," Bea teased.

"I am not. You kept all those vinyl albums, and we don't even have a turntable, so I think you win the hoarder contest."

Chelsey giggled. "No, I think Grandpa wins, hands down. I swear he had those ugly oil paintings in every room the last time I visited, including the laundry room. I don't even know what colors the walls are because there is literally no open space anywhere. I feel sorry for the housekeeper with all those figurines. Grandmom would roll in her grave to see what he's done to the place. She was such a neat freak."

"Oh, they don't dust the figurines. But, I'm sure it's challenging to clean Dad's house." Lucy shook her head. "He used to have these ghost ants all over his kitchen counters, so we bought traps for them. But this year, it was so disgusting, even the ants left. Cockroaches don't have the same standards. He leaves everything for the housecleaner, including his grimy dishes with caked-on food. I might have to send them every other week now. Because once you have cockroaches, they're damn near impossible to get rid of."

"Will you have time to look for the old photo?" Saville asked. "It would be interesting to see it. You could bring it to the site tomorrow."

"We can go to the storage unit tonight and grab the two boxes full of the family albums. If it's there, I'll find it." Lucy stood. "We should probably call it an evening if I'm going to scrounge through all those albums to find the picture."

"What about the last letter? I'm dying for you to read that," Saville said.

"I guess you'll have to live with a little delayed gratification for once, Miss Read The Last Page." Fi stuck out her tongue.

"At least I do more with my tongue than act like a five-year-old. Do we need to have another session on the proper use of one's tongue?" Saville smirked.

"Well, I'm definitely coming back tomorrow to help. First, I want to see that picture and have Lucy read the rest of the letters," Chelsey interrupted.

Saville wondered if her last comment was out of line. Maybe she would ask Lucy. She'd been serious about reining in her jealousy after Lucy gently took her to task. Or maybe Chelsey was a bit of a prude and uncomfortable hearing anything about Saville and Fi's hook-up. Saville frowned. Hook-up wasn't precisely the correct term to use. Regardless, it seemed as though Chelsey intended to ingratiate herself into their ghost-hunting adventures, which meant more time with Fi. Saville did not like how this was turning out. No, she did not like one bit of it. *Would it be horrible if I gave Chelsey the dirtiest jobs to accomplish? Maybe something very tedious, like cleaning the chandelier in the hotel. That would take some time to complete and keep her away from Fi.* An evil grin appeared on Saville's face.

"What are you grinning about?" Fi asked. "I thought you'd internally combust, knowing you have to wait another day to read the last letter."

"Oh, no, I have the patience of Job. I'm just happy to have another body to help. Chelsey can clean the chandelier at the hotel tomorrow while the rest continue working on the saloon. We can order pizza for tomorrow night, then finish reading the letters. Of course, it won't be convenient for you to go home and primp after work. Are you okay with that?" Saville directed her question to Fi.

"Fine with me. Sounds like a plan." A forced smile appeared on Fi's face. When the smile did not reach Fi's eyes, Saville knew it was anything but fine with her. Saville thought Fi was stunning, even covered in dust. She didn't need to shower and change for Saville to believe Fi was the most striking woman she'd ever met. And that was saying a lot since she'd met a fair number. Would Chelsey feel the same way?

Lucy gathered her letters. The rest of the group quickly cleaned the area, folding the camp chairs and helping Fi carry them to her truck. After the rest of the group had left, Saville leaned against Fi's truck and asked, "So, did Chelsey ask you out?"

"None of your business," Fi responded.

"I'll take that as a yes."

"For your information, she thinks we have a thing for each other. She only gave me her number as a friend."

"Sure, she did. You are so oblivious to other people hitting on you."

"She did not hit on me. We had an enjoyable conversation that did not include, 'Hey, why don't you come over later and we can fuck like bunnies.'"

"I never said anything like that to you. Look, I know I told you it was a mistake, but I regret how I phrased everything. I could have been, uh, more diplomatic. I'm sorry."

Fi raised her eyebrow. "You're just jealous because one of your play toys found another woman attractive and interesting."

113

"Aha, I knew it. You want to date Chelsey. She looks fourteen, you know. How can you sleep with someone who looks so young? By the way, you are not and have never been one of my play toys."

"No one said anything about sleeping with her, and I find her dimples and freckles adorable. She does not look fourteen. Can we not do this right now? It's late, and I want to get another early start tomorrow."

"Fine. Okay. But can we have dinner this weekend? Just the two of us. I want to have an adult conversation with you about, you know, what happened between us. Clear the air, once and for all."

"Fine. We can have dinner on Sunday. I'd like to keep that day open and not come out here to work."

"I'll bring something to grill. Do you want beer or cider?"

"You don't have to always bring the food and alcohol. I'll get beer and cider for us."

"It's a date." The words flew from Saville's mouth before she censored them.

Fi opened, then closed her mouth and simply nodded.

CHAPTER EIGHT

Fi and Saville worked without incident for three hours before Chelsey, Lucy, and Bea arrived at the worksite. The way Lucy wiggled around with excitement suggested she was bursting at the seams to share something with Saville and Fi. She carried the stack of letters on top of a box of donuts, while Bea brought the Coffee Traveler from Starbucks—ninety-six ounces of pure black gold. Fi needed a small pickup with hot coffee versus the lukewarm cup that remained in her thermos. She silently thanked the coffee gods and mumbled a quick thanks to Lucy.

Fi wanted to put Lucy out of her misery since it was apparent Bea was having a hard time keeping her from spilling whatever news she had. "Saville and I were just about to take a break."

"We were?" Saville asked.

115

Fi gestured toward Lucy, with a subtle tilt of her head in Lucy's direction.

Lucy's smile grew wide. "I brought the picture. Although it was a little water damaged, the date marked on the back is March 27th, 1909, and I can clearly make out the name Clara. The rest of the writing is blurry."

Fi reached for the box of donuts and carried them to the bar. "I'll grab the camp chairs and table, and we can dig into this box of pure sugary goodness. Then I would love to see that picture. And maybe we can take a few minutes and have you read the last letter."

"I'm so sorry, but after I found this picture, the coincidences were far too great to ignore, and I read the last letter. We also looked up Wellesley College, and the building Nona and Clara are standing in front of is College Hall," Lucy frowned, then continued, "which burned down in 1914. I imagine Nona would have completed her education prior to the building catching fire, but the trauma of learning about her old hall would have been nothing compared to learning the fate of her parents."

"Wow! I agree. Everything seems to line up. Oh my God, you're George's great-great-granddaughter, Lucy. No wonder he keeps trying to touch you," Saville exclaimed. "What's in the last letter? Any clue about what happened when Pearl returned home to learn about the fate of her parents?"

"Sort of. I have my theories, but nothing definitive," Lucy answered.

"Will you help me with the chairs?" Fi asked.

"Sure," Chelsey and Saville said in unison.

Uh oh. Fi wondered if she would need to play referee today between the two women.

116

After Fi, Chelsey, and Saville retrieved the camp chairs and table from Fi's truck, Bea set the Coffee Traveler on the table along with cups, sugar, and cream. Lucy set the donuts on the table next to the coffee, then pulled a picture from the stack of letters and handed it to Chelsey. The group settled into their chairs, each grabbing a donut and a cup of coffee.

"Wow! Nona looks a lot like you, especially when you were younger. Grandmom also looks a lot like Nona. I wish I'd gotten those same genes. Your beauty is timeless. I hope to look half as good as you when I reach my golden years, Aunt Lucy." Chelsey handed the picture to Fi's outstretched hand.

"They look so happy," Fi noted as she turned over the picture to inspect the back. "The resemblance is uncanny." She handed the picture to Saville.

"Oh yeah, I can see the family resemblance to the woman on the right. Damn, they're both total hotties," Saville exclaimed. "Okay, the suspense is killing me. Can you please read the last letter now?"

Lucy smiled and then began. "'Dear Papa and Mama. I grow more worried each day that passes without a letter from home. Since my last three letters have gone unanswered, I fear that one or both of you have taken ill. I do hope that whatever is causing the delay in your response resolves itself quickly.'"

"Oh, no! She doesn't know that her parents died. How sad," Fi remarked before biting into a donut. "Sorry, please continue," Fi said around the bite of her donut, covering her mouth to hide her absence of manners.

Lucy sipped on her coffee and then resumed reading. "'My other fear is that I have upset or disappointed you with

117

my prattling about options for the summer break. Did you wish for me to accept Joseph's marriage proposal and suggestion to vacation abroad for the summer? Joseph is a fine man that I am sure both of you would approve of, yet I believe his proposal is premature.'"

"Smart woman. There is no way I would have accepted a marriage proposal at eighteen or nineteen," Saville interjected.

"You wouldn't have accepted a marriage proposal from a man or woman at any age," Fi noted.

Saville shrugged. "Just saying, she was too young to get married."

"Not really," Chelsey said. "Back in the early 1900s, some women married even younger than eighteen. A woman was an old maid at twenty-five. Sorry, Aunt Lucy, we keep interrupting."

Lucy adjusted her reading glasses before continuing to read. "'I have not given an answer yet, but I am inclined to refuse his offer to marry until I have completed my studies. I wish to accept Clara's offer to accompany her and her family on their annual journey to Europe for the summer months.'"

"Do you think Clara and Pearl had something going on between the two of them?"

"Maybe. Pearl talks about her fondness for Clara in the letter. But I don't think they ever entered into a Boston marriage. She married and had five other children besides my grandmother. So maybe they had a fling," Lucy suggested. "They do look cozy in the picture."

"Oh yeah, that would have been more common," Chelsey noted. "I suspect even if she was a lesbian and insisted on finishing her degree, she probably capitulated to what society expected of her. Marriage and family."

Lucy grinned. "Shall I continue, or would you like to resume your discussion of lesbianism in the 19th century?"

"Sorry, Lucy. Please go on," Saville directed.

"'I've grown quite fond of Clara, and she insists I would do her a great favor should I decide to accompany her and her family on their European vacation. However, if you would prefer that I return home after my examinations, I remain your loyal and loving daughter and will do as you advise. I hope you find the time to respond before the end of the school term. Mama does not need to make the journey east, as I can make the arrangements to travel on my own. I eagerly await your response. Your loyal and loving daughter, Pearl.'" Lucy finished reading and then relaxed into her chair.

"So, I'm dying to hear your theories." Saville leaned forward, propping her head on her hand.

"Well, I don't believe that Pearl ever came home. Otherwise, surely she would have found the gold and the stack of letters."

"No way would she have stayed in Boston while receiving radio silence from her parents. Clearly, she loved them both," Fi noted.

"They had telegrams back then. Maybe someone intercepted the last letter from Pearl and sent a telegram to let her know what happened. If at least one of the dance hall girls knew George's secret and supported George and his wife, surely she would have told Pearl what occurred."

"But then why wouldn't Pearl have gone home to lay her parents to rest?" Saville asked.

Lucy shrugged. "I don't know. My guess is that it was a pretty gruesome sight. And whatever kind soul sent the notice did not want Pearl to hear the entire story. Perhaps she was protecting Pearl from the truth about her father."

"That's a pretty big secret to keep." Bea finally entered the conversation after remaining quiet during the earlier discussion and reading of the letter.

"Unless we find a journal or this telegram you theorize some random saloon girl sent, we'll never know," Chelsey said. "Most Old West towns did not keep careful records, other than official court or land records. Letters and journals contain most of what we know about the Old West."

"Mom had a stack of old documents that I threw into one of the boxes with the old picture albums. I've never gone through that because I was more interested in the family photos. We could get lucky," Lucy stated. "I'd pay a hundred thousand dollars for a journal recording what happened back in 1909."

"You never know. Maybe George has something up his sleeve and will lead us to another incredible discovery," Fi suggested.

"I love research. If there is a museum or historical society near here, I'll try to find anything related to George and his family. How did you first learn about George?" Chelsey asked.

"Amelia, our real estate agent, 'fessed up,'" Bea answered.

"I'll ask her about it. I planned to have dinner at Darcy and Amelia's place on Saturday to catch up because I've been so busy I haven't talked to them lately," Fi said.

"They invited you to dinner, but not me?" Saville pouted.

"Oh, um. I called Amelia last night to tell her about the gold and letters we found. I thought she might be interested."

Saville whipped out her phone and violently poked at the screen. "Hey, I'm trading you in for another best friend and inviting myself to dinner on Saturday."

"You heard, huh?" Darcy said.

"Yeah, dumbass. We work together every single day now. How come you didn't invite me? I'll bet you're serving Amelia's famous barbeque chicken and ribs. You know that's my favorite."

Darcy sighed. "Yeah, the chicken is Fi's favorite, too. I didn't do the inviting. That was Amelia," Darcy defended.

Saville glanced over to Fi. "Things are cool between us, right?"

Fi shrugged. "Yeah, I guess."

"You better pick up more food. We're bringing a posse with us. I think the whole gang should swarm your farm, and we can all go on a treasure hunt for more information about the big mystery behind George the ghost, who I might add has popped in on us several times already."

"What whole gang? And yeah, I heard," Darcy responded.

"Lucy, Bea, and Lucy's niece, Chelsey, the wonder dyke." Saville whispered the last part into the phone, audible enough for Fi to hear, but hopefully not Chelsey. That had earned Saville a dirty look from Fi and a quick retort from Darcy.

"I see you're exhibiting your best side again. Jealous much?"

"I wish everyone would stop saying that."

121

"We can't help it if you're so transparent. Fine. Tell everyone to come around six, and you're supplying the wine," Darcy said.

"Deal." Saville turned to the group. "Okay, we've all been invited to Amelia and Darcy's farm for dinner on Saturday. Bring everything you can dig up, and we'll piece this mystery together once and for all. Thanks, Darc, see ya on Saturday."

"Please tell me you did not just worm your way into a dinner invite for not only yourself but everyone else." Fi wrinkled her nose in displeasure.

Saville grinned. "Not everyone. You already had an invite."

†

Not that George's sudden appearance again unsettled her, but Lucy felt an icy breeze at the back of her neck, and that had startled her. Lucy studied the picture again, trying to glean anything from the expression on their faces.

"My sweet Pearl, when you were young. Do you have more pictures?" George asked in a pained voice, as if every word took effort for him to get out.

Lucy turned in her chair to find George so close, leaning over her shoulder. She sucked in air to compose herself. She didn't believe George was capable of violence, but one never knew about these types of things. Lucy had never met a ghost before. But Lucy was kin, and she'd make that clear to George.

"Well, hello George. I'd offer you coffee and donuts, but I don't know if ghosts can actually consume food. I don't think you had donuts back in your time. They're absolutely divine."

"Actually, Aunt Lucy, a man named Hanson Gregory invented donuts in 1847," Chelsey corrected.

"How in the world does she know so many inane facts?" Saville mumbled under her breath.

"My Pearl," George repeated.

"Oh, sorry. That's my mother's Nona, or rather my great grandmother. Surprise, I'm your great-great-granddaughter. I think it's absolutely divine intervention that we bought this town." Lucy smiled at the ghost who had tilted his head, scrutinizing every word out of Lucy's mouth.

"Yeah, George. So be nice to all of us, or you'll be offending your great-great-granddaughter. By the way, want to do us a solid and fill in the blanks? Like, for starters, did they really hang you? And we have to stop calling your partner the wife. What was her first name? Couldn't you or your wife have kept a journal for us to read? Inquiring minds, you know." Saville relaxed into her chair, linking her fingers together and clasping her hands behind her head.

George turned his attention to Saville and glared. "You are not my kin." He glided in Saville's direction, bending his tall form in an unnatural pose as he brought his face directly in front of Saville and rearranged his face in the most menacing show of aggression that Lucy had seen since they'd first met George. Saville had nowhere to go, as her body was already as far back in the chair as it would go. Perhaps George wouldn't be so tolerant of Saville's smart-ass remarks.

"I think that means none of your effing business." Fi smirked.

"I would be very interested in learning my great-great-grandmother's name," Lucy added.

George rearranged his form again, returning to a standing position but with much less intimidation. "Ruth," he answered with a sigh and then disappeared again.

"Well, alrighty then. One tiny mystery solved. Do you think it takes a lot of effort for George to appear and like move shit around?" Saville asked.

"Seems like it. Odd. In the *Sixth Sense,* that psychologist had long conversations with the kid who saw dead people. How come he could talk with him, but George can barely string together three words?" Lucy asked. "Do you think George knows he's dead? That psychologist didn't. Maybe after we get our answers, we can enlighten George and help him pass to the other side."

"That's the most ridiculous thing I've ever heard. I don't think a Hollywood movie knows any more than we do about ghosts. In fact, we probably know more than the person who wrote that script. I'll bet they never met a real live ghost," Bea grumbled.

"I don't think there is such a thing as a real live ghost, dear. That's the point. They're dead."

"Figure of speech," Bea amended.

†

"Right, then. Shall we get back to work?" Fi had decided they'd had a long enough break. She was determined to stay on track, no matter what new and exciting discovery they'd found.

Lucy popped up from her chair and eagerly responded, "I'm ready, boss. We can stay all day today. No afternoon showings. Where do you want us?"

"If you don't mind finishing the stools, then you can start on the bar. Ideally, I want every inch stripped and sanded, but don't sand too vigorously. A few dents or scratches will give the bar character. If you have to grind to the point where you create a divot, that's too much," Fi directed.

"Aye, aye, Captain." Lucy gave Fi a sloppy salute.

Fi smiled as she shook her head.

"And I'm on chandelier duty, right?"

"Um, yes, are you okay with that? I have some natural cleaning solutions I prepared that are safe on the metal, glass, and crystal that I set on the floor below the chandelier." Fi furrowed her brow, remembering how George had rattled the ladder the other day. "But I'm a little concerned about you being on a ladder by yourself in the hotel. You should stay here in the saloon and help Bea and Lucy with sanding the bar."

"I need to rewire all the lighting in the hotel, so I'll climb up there and remove the chandelier and bring it to the ground. That should make it easier to clean. It shouldn't take me too long," Saville offered.

"Okay, but you should probably have Chelsey hold the ladder. I don't want a repeat of what occurred before when George made his presence known."

"Nah, that's unnecessary. I think George and I have an understanding now. Two alphas learning to co-exist. We're almost there. I can feel it." Saville grinned.

Fi marveled at how casually Saville always seemed to deal with George, who, in her mind, could be pretty intimidating. Maybe that was the way to handle angry, frustrated ghosts. Lucy had the same nonchalant posture as well. But, of course, Lucy was George's great-great-granddaughter. Now that Lucy had confirmed what was probably George's suspicion from the first time he met Lucy, Fi hoped George wouldn't be as aggressive with their group. Unless Saville continued to poke that bear.

"If George pops in again, don't piss him off. I can't do the electrical part, so you need to remain in one piece. I'd rather not take the time to drive you to the hospital."

"Wow, Fi, your concern for my well-being is overwhelming. It almost brings a tear to my eye." Saville swiped at the non-existent tear. "I'm not so sure George can leave the saloon. We've never seen him anywhere but here."

"Well, I'd prefer not to test that theory with either your or Chelsey's safety. Ultimately, I feel responsible for everyone here. That reminds me. I've decided to add everyone to my worker's compensation policy, except Saville, because she has her own. But I haven't done that yet, so everyone needs to be especially careful today."

"I'll get the ladder. Give me about thirty minutes. I should have the chandelier down by then."

"Okay, I'll help Lucy and Bea with the bar until then," Chelsey responded.

"We'll take another break for lunch at around twelve-thirty. Is that okay?" Fi asked.

A combination of head nods, yeahs, and yeses was the response.

"I know it's a little anti-climactic, but I'd love for Aunt Lucy to read the earlier letters when we break for lunch. I always like a complete perspective when studying historical events or ancestral research. Now that I'm here and around this rich history, I feel invested in developing a conclusive picture. It's kind of my jam."

"Sure, that sounds good. I'm curious as well. Thanks for the suggestion, Chelsey." Fi smiled at the young woman.

"Well, I guess that means no pizza and beer tonight," Saville grumbled as she climbed the stairs.

"Why not?" Fi asked.

Saville turned her head. "Because, besides those letters, until Lucy checks that other box of documents, we won't have anything else to unravel for tonight." She continued her path up the stairs.

Lucy grinned. "I think Saville enjoys hanging with us old folks."

"I think she's looking for an excuse to spend more time with Fi," Chelsey remarked.

Fi blushed. "Doubtful."

Lucy opened her mouth to challenge Fi, but Saville, yelling from above, interrupted her response.

"Hey guys, I think you better come up here."

†

Saville grumbled to herself as she savagely grabbed the ladder, hoisting it under her arm. It startled her when pieces of the wood flooring began flying in all directions. George pulled at the wood floor, tossing the weathered floorboards aside like they were tiny toothpicks.

Saville blinked as another apparition appeared and laid her delicate hand on George's shoulder. Dressed in a ruby red dress with ruffles on the hem, the plunging neckline verged on scandalous, especially for what Saville expected was the time this ghost lived. *Could this be the infamous Ruth?*

"George, I don't need protecting. Let them find everything. They won't judge."

George seemed to melt under the new ghost's touch. The beautiful woman, who had a striking resemblance to Lucy, lowered herself to George's level and stroked his cheek.

Saville found the voice both soothing and commanding. The delicate tone reminded her of woodwind instruments in a symphony. Saville shook herself from her stupor and called downstairs. The rest of their merry band of historians needed to see this.

It didn't take long for the rest of the crew to climb the stairs and find Saville, who remained transfixed by the new ghost. Fi was the first to break the silence.

Fi blinked her eyes rapidly and noted, "There's two of them now?"

"Um, yeah. If I had to take an educated guess, you're looking at Ruth, George's wife."

Lucy clapped her hands and bounced on her feet. "Oh, goody, goody. I get to meet my great-great-grandmother."

"You two could be twins," Bea exclaimed.

"I believe George was in a right state of panic, trying to find something that he doesn't want us to see, but Ruth here has a different view."

"Dammit, look at this mess. I just secured those boards to prepare the floor for the reclaimed wood I have specifically selected to blend well with the rest of the wood. That will keep the historic feel of the place," Fi grumbled.

That melodious voice filled the air again as Ruth calmly directed, "George, please offer your apologies to these women."

"Someone's got George wrapped around her little finger," Saville teased. "At least she's more communicative than George. I suppose George is the strong silent type."

George glared at Saville. "You go. Everyone leave but you." George pointed his finger at Lucy.

Ruth glided her hand down George's arm. "Do not be rude, George. I trust these women to tell our story." Peering into the large hole in the floor, Ruth reached in and pulled a leather-bound book from below. She held the prize out, but only Lucy was brave enough to snatch the treasure. Lucy ran her hands over the worn leather, and the joy on her face seemed to lift at least twenty years from her age. Already youthful in appearance, Lucy looked like a woman in her thirties who had just discovered the meaning of life.

Ruth pulled on George's arm. "Time for us to go, my love."

"No, please don't," Chelsey exclaimed in desperation. "What if we have questions? I'm an amateur historian. I'd love to write your story."

"Oh, yes. A book about George, Ruth, and Pearl that we can have available for future residents. You can also sell it at the local bookstore. That's a grand idea," Lucy remarked.

Saville couldn't tell what either Ruth or George thought about that idea, because the two ghosts faded from view before Lucy had finished her suggestion. "Ruth might be down for you writing a book, Chelsey, but I don't think George is as fond of you learning all his dirty little secrets."

Lucy gently opened the leather book. "It's a diary. But I'm not sure if it's George's or Ruth's."

"As much as I'm curious about that journal, I'm further behind than before with George tearing up this floor. Can we powwow on this tonight? I'm sure the journal will hold until then."

Lucy sighed. "I suppose."

"I put the hand sander and sanding blocks on top of the bar," Fi said.

Saville's smile widened. "Well, at least pizza and beer are back on." She pumped her fist in the air.

"Glad you are so easily mollified." Fi rolled her eyes.

CHAPTER NINE

Fi had acted like a whirling dervish, accomplishing a lot more than she hoped. She'd repaired the disaster created after George's mini rampage, using the reclaimed wide plank wood she'd found that had arrived around noon. Sitting on her legs, Fi stretched her aching back. Exhausted by the day, the last thing she wanted to do was have pizza and beer. Instead, Fi longed to slip into her claw-foot tub, filled to the brim with lavender bath oils.

Saville had worked alongside Fi, but she had her own work to accomplish, and by the time they broke for the evening, Saville had almost rewired the entire upstairs. She looked as fatigued as Fi felt.

"Do you think the rest of them are as tired as us? I might want to beg out on pizza and beer tonight. My tub is calling me." Fi stood, continuing to stretch her back.

"Speak for yourself. I could go another several hours. Unless that tub is big enough for two." Saville winked.

"I wasn't inviting you to take a bath with me," Fi answered with crisp precision.

"Darn, must have read the tea leaves wrong. But, come on, don't be such a wet blanket. Aren't you dying to learn what's in the journal?"

"Not really. Sure, it's interesting, but my first priority is to complete the job on time."

"One hour, and then I'll follow you home to make sure you don't fall asleep at the wheel." Saville batted her eyelashes. "Pretty please, with cinnamon sugar on top. It's your favorite."

"A woman who rides a Harley can never pull off that femme look. Never bat your lashes again," Fi teased.

Saville pulled her long hair from the messy ponytail and then flicked it over her shoulder. "How about this? It always seems to work in the movies."

Fi laughed. "Nope, not that either."

"Mission accomplished. I got you to laugh. Since laughing and embracing joy are good for the soul, you need to take the next step and have a nice dinner with friends."

"I wouldn't exactly call Lucy and Bea friends, more like my employer."

Saville lifted her eyebrow. "So, Chelsey is a friend now?"

"She could be. She's nice, my age, single, and a lesbian. Yeah, I could definitely see us hanging out after work sometimes."

"What about me? Am I chopped liver or something?"

"No, of course not, but you're danger on a stick."

Saville wiggled her brows. "You mean like a popsicle. You can lick me anytime you want."

"I thought it was a big mistake."

"Yeah, about that—"

"Girls, the pizza just arrived," Lucy called from below. "I thought I would order now because I'm starved. Bea ran to the store to pick up some beer."

Saville linked her arm inside Fi's. "To be continued. Time to suck it up and have some well-deserved pizza. It would be rude to leave now, considering Lucy and Bea went to the trouble to order and have the food delivered."

"Fine, but I'm planning to start a little later tomorrow. These late nights are killing me. I know you're used to it with your carousing around at night, but I'm more of a 'take a bath and curl up with a good book' kind of gal."

It was not the time or place to start a discussion about what the hell was going on. Saville kept dropping hints about the two of them, but Fi hadn't the foggiest idea where those dangling threads were leading her. She was afraid to pull any of them. But unless Fi was reading the clues all wrong, it almost sounded like Saville didn't believe their one night of passion had been a mistake. *Could Lucy and Chelsey be right, after all? But am I willing to take a chance on someone who clearly wants different things from a relationship?*

†

As Saville and Fi walked down the winding staircase to join the others, Saville noticed an almost pained expression on Fi's face. At first, she thought it might be related to Fi's sore back and her exhaustion after a very full day, but studying her carefully, she concluded, something else was going on in that beautiful brain of hers. It was almost like Fi was trying to figure out an impossible puzzle.

As Saville cataloged her life over the past couple of days, she had started to reassess everything. She'd thought she'd been happy with her casual and carefree love life, but it was becoming increasingly clear that spending time with Fi was something which she wanted to do a great deal more of. If Saville was completely honest with herself, nothing had been the same since she'd slept with Fi.

Saville kept trying to reconstruct with other women the same hunger she felt at the most fervid point in her lovemaking with Fi, but all her encounters seemed like washed-out clothing, devoid of any vibrancy. The sex was mediocre at best with anyone who wasn't Fiona O'Reilly.

The damn woman had somehow burrowed under her skin and not let go. Saville could either listen to her heart and go for it, or try to excise her without causing pain to herself or Fi. As soon as Chelsey had come onto the scene, Saville's path was suddenly crystal clear. She didn't want Chelsey stealing this wonderful woman from right under her nose without a fight. But did Saville deserve to have someone like Fi in her life? That was the ultimate question she hadn't reasonably answered for herself. She just knew she had to go down swinging because the reward was worth the risk.

"What's that look on your face about? If you really want to go home and take a nice, long, hot bath, I promise not to give you any shit. I'll even defend you from the grief the others will surely send your way."

Fi shook her head. "No, it's okay. I was just thinking about stuff."

"Stuff? Want to be more specific? Is there anything I can help with?" Saville asked.

"No. I need to work this out on my own."

Before joining the rest of the women, Saville pulled Fi to the side and grabbed her hands, turning Fi to face her. Continuing to hold both hands, she caught Fi's eyes and began with a level of seriousness she wasn't sure she could pull off. "Before I fucked everything up, we used to be close friends. I want you to know that I would do anything for you. I care a great deal about you, Fi. I hope you know you can come to me with anything, and I'll listen, advise, be a shoulder, whatever you need."

Fi carefully withdrew her hands from Saville and swiped angrily at the tear that had escaped. "Why do you have to be so sweet sometimes? We better join the others before they think we've fallen through the floor."

"Deflection. That's okay. I'll wrangle it from you when we have dinner together on Sunday. Just the two of us without our merry band of amateur historians."

"We'll see."

The squeak of the saloon doors reverberated in the room, interrupting their talk, and they peeked around the corner to see Bea laying two six-packs on the bar.

"Do you think Bea has good taste in beer, or will it be some popular piss water? I should have zipped out and gotten your favorite organic beer."

Fi lightly smacked Saville on the arm. "There you go again with that kindness where you definitely are not only thinking of yourself." Fi started making her way toward the other women hanging at the bar.

Saville grinned and, following close behind Fi, whispered, "Oh, I think you know firsthand how attentive I can be with a laser focus on my partner."

As Fi reached the group, she turned her head and replied, "Now there's the Saville I know and love. You're like that commercial for SweeTARTS Rope Bites."

"Yeah, well, as I remember correctly, everyone seems to say, 'why wouldn't I want both?' There's where my charm lies. I'm both sweet and tart. Don't you want both?" Saville teased.

"SweeTARTS? I loved those candies when I was younger, but I haven't tried the Rope Bites yet. Are they good?" Lucy asked. "Do you have some? I'm not sure how well they'll go with pizza and beer, though. Maybe we should go out for ice cream later."

Saville laughed. "Ice cream sounds awesome. No, we don't have any candy. Fi was just talking about how I'm both sweet and sour, like the candy."

"Sweet and tart," Fi corrected.

"Right, right. I suppose that's an apt description," Saville admitted. "I'm like a delicious pastry, maybe a little flaky at times, but still lusciously yummy."

"There is another definition for tart. In the late nineteenth century, tarts were also a name for prostitutes or women with multiple sexual partners," Chelsey added.

Fi laughed. "Yup, that fits too."

Saville glared at Chelsey. "So sexist. We call women tarts, but we label men who have a lot of sexual partners, studs. Surely, we are all enlightened women and aren't prone to judge our fellow sisters more harshly than men."

"I don't call men studs. I'd more likely use the term man-whore." Chelsey shrugged. "But, to each their own, as my grandmother used to say."

"Mom did say that, didn't she?" Lucy responded. "There is nothing wrong with a healthy sexual appetite.

Don't you let them make you feel bad for it, Saville. But I will tell you from experience that the best sex you'll ever have is with someone you love. Nothing compares to that." Lucy offered Saville a brilliant smile. The subtle message was not lost on Saville. Making love to Fi had been a mind-blowing experience. Could that be because she was in love with Fi?

†

Lucy mentally patted herself on the back for her restraint. She'd desperately wanted to open the leather-bound book and simply take a quick peek, but Bea had grabbed the journal and placed it inside her sling pack. Lucy hadn't even determined which ghost had written in the journal. Now, her wife and the journal were out of reach. Lucy had no choice but to wait for Bea to return with the beer.

The pizza had arrived, and she'd called upstairs for Saville and Fi, who were tidying up. Chelsey quirked her eyebrow, and Lucy turned her head and caught Saville pulling Fi into a dark corner. Something was definitely brewing between the two of them, and Lucy took credit for that. Introducing Chelsey into the mix was a brilliant move, in her humble opinion. Bea hadn't agreed. And Chelsey had acted a little off ever since Fi and Chelsey had taken that tour. Bea had warned Lucy to stay out of it because her favorite niece would be collateral damage in her matchmaking venture if she wasn't careful. Lucy would simply need to find a suitable partner for her niece that wasn't Fiona O'Reilly because, from everything she'd witnessed, that love boat had sailed.

Finally, everyone had settled into her respective camp chair, with beer and pizza in hand. Setting down her beer and a slice of pizza on a napkin, Lucy wiggled her fingers in front of Bea. After over thirty-five years together, her wife understood the gesture and retrieved the journal from her pack.

"Can we at least finish eating before you crack open the journal?" Bea pleaded. "The damn thing will not spring legs and walk away."

"Maybe not, but what if George has second thoughts and tries to steal it back?" Lucy lamented.

"I think Ruth wanted us to find everything. She won't let George misbehave," Fi assured.

"Yeah, right. Where was Ruth when George tried to kill you?" Saville grumbled.

"I don't believe he was trying to kill me. Just rattle me a bit," Fi answered.

"Not that I'm afraid of his pathetic attempts to scare us, but I wish there was some way to fight an irritating ghost," Saville mused. "It's not like I can punch him or anything. My fist would merely move through thin air. Completely unsatisfying. Hey, Chelsey, in all your historical research, did you come across any rituals or chants or something to rid the world of ghosts?"

"Um, no. I'm not an expert on the occult," Chelsey answered.

"I don't want to get rid of Ruth and George. They have as much right to live here as we do. Maybe more. They were here first. Besides, they're my kin," Lucy declared.

Bea rolled her eyes. "I'm eating before the pizza gets cold. It's not like this saloon has a microwave to heat our dinner while we sit around the campfire and tell ghost stories."

"Don't be such a curmudgeon." Lucy couldn't wait one second longer. She opened the journal to the first page and began to read, "'January 5th, 1889. The vultures have declared their intentions, but I have no interest in becoming another man's property. I do not know what I shall do if I cannot keep the saloon going. The other ladies depend on the dance hall to make a living. The small stash of gold Josiah left will not be enough. Josiah was a good man, but his insistence that women shall not enter the affairs of men has left me ill-prepared to run a saloon. If I have to become a dance hall girl, I shall embrace this new life. I will not let my unborn child starve.'"

"I can't imagine George as a dance hall girl. It's probably Ruth's diary. Do you think Josiah was her first husband?" Fi asked.

"Probably," Saville flipped the top on her beer, and after taking a huge swig, continued, "I'm sure we'll know more after Lucy reads the entire journal. Maybe she should do that on her own, and then we could skip to the end after we get a better sense of the characters?"

"This isn't a mystery novel, you know, where you skip to the end to find out who killed Josiah." Fi made a tsking sound before taking a bite of pizza.

"Ooh. Do you think someone murdered Josiah? Maybe it was George because he set his sights on the lovely Ruth." Saville leaned forward, her eyes bright with excitement. "No wonder they hanged him."

Lucy continued to read on, skimming through the journal until she came to a passage where Ruth wrote about

George. "Hey, I found a passage where she mentions George."

"Read it out loud, Aunt Lucy."

"Okay." Lucy began reading. "'May 1st, 1889. I cannot understand how the men still wish to dance with a woman swollen with child. I continue to spurn Abraham's advances. He is not one to accept the declination of his marriage proposal. Tonight, he was notably aggressive, and the new sheriff, George Thompson, intervened. There is something very different about George. I find myself drawn to him. He is quiet and polite and has not once asked for special favors from any of the girls. Most men do not consider us painted ladies, but nearly all have tried to take liberties not offered in the saloon. I have reminded them more than once that should they seek that kind of companionship, they are welcome to spend their time and money in the brothel. I do not judge the painted ladies, for that could have easily been my fate after Josiah died. I wonder if George visits the brothel. He seems to have a soft spot for Mae, treating her no different from my dance hall girls.'"

"Now we're talking. A little love triangle." Saville rubbed her hands together.

Lucy continued her exploration of the journal until the words *scarlet fever* caught her eye. Silently reading the passage to herself, she decided the group would be very interested in this entry. "Hey, listen to this. 'June 30th, 1889. Mae ran into the saloon today. Her eyes were wild as she approached, pleading for me to come with her. Abraham was not pleased with the interruption and tried to prevent me from following Mae. Mae's frightened eyes were enough to refuse his offer to accompany me. I do not know why Mae has entrusted me with George's secret, but this burden is one I intend to keep until my dying day.'"

"Do you think Mae and George were lovers before he married Ruth?" Chelsey asked.

"Possibly. Let me finish this passage." Lucy continued to read. "'I've agreed to help nurse George back to health. Scarlet fever has already taken the lives of too many. George seems strong. I believe he will survive this illness. I owe George a great debt for always taking the complaints of my girls seriously. Since George has been sheriff, the men do not take liberties, nor does George allow the men to get rough with my girls after too much whiskey. George's weak protests nearly broke my heart. At first, I thought he feared I would reveal his secret to others. As I wiped his fevered forehead, I assured him I would not. Yet, his concern was not for himself but for my unborn child and me. He is more of a man than Abraham will ever be.'"

"Wow! Even after learning George is a woman, Ruth uses the pronoun he. Ruth must have been quite a woman. So ahead of her time," Chelsey noted.

Fi finished her beer and crumpled the can. "As much as I would love to listen to Lucy read more of the diary, I am completely done for the evening," Fi said around a yawn. "Do y'all mind if I head home and you can fill me in tomorrow?"

"Damn, it was just getting good, too. I was hoping the steamier passages might be a few entries away. I'll follow you home. I wouldn't want you falling asleep at the wheel. I'm sure the purr of my Harley will keep you awake," Saville offered.

"No, no, you stay. I'm not that tired. We can leave the chairs set up. I feel like it's Girl Scout camp, and we're all sitting around the campfire, without the fire, of course." Fi stood grimacing as she stretched her back.

"You sure?" Saville asked. "You look like you're in pain."

Fi nodded.

Saville stood. "I'll walk you out."

"Really, I'm fine. I'd be more worried if my back wasn't a little sore. It just means I got a lot accomplished today." Fi gave the group a weak smile.

Saville slung her arm around Fi's shoulders. "Come on, my legs need stretching, so don't fight with me. Besides, it's pitch-black outside. Two phone lights are better than one."

Lucy had paused, skimming over the words in the journal. Although the bits and pieces she read filled in a few blanks, she reveled in the notion they would all have a front-row seat to Ruth and George's love story. Lucy mused about the privilege of watching another love story unfold before her eyes. She predicted it would not be long before Saville realized her feelings for Fi went well beyond carnal attraction or mere friendship. The barriers Ruth and George had to overcome, overshadowed by the big secret, did not exist for Saville and Fi. Yet, here Saville and Fi were, dancing around love as if a crazy mob would come gunning for them should they dare to reveal their true feelings.

CHAPTER TEN

"Ah." Fi slipped into her old-fashioned claw-foot tub that she'd spent months searching for after her bathroom remodel. The soapsuds encased her in the tub like a warm blanket in a field of lavender. She lifted a handful of bubbles to her nose and breathed in her favorite scent. Beer or cider was her preferred adult beverage, but tonight she opened one of the few bottles of wine she stored in her refrigerator, just in case she had a guest who preferred wine. *Oh, who am I kidding?* No one except Amelia and Darcy ever came to visit. Her social life was practically nonexistent. For now, she convinced herself it didn't matter. If she was going to give it a go with her remodeling business, she needed to work hard and not have anyone, least of all Saville, distract her.

Flicking the bubbles and then blowing them away from her body, Fi luxuriated in her bath, giggling as she played in her tub like when she was a small child. She knew it was silly for an adult to have rubber duckies, but they were a lot like those stress balls that were so popular as she moved them around in her tub and squeezed them, squirting bathwater everywhere.

When Fi's doorbell rang, the noise startled her so much that she slipped under the water and began coughing as bubbles and water entered her mouth without her permission. She contemplated not answering, but the buzz kept interrupting her peace and quiet. Whoever was at her door was not going away.

Reluctantly, Fi climbed from her tub, quickly drying off and wrapping the towel around her head before donning her fluffy white robe. The incessant intermittent buzzing was giving her a migraine. Distracted by her discomfort, she accidentally kicked over the wine that she'd set on the floor within reaching distance while relaxing in her tub. Grabbing a wad of toilet paper, she quickly mopped the wine and set the glass upright next to her tub.

"Fuck a duck," she swore, then looked at her innocent rubber duckies floating in the tub. "Sorry, sorry, not you guys." The ridiculousness of what she'd said caused her to break out in a fit of laughter as she made her way to the front door, where apparently whoever was here felt the need to lean on the doorbell, turning the intermittent noise into a constant irritating buzz.

"All right, already. I'm coming," Fi yelled at the door before yanking it open. "Saville? What are you doing here?"

"Do you think we're lucky to be born in this time? You know, to have the way paved by courageous women who literally gave their lives for love?"

Fi wrinkled her nose. "I don't know, Saville. Why is it so important for you to have this question answered for you at"— she glanced over her shoulder—"eleven o'clock?" Fi had never seen Saville look so serious. She sighed and then opened the door. "Well, come on in. Even though it's late, you look like you need a friend tonight." Pulling the towel from her head, she rubbed vigorously, then shook her hair out. After finger-combing her hair, she tossed the towel into the basket in the laundry room and continued on into her living room.

Saville followed Fi like a lost puppy. "Something Lucy said tonight kind of hit me. Plus, the passages she read after you left were heartbreaking because we know things ended badly for Ruth and George. I'm almost thirty, and what the hell do I have to show for my life? I live in a crappy place with shitty neighbors who mistreat their dog. No love in my life. There might not even be passion. Even the sex has been mediocre of late."

Fi raised an eyebrow.

"Oh, not with you, um, with others."

"Would you like some wine? I opened a bottle to have a glass while relaxing in the tub."

As if something had finally registered in Saville's brain, she scanned Fi's appearance. "Oh, God, I'm sorry. I interrupted your bath. How's your back?"

Fi rocked her hand. "So so. I guess it could be worse. The bath was helping."

"Damn, sorry again. I could rub your back for you," Saville offered.

Fi pointed to the couch. "Go, sit. I'll get us both a glass. Unfortunately, I kicked mine over, running to answer the door after your incessant buzzing. You'd think the world was ending," Fi teased.

"The world *is* ending," Saville drily remarked. "Since when have I ever gotten philosophical? I'm the happy-go-lucky one who never takes anything seriously, including myself. What the hell is happening to me?" Saville sat heavily on the couch while Fi retrieved the wine.

The two women remained silent while Fi poured the wine and then handed a glass to Saville. "Adulting is hard, isn't it? But, you know, maybe things didn't end that badly for Ruth and George. They were together for a long time. Raised a daughter. And it looks like they're still together."

"Did you know that Ruth barely agonized over her love for George, despite all the societal pressures to marry again?"

"She did marry again," Fi noted. "It's not like everyone knew about George. At least, not until the end. They were married for many years, right?"

"Yeah, three months after George recovered from scarlet fever, they married."

"Wow, you must have gotten pretty far into the journal."

"Not really. Lucy skipped ahead, looking for the steamy passages." Saville smiled. "You know, I had a girlfriend once."

Fi turned her body to face Saville. "No, I didn't know that."

"I used to work in Seattle. I met her when she hired my company to wire her new hot tub. Katrina was a high-powered lawyer. After two years of never being invited to accompany her to events, I finally realized she was embarrassed to be seen with a lowly electrician. She swore she had to go to them but wanted to spare me the pain of attending something so excruciatingly boring I'd want to pluck out my eyeballs for fun. In reality, she didn't think I could hold my own in a conversation with her colleagues. I've always been good for a romp in the hay, but nothing more serious."

"That's bullshit."

"You have that fancy architectural historic preservation degree from the University of Oregon. I went to tech school. They are hardly in the same stratosphere. You probably have more in common with the history scholar."

"Chelsey?"

"Yeah, Chelsey. She's irritatingly nice and intelligent. I wouldn't be able to keep up, even if I tried. Animal magnetism fades, intelligence and genuine kindness do not. You should go for it. She's clearly into you."

"How magnanimous of you," Fi said with a healthy dose of sarcasm. "And to think that all I needed was your permission to pursue dating someone. Well, news flash, I don't see myself settling down with Chelsey and having two point five kids. I hope we'll continue to develop a friendship, though. I can always use more friends."

"Are we friends?" Saville asked.

"Yeah, I think we're getting there," Fi answered.

"Do you think it could ever be more?"

"I thought we'd already determined that ship has sailed."

"Maybe I'd like to reconsider sailing back into port, but I can't shake this feeling that, just like Katrina, you're too good for me."

"Double bullshit, but I don't know, Saville, you really hurt my feelings that night. Maybe we were destined for friendship, but nothing more. No matter how much I enjoyed our time together, and not only that fateful evening, I think it's going to take some time for me to heal my bruised ego."

"But you said it was a mistake, too. I thought you'd come to the same conclusion."

"What else was I supposed to say after you rolled away and said it was a mistake? I needed to hold on to the small amount of dignity I had left."

"Oh." Saville nervously gulped her glass of wine. "I better go, huh?" Saville stood. "I'll see you tomorrow, bright and early then."

"Not too early. I'll probably get there around seven instead of six." Fi followed Saville to her front door. Before she could stop herself, she gathered Saville in a hug and murmured, "Friends hug friends goodbye."

"Yeah, they do."

As the two women pulled apart, both seemed reluctant to break their embrace. Fi noticed Saville had a genuine smile on her face. Fi matched her smile and then spontaneously kissed her cheek.

"See you tomorrow, Saville."

†

Saville had tossed and turned all night, thinking of what Lucy had said to her. As the small party broke apart, Lucy had pulled Saville aside and said, "You know, Saville, I don't see an angry mob trying to keep you and Fi apart. You're doing a fine job of that all on your own. I suggest you grow some tits, stop being an ass, and not let one more minute pass. We only get a finite amount of minutes on this earth, and trust me, they gallop along without your consent. Don't waste the time you have left. Before you know it, you'll be as old as me, and Fi will have moved on." She had shrugged, then added, "Maybe with Chelsey, which from my perspective wouldn't be that horrible for her or Chelsey."

Glancing at her phone, Saville noted it was still early. She sighed as she flipped the covers off and made the trek to her bathroom for a quick shower. She might as well make a stop at the bakery for one of those stuffed croissants she used to bring for Fi. The childlike delight never seemed to get old. Fi would attack the croissant and moan in appreciation, as if this would be the last croissant on the planet, and Saville had saved it just for her.

Saville reached the worksite fifteen minutes before seven. It surprised her that Fi wasn't there already. She carried the hot coffee, made precisely the way Fi liked it, and set it along with the croissant on the floor next to the spot where Fi would resume her work on the flooring. She smiled, thinking about Fi's joy at finding the small gift.

"I'll bet Chelsey doesn't know your favorite breakfast food, the ones that cause your beautiful green eyes to light up," Saville mumbled under her breath.

Saville hadn't heard the squeak of the saloon doors or footsteps on the curved staircase. She turned around when she felt a presence behind her, but it wasn't Fi. Instead, a translucent Ruth stood in the doorway, beckoning her to follow. Saville stood and brushed her hands against her pants before tagging behind the less threatening ghost. Neither Saville nor Fi had touched the farthest bedroom in the back after assessing the size and determining it would make a perfect guest bedroom. Fi had wanted to tackle the larger areas first, leaving the small bedroom for the end.

As Saville looked at the room that just the other day was in fine shape, she swore, "Fucking hell, George. What new bug crawled up your ass?" To Saville's surprise, Ruth chuckled, then pointed to the large hole in the floor.

"George and I do not agree, but I do not wish to hide from our story. History cannot be rewritten, but the facts should be told without judgment. Perhaps you will learn something important. Jealousy is a destructive force that you should never allow to grow and fester. The final piece is there." Ruth pointed to the hole and then disappeared.

Saville carefully navigated the discarded floorboards strewn all over the room. Peering into the hole, she spied another leather-bound book. Certainly not as fancy as the diary from which Lucy had read the prior evening, but Saville suspected this was another journal. Perhaps George kept his own thoughts in a diary. She was so excited to crack open this new discovery, she wasn't watching where she was going and stumbled, cracking the subfloor and falling partially through the unstable wood. At least Saville had grabbed the book and held it in her hands. She imagined how ridiculous this might look with the bottom half of her body dangling in the air above a remote corner of the bar.

The squeak from the saloon doors alerted her that Fi had arrived. She was glad she hadn't oiled the doors yesterday like she'd meant to do before leaving.

"Help! I need a little help here," she called.

Saville couldn't see Fi but was happy when she heard her approach from below. She imagined it was quite humorous with her legs dangling from the ceiling.

"Oh, my God, Saville. Are you okay?"

Saville groaned in embarrassment. "Yeah, I'm fine. Just a little stuck."

Fi giggled. "Yeah, you give new meaning to the moniker, 'stuck-up.' Now, this is an interesting predicament

150

you have yourself in. Maybe I should wait until the others arrive. This is just too good not to share with them. Hmm, I don't suppose they'd want to keep you there as a special attraction. You do have a particularly fine butt. That could be quite the draw."

"Not funny, Fi. Ruth led me to another journal which I have in my hand and will not share unless you help me out." Saville wiggled her legs to emphasize her need. "Besides, what if the floor gives way and I break my leg on the way down?"

"It's like five, maybe six feet to the ground. I think you'll survive the fall," Fi answered from below.

"Maybe, but the indignity might kill me. It's bad enough you found me like this."

"A dose of humility is just what the doctor ordered. Hang on, don't go anywhere." Fi laughed. "Oh right, hanging on is about all you can do right now."

Saville heard Fi's footsteps on the staircase and mumbled, "I'm never going to live this down."

As Fi approached, cocking her head as if to assess the situation, Saville heard a commotion below.

"Don't come upstairs, this room is not stable," Fi yelled down.

"Oh, my. Is that you hanging from the ceiling?" Lucy asked.

"Nope, it's Saville. She's training for the construction Olympics. One event is floor gliding," Fi called to the people below.

Laughter from below floated through the hole in the ceiling

"You are not funny," Saville grumbled.

Annette Mori

"They think I am. Okay, hand me the book and take my hands. I'll pull you out."

"Maybe you should get a rope or something. I'm not sure how stable this floor is. While it wouldn't be the worst thing to be stuck together, I can think of a more pleasurable position to be in, where all parts of our bodies are accessible to the other."

"Oh, so you can joke about this, but I can't. I see how you are," Fi teased. "But you may be right about the rope. I think I have some in my truck."

"Thanks, Fi." Saville flung the journal into the center of the room, and Fi snatched it and left the room as carefully as she'd entered.

Saville tried to listen to the murmuring below, but she couldn't quite understand what they were saying. She heard her name but wasn't sure if they called her a dumbass or expressed concern for her predicament. Finally, after a few minutes, Fi returned with rope and a long chain in her hand.

"I wasn't sure which was better to use. The chain may be sturdier. I've hauled many cars out of ditches with this chain. It works better than the rope. Not that you weigh as much as a car. Or that I plan to hook this to my truck. How do you want to do this? One hand or two?"

"Do you have anything to wrap the chain or rope around while you pull?"

Fi looked around the empty room. Unlike the other rooms, they hadn't removed a wall, leaving any part of the frame exposed. She shook her head. "No, but I'm stronger than I look."

"Okay, how about I wrap one hand around the chain, and you can pull while I push with my other hand? Are you sure you don't want to get Chelsey or someone else to help?"

152

"Nope, I don't want anyone else getting injured. Besides, I thought you wouldn't want to suffer the embarrassment."

"A little late for that now. I heard you all laughing and talking about me." Saville wiggled again, trying for better leverage.

"Where has that famous sense of humor gone?" Fi quipped.

Saville wiggled her fingers. "Just toss me the chain."

"Should I mention I was never very good at softball?" Fi tossed the chain, and the heavy metal smacked Saville's head.

"Ouch," Saville said as she grabbed the chain and wrapped it around her hand.

"Sorry. You ready?"

Saville nodded.

"Okay, on the count of three, I'll pull and you push. One, two, three."

Saville grunted as she pushed against the board, hearing it crack. "Pull harder, or you and I are going to end up on top of one another if the entire floor gives way."

"I'm doing the best that I can. Unfortunately, you're a lot heavier than you look."

"It's all muscle. It weighs more than fat, you know."

Finally, Fi pulled hard enough for Saville to gain her footing, enabling her to scramble away from the hole.

"You girls okay up there?" Lucy called from below.

Without getting too close to the hole Fi had just pulled her from, Saville answered, "Yup, all good now. Thanks. Nothing to see here. Move along." She turned to Fi. "I'll help you fix the floor today." Holding out her hand, she pulled Fi into the other room, where she had set out the coffee and croissant. "I'm glad I thought to get those for you. Consider this an offering of sincere gratitude."

Fi hurried to snatch the treats and squealed, "Is that my favorite croissant from the bakery?"

"Uh-huh." Saville smiled shyly.

"Did you bring some for everyone? They're going to love it. Hopefully, you won't offend Lucy. I saw a box of donuts and coffee on the bar."

"Um, no." Saville mentally chastised herself for not thinking of the others. "I only brought that for you. I didn't even get one for myself."

"Oh, okay. Maybe I'll keep this here and eat it after we've assigned everyone their daily tasks. There's plenty of sanding left to do. I thought I might ask Chelsey to help me with the floor. It'll go a lot faster with two." Fi looked lovingly at the croissant. "Maybe a small bite, and then I'll go downstairs." Fi took a bite of her croissant and moaned in delight.

Saville closed her eyes, enjoying Fi's reaction to her small gift. However, there was not a chance in hell she would let Chelsey and Fi work together all day. She quickly offered to help. "I nearly finished the wiring of the upstairs yesterday, so I can help. I wouldn't want Chelsey to hurt herself. As you discovered, not every room is safe and secure."

Fi wrinkled her nose. "Okay, if you're sure you can spare the time."

"I can spare the time. By the way, what did you do with the new journal?"

"It's on the bar. Lucy did her bouncy thing. She was so excited to see the book. She had already cracked it open and learned that it was Mae's diary. You know, the painted lady we suspect was George's lover at one point." Fi sipped on her coffee and took another large bite of her croissant.

"Hmm. I wonder why Ruth led me to that journal?"

"Ruth was here this morning?"

Saville nodded. "Yeah, and get this. She wants us to tell their story. I'm sure that diary has some missing pieces." Saville deliberately left out Ruth's warning about jealousy.

"Wow! That's almost enticing enough to play hooky and read all day, but I need to finish replacing the damaged floorboards. Bea and Lucy plan on living upstairs, but they aren't too fond of wallpaper, so we talked about modernizing the walls. I need to finish hanging and taping the drywall well before the appliances and cabinets arrive. Besides, after Chelsey, Bea, and Lucy complete the sanding downstairs, painting the walls will be a simple task to assign." Fi finished her croissant and then brushed off the crumbs from her ratty T-shirt and overalls.

"Sounds like a plan. Guess we'll have to consider what to order tonight for our third meeting of the Georgetown Glen historical society. It's getting to be quite the habit for all of us to gather in the evenings. Honestly, I'm looking forward to it. This has been a lot more entertaining than what I normally do after work."

A raised eyebrow was all Saville received in response. Perhaps it was not the best thing to remind Fi that Saville spent most of her time at the local bar hoping to pick up women. If she wanted to change the dynamic between the two of them and have any chance at something more than friendship, she'd need to change the script, and reminding Fi of her past escapades was not the slickest move.

†

It surprised Fi that the project had moved along despite the relatively minor inconvenience of fixing the floor that George seemed insistent on tearing apart. Miracle of miracles, the sheetrock had arrived at nine, just a few minutes before Fi replaced the final subfloor plank. She couldn't have done it without Saville, who proved to be an efficient partner. She preferred to get in the zone, which meant no chatter while working. A bit of music, and she was good to go. Saville respected her need to concentrate.

Fi had to shake herself back into motion as she stood watching Saville's straining muscles while she carried several wallboards up the winding staircase. After laying the boards on the floor, Saville lifted her T-shirt and wiped the sweat from her brow. Fi's eyes riveted to Saville's glistening muscles. A sardonic grin appeared on Saville's face.

"Like what you see?" Saville leaned against the wood frame.

"Now, why did you have to ruin a perfect morning with that false bravado?"

Saville shrugged. "Sorry. Old habits die hard." When Saville's stomach grumbled, she placed her hand on top and announced, "I think it's time for lunch."

"Agreed. We are at the perfect breaking point. Um, I didn't know if you brought lunch or not, but I made plenty of chicken curry salad if you want some. It's in the cooler in my truck."

"Sold. Much better than cold pizza. I think Lucy made sandwiches for everyone, but you know how much I love your chicken curry salad. Thanks. I'll bet Lucy can't wait to share a few passages from the new journal. Or maybe she'll continue reading from Ruth's diary. Either way, I look forward to our gatherings. It's kind of hard to tear myself away. Like a train wreck, you know it's coming, but you want all the sordid details, anyway," Saville said.

"Oh, I don't know. It feels more like an epic love story than a train wreck." Fi absently pulled her hair from the tie and refastened it into a neat ponytail.

"Uh, news flash. They hanged George and Ruth."

"I know, and that was the tragic part, but they had nearly twenty years together before the town lynched them. That's a long time. Plus, they're both ghosts now and get to spend their afterlife with one another like true soul mates. I hold on to the romantic notion that even if they knew what was going to happen in the future, they still would have spent their life as one."

"It's a nice thought, but reality sometimes gets in the way of fantasy. I can't imagine all of those years were perfect. Every relationship has challenges." Saville brushed a speck of dirt from her pants.

"Such a cynic for one so young."

"I'm not that young. Remember, thirty is just around the corner. Besides, I'm a realist, not a cynic."

"Cynic. Realist. Same thing. You say *puhtaytow*, I say *potahtow*." Fi grinned.

Saville pulled her phone from her pocket, her thumbs flying over the screen. "Interesting."

"What's interesting?" Fi approached and tried to look over Saville's shoulder.

"While cynic is a synonym for a realist, unrealistic, impractical, and sloppy are all synonyms of romantic."

As Fi peered over Saville's shoulder, she added, "And so are adventurous, charming, exciting, passionate, and enchanting. If I'm a romantic, so be it. I'll take passion over"—Fi grabbed Saville's phone and typed in synonyms for realist—"fatalist, nihilist, or defeatist."

Saville laughed. "Well played. Now give me my phone back." She held out her hand. "My mouth is literally watering as I imagine my first bite of your awesome chicken salad."

†

Lucy pulled out the two journals with the multicolored flags she'd placed in both books. She tried to select the most explosive passages. She was excited to share her findings. After everyone had taken their place in the camp chairs, she began. "So the old story isn't quite accurate. Good old-fashioned jealousy caused the demise of Ruth and George."

"Mae?" Chelsey guessed.

"Yup. Listen to this. 'April 2nd, 1909. What have I done? Oh dear Lord, what have I done? The mob has come for George and Ruth. I fear they will take the most extreme justice. Abraham and the stranger carry a rope in their hands. Banishment from the town will not be enough. Abraham felt Ruth's spurn of his advances as keenly as I suffered George's rejection. I only wanted George to seek comfort in my arms while Ruth was away, and she acted as if I was vermin to suggest such a thing. I am not the one who has deceived this whole town, but still, I must make this right. Pearl must never know what happened.'"

"You think Mae ratted them out?" Saville asked.

"I believe so. Mae did not have a good life after the town hanged George and Ruth. Apparently, led by Abraham and an unnamed gambler, the two men took over the saloon and destroyed the place. Not only did Mae lose George as a friend, but she lost a protector. The painted ladies and dance hall girls had depended on George to keep them safe. With George gone, the town spiraled downhill." Lucy shook her head. "I'm still searching for how Mae made things right. I hope she buried the answer in one of her passages."

"On that depressing note, any chance you can read something more cheerful or salacious?" Saville waggled her brows. "Any naughty bits mentioned in either journal?"

"Well, it isn't erotica, but there are some passages that might be of interest," Lucy answered.

Saville finished chewing the bite of chicken salad and glanced at Fi. "Please tell me we have a little more time to hear one of those before we have to go back to work."

Fi held up one finger. "One or two."

"So this one is tame but sweet. 'It had been a full day since we settled George into my bedroom at the saloon. Summoning the doctor was not an option lest his secret became known to the rest of the town. As I run a cool cloth over his forehead, I am amazed that I did not see it earlier. The delicate curve of his nose and the absence of facial hair. I had always assumed he took great pride in his appearance, preferring to always remain clean-shaven as he made his rounds.'" Lucy paused.

"Well, go on. I'm guessing it gets a lot better." Saville grinned.

Lucy continued, "'My girls believe I am having an affair with the handsome sheriff, and Abraham has not taken this news well. This is so absurd, considering how much worse George's fever has become. But I cannot deny the strange feelings I have when touching his smooth skin. He seems more comfortable after bathing his body and putting

159

on a fresh shirt. I am now used to seeing his breasts under the bindings that hid them so well. The pain in his eyes when he awoke earlier nearly broke me. He tried to explain and apologize for his deception. I placed a kiss on his forehead, hoping to calm his fears. I wonder if I am unnatural for wanting to put my lips on his. I long to feel their softness. I imagine that being so unlike the rough kisses of Josiah. This thought keeps me awake at night.'"

"Okay, that's like the PG-13 version of lesbian romance. Does it get any steamier?"

Lucy nodded.

"I say we save the racier passages for tonight. We can get a lot done in the next four to five hours and then knock off early if we hustle. I like to be done by five on Fridays to pretend I have a social life. I might even let loose and have two drinks tonight." Fi picked up her container of chicken salad and placed it back in the cooler. "Ready to lug more sheetrock up the stairs?"

Saville saluted. "Yup! Lead the way."

CHAPTER ELEVEN

"I can't wait to finish this room. The sooner we have a working sink, the easier it will be to wash up. At least the previous contractors connected most of the plumbing network. Do you want to help me run pipe into the kitchen before we finish the drywall? It'll give your sore muscles a break." Fi pushed her hair from her face with the back of her hand. White dust particles floated to the ground.

Saville knew that before the evening was over, Fi would drag out her shop vac and clean the floor, only to have to vacuum again tomorrow. If it were up to Saville, she would leave her tools and not tidy up every evening, but Fi insisted on an orderly workspace. She abhorred clutter, including worksite chaos. Immediately after using any tool, she would methodically put the device back in her toolbox, lugging the large box up and down the stairs every evening and every morning. Saville thought that added extra work, but Fi insisted she couldn't think amidst the disorder and needed to perform this ritual every evening.

George or Ruth would appear and simply watch the activity throughout the day but had shown no aggression, nor had they said a word. The ghosts simply hovered for a few minutes and watched. Saville was getting used to their intermittent presence. At one point, Ruth had smiled and nodded at Saville when she caught Saville staring at Fi as she worked.

Saville couldn't help herself when she ran her thumb across Fi's cheek to remove the large smudge of drywall dust. Normally, she hated helping with one of the dirtiest jobs, but all Fi had to do was ask, and she was eager to help.

Electrical work was far less taxing than nearly every other subcontracted work. The fact that Fi had agreed to take on the entire project, performing all the work herself, minus the electrical, was a testament to her talents with restoration work.

Saville was so close to Fi that all she had to do was collapse the distance. Two inches, maybe three, and her lips would be on Fi's. Fi met her eyes. A confused look on her face.

"You were wearing part of the sheetrock," Saville said as a way of explaining why she'd touched her face. If Saville were honest, it probably felt more like a caress than simply removing the white dust.

"Oh. Yeah, this is a dirty job. I really appreciate your help."

"Sure, no problem." Saville flicked her hand. "Name the date or place, and I'll get dirty with you any time you want."

Fi frowned and answered, "I'm not going to even respond to that. For once, can you just accept my gratitude without turning it sexual?"

And just like that, Saville lost the moment. Maybe that was for the best, because Saville was dangerously close to kissing Fi. Unfortunately, the confusion in Fi's eyes did not divulge how she might have reacted. Fi was as likely to slap her face as to lean into the kiss.

"Sorry. I am trying to change my spots, but the old Saville keeps popping up."

Fi grimaced. "I'm not asking you to change, Saville. I'd just like to know the part of you that you try so hard to hide with jokes and snarky side comments. It's like you feel the need to bring out that Saville even more after we slept together. Maybe a better balance, less tart, more sweet."

Not thinking about how vulnerable it would seem, she blurted, "We're still on for dinner on Sunday, right?"

Fi furrowed her brow. "Of course. Why do you ask? You're not getting out of dinner so easily with a few raunchy jokes." Fi smiled.

Saville sighed in relief and then changed the trajectory of their conversation. "I'll get the shop vac and help you tidy up. It's almost five."

"As much as I want to hear more of George and Ruth's story, I would kill for a shower right now. I feel disgusting." Fi wiped her hands on her pants.

"You don't look disgusting. In fact, you're kind of adorable right now. You'd look good in baggy overalls, caked in mud."

Fi blushed. "Um, thanks. Do you think I could convince the gang to come back to my place tonight?"

"I'm sure they would, but then you can't bug out early, and they might overstay their welcome. Although, none of them have seen your home. They're going to flip out. Your place is amazing. I'll bet even Bea will be impressed. They certainly chose the right woman for the job."

"I hate ordering pizza again, but I have nothing to offer for dinner unless I stop at the store." Fi collected her drill and saw, methodically wiping both tools with a neatly folded rag.

"Don't worry about dinner. We'll come up with something. Any chance I could shower at your place rather than going all the way home?"

"Um, sure. You can use the guest bath. My home might be old, but I made sure the water pressure is enough for two people."

Saville grinned. "I knew that. I wasn't suggesting I shower with you. Although if that's an option, I'm all for it. Saving water and all is the right thing to do because I care about the planet." Fi opened her mouth to respond, and Saville held up her hand. "Just kidding. Sorry, this shit just pops in my head, and it's out before I have a chance to edit my thoughts."

"Well, I do care about the planet..." Fi let the rest of the sentence dangle, chuckling as she walked away with her drill and saw, and placed them in her toolbox.

"Wait. What? Was that an invitation?" Saville asked.

Fi simply laughed as she continued to clean.

†

Fi frowned as she looked in her rearview mirror and saw that Saville had turned as if she were heading home. She

164

wondered why Saville had asked if she could shower at her place if she was just going to go home? *Whatever. If I have fifty more years with her, I'll never figure that woman out.*

The second Fi opened her front door, she shed her clothes in the entryway, not wanting to track drywall dust all over her shiny wood floors. She took great pride in keeping her home showroom quality. The recycled wood had been lovingly hand-sanded. After she added the clear satin finish, the beauty of the wood grain popped to the surface. She still cringed when Sassy would run and play on the bare wood, fearing that her cat would scratch the finish. So far, she'd been able to lead Sassy to the carpeted sections to play, and during the day, the cat usually took a long nap. Sassy also spent a considerable amount of time outside stalking her prey.

On cue, Sassy sauntered into the foyer, stretched her paws in front and yawned. She sniffed at the pile of clothes on the floor, then turned away. Fi crouched in front of Sassy, running her hand over her head, then scratching under her chin.

"Did my baby miss me?"

"Meow."

"Yeah, I know, Sassy, I haven't been home a lot lately. Maybe I should go to the shelter and get you a new playmate?" Fi continued to pet her cat, who placed her paws on each shoulder, giving her owner a kitty hug. Fi loved how affectionate her shelter rescue cat was.

"Meow."

"You like that idea, huh?" Fi kept scratching Sassy's ears and chin, and then she smacked her head. "Damn, I almost forgot about Saville's asshole neighbors and that poor dog they have chained up. Don't let me forget to have a serious talk with Saville. We need to make plans for a dognapping."

"Meow."

Fi walked naked into her kitchen and retrieved a plastic garbage bag for her clothes. Stuffing the dust-filled pile into the bag, she promptly dumped them into her washing machine before heading to her master suite. Although Fi expected the rest of the gang to arrive in the next hour, she continued to walk naked around her bedroom, pulling out various outfits and then promptly discarding them on the bed. She'd have to clean the mess before everyone arrived. Finally, she had decided on what she would wear and was about to walk into her master bath when she heard three sharp knocks.

"Hello," Saville called. "I hope you don't mind. I let myself in."

"Shit, shit, shit." Fi quickly shook her head over the sink, attempting to loosen most of the plaster dust in her hair. "I'll be out in a minute." She grabbed her robe before greeting Saville.

Saville had carried several bags into her home and set them on the kitchen counter. She looked particularly pleased with herself.

"What's in the bags?" Fi tried to ignore the small amount of dust that Saville tracked in.

"Dinner. I bought supplies for tacos. It isn't Tuesday, but I thought it would be an easy meal to make. I got ground turkey for you and anyone else who might have an aversion to beef. But, I couldn't bring myself to buy tofu. I hope there aren't any pure vegans or vegetarians in the group. I also got limes for margaritas because I know you have that nice bottle of tequila. I called Lucy and asked her to bring some

Cointreau. She sounded excited for Taco Friday, especially with the prospect of having a true margarita instead of that shitty mix they use in most bars."

"Oh, okay." Fi glanced at her gleaming floor with a trail of white particles to the kitchen and grabbed her broom and dustpan to sweep them up.

Saville stood frozen in the kitchen. "Oh, shit, I'm sorry I tracked that crap into your beautiful home. Maybe I should have stripped the minute I entered. I thought I'd shaken most of it off on the ride over."

Before Fi could stop herself, she'd answered, "That's what I did."

"Damn. If I'd known that, I wouldn't have stopped at the store first. I would have followed you home." Saville winked.

Fi pulled another garbage bag from the cabinet below her sink and handed it to Saville. "You can put your clothes in here, and I'll add them to my load."

Saville began to strip, and Fi looked away. "Um, I'm going to jump in the shower now. Do you need me to get you a towel?"

Saville laughed. "It's not like you've never seen me naked before or that I haven't been to your house. I know where you keep your towels. But, if you don't mind, can you spare shorts and a T-shirt, so I won't have to sit around in a towel waiting for my clothes to dry. I suppose I didn't plan this well because I don't have an extra change of clothes."

Fi kept her body turned away from Saville and mumbled, "Yeah, I'll set them outside the bathroom for you after I finish my shower."

As she walked away, she heard Saville chuckling, and then her affectionate cat must have come to check out the new person because she heard Saville having a conversation with Sassy.

†

Saville grabbed the beef, ground turkey, and cheese from the bag and placed the food in the refrigerator. She left the rest of the ingredients on the counter when she felt a tickle on her leg. Looking down, she found a fluffy tortoiseshell cat weaving in and out of her legs.

"Well, Sassy, you certainly don't live up to that name. You're an affectionate little girl, aren't you?"

"Meow."

"Yes, and just as beautiful as your mommy. I think I shocked her when I stripped in the kitchen." Saville snorted. "I don't think she remembers how immodest I can be."

Saville collected her bag of clothes and dumped them into the washer to mingle with Fi's work attire. Sassy had followed her to the laundry room, so Saville leaned down and scratched her behind her ears.

"Ooh, you like that, don't you? Do you think it's strange that I'm jealous of my dirty clothes?" she asked, laughing at how ridiculous that would sound to someone who might overhear her talking to the cat. "Don't look at me like that. I just meant that my clothes get to take a bath with her adorable overalls, and the owner hasn't invited me to get all slippery and soapy with her. That seems unfair, doesn't it? Let's go find me a towel before your mommy gets done and sees me lamenting over another missed opportunity to get naked with her."

Opening the hall closet, Saville lifted a fluffy sage green towel, perfectly folded, which sat on top of the other flawlessly stacked linen. "I wonder if Fi uses a tape measure when she's folding her towels," she mused. "God forbid they don't stack perfectly. No wonder she's so good at what she does. You'd never see your mommy cutting any corners. She takes the maxim, 'measure twice, cut once' to brand new heights."

The door to the master suite opened, and Fi gasped, "Oh my God. I'm sorry, I was going to lay these on the bed for you. I thought you'd be in the shower by now." Fi looked anywhere but at Saville, who made no effort to hide her naked body. Fi had a towel wrapped around her own body, barely covering her intimate bits.

"Nope, not yet. I was getting to know Sassy. She's lonely. You should get her a playmate. Hey, were you serious about stealing my neighbor's dog?"

"Um, yeah. I was going to talk to you about that. But can we please do that after we both have clothing on?"

Saville laughed. "You at least have a towel. My titties are hanging out for all to see."

"Yeah, I see that."

"Um, no, you don't, because your eyes have been everywhere but on my body. I'm starting to get a complex. Doesn't my body turn you on anymore?" Saville teased.

"No, I mean, yes it does, but I don't think it's appropriate to stare," Fi sputtered.

"You were far from staring. More like avoiding catching even the tiniest glimpse."

"Will you please just jump in the shower? It was your idea to bring taco ingredients, so you're cooking. They'll be here soon, and if I'm starving, I'm sure they're hungry as well."

"Okay, okay, don't let that towel bunch in your pussy."

"What?" Fi gasped.

"Well, you aren't wearing panties, so I couldn't very well say—"

"Just go."

Saville brazenly approached Fi and took the offered clothes from her, hearing Fi's breath hitch as she kept her eyes on the floor. Chuckling, Saville made her way into the guest bathroom as Sassy followed closely behind.

†

"I'm too sexy for my clothes, too sexy for my clothes, yeah too sexy without my clothes," Saville sang loudly in the echo chamber of the shower. Hearty laughter reverberated inside the shower, making it possible for Fi to hear Saville clearly sing the revised words to the famous song.

"I can hear you," Fi said through her laughter.

"You're too sexy for your towel, too sexy for your towel so sexy…And we're too sexy for our clothes, too sexy to wear clothes, too sexy for our clothes," Saville crooned. Badly, but that was all part of Saville's charm.

Fi couldn't help herself. Saville was clearly bonkers, but she loved that about her. The flirting. The teasing. The innuendoes. Fi loved every single one. She couldn't fool herself anymore. No matter what came out of Saville's mouth, unfiltered and raw, she loved it.

The doorbell interrupted Saville's singing as Fi hurried to answer the door. Opening the front door, Fi waved Chelsey, Lucy, and Bea inside while placing her index finger on her lips and beckoning them to follow. As they made their way to the hallway just outside of the guest bath, all four women doubled over in laughter as Saville's singing turned to rap.

"I like big boobs. I cannot lie. Yeah, those soft pillowy globes. They make me smile."

When Fi heard Saville turn off the water, she gestured for the small group to follow and headed to the kitchen, pulling her bottle of tequila from the refrigerator.

"Margaritas, anyone?"

"Hell, yes," Lucy answered. She held up the bottle of Cointreau. "Saville called because she wasn't sure you had any."

Chelsey nodded and said, "Sure, why not, but only one. Too much tequila makes me a little goofy and hung over."

"This is the good stuff. It won't give you a hangover. I had a friend show me the error of my ways and bought me this bottle of Dobel. The trick is you have to buy one hundred percent blue agave tequila."

"Good to know."

"I'll have a tiny bit." Bea demonstrated the amount with her thumb and forefinger. "Someone has to drive these two home."

"So, Saville's in your shower," Chelsey noted. "Is there a recent development with you two?"

"What? Oh no. God, no. Although, the arrogant little minx stripped right here in this kitchen." Fi pulled her cutting board from a drawer and began rolling the limes.

Lucy laughed. "Did she think she'd have time for a quickie before we arrived?"

"Yeah, right." Fi grunted. "No. Saville was just showing off with her perfect body. I might have pulled out a broom and dustpan when I saw a minuscule amount of dust on my wood floor. Her response was to strip where she stood so she wouldn't track anymore of the worksite on my floors on her way to the shower."

"And she was taking a shower because…" Chelsey left the question for Fi to fill in the blank.

"Her place is way on the other side of town." Fi cut the limes in half and then pulled her manual citrus press from another drawer.

"Smart." Lucy grinned.

"Yeah, convenient," Chelsey added.

"What? Nothing is going on."

"Yet. Saville is making her play. The question you need to grapple with is, will you let her?" Chelsey asked.

"Now, that is an excellent question." Fi methodically pressed the lime juice into a cocktail mixer, then added simple syrup, Cointreau, and the Dobel. Fi pushed the top of the spinner several times, using the device to blend the four ingredients thoroughly. "Who wants to be my first taste tester?"

Lucy raised her hand.

"Salted rim?" Fi asked.

"No. Better not."

Fi filled a glass with ice, then poured the margarita she'd just made into the tumbler, handing it to Lucy as she waited patiently for her assessment of the drink.

Lucy took a sip of the drink. "Mm, this is heavenly. Best margarita I've ever tasted. Bea, you're going to love it."

Fi poured the last bit into a small glass and finished the remainder of the drink, nodding her agreement that it was good.

Saville sauntered into the kitchen, towel drying her hair. "I see you've started the party without me. Fi, you want me to put this towel in the washer with our clothes?" She side-eyed Chelsey while smirking at her.

"Yeah, thanks. You want a margarita, right?" Fi asked.

"Of course. But I can wait until you fix everyone else one. I need to cook the meat. Anyone a vegetarian?" Saville asked.

"I don't eat beef," Chelsey answered.

"Of course you don't," Saville mumbled. "Don't worry. I bought ground turkey for those who wish to ruin a perfectly good taco."

Fi stopped pressing her lime and raised her hand. "I'll take one with ground turkey."

Saville rolled her eyes. "Yeah, I already know that. I still don't understand how you can eat chicken and fish, but not beef. When did you decide beef was the enemy?"

"Since I saw that documentary on the beef industry," Fi answered.

"Don't tell me anything about it. I want to preserve my sacred taco," Saville joked. "Okay, anyone else for the inferior replacement meat?"

Lucy raised her hand. "Sorry, Saville, I'm with Chelsey and Fi, but Bea will eat the beef tacos with you."

"Alrighty then. The quicker we prepare the taco fixings, the sooner we can eat. Anyone willing to help grate cheese and cut up the tomatoes, onions, and lettuce?"

"I can do that after I finish making margaritas," Fi offered.

"No, dear, you just keep those drinks coming. We'll all help Saville."

Fi held up the cocktail mixer. "Who's next? Salt or no salt?"

CHAPTER TWELVE

"Compliments to the chefs." Fi held her glass in the air.

Bea had switched to water, but the rest of the group held up their margaritas and clinked glasses. Everyone except Bea was on her second or third drink, and Lucy noted the increase in laughter as everyone loosened up.

"Hey, after Lucy reads a few more passages, you guys wanna join Fi and me for an adventure tonight?" Saville grinned.

Fi scrunched her nose. "What adventure?"

"Project dognapping."

"I'm in," Lucy and Chelsey answered in stereo.

"I don't think that's a good idea," Bea warned.

"Aw, come on, Bea. You can drive the getaway vehicle since you're the only sober one here." Lucy giggled. "Besides, we can't leave that poor dog chained outside."

"Exactly." Saville slapped her hand on her knee.

"Maybe you all should sober a bit before we attempt to rescue, not kidnap, the dog," Bea suggested. "No more margaritas."

"I like how you reframed that, honey. Yes, let's call it a rescue, not a kidnapping. Surely they won't put us in jail for helping that poor animal." Lucy gulped her margarita. She decided not to respond to Bea's other suggestion. One more drink wouldn't kill her, especially if the good tequila didn't cause a hangover. That was a welcome bonus.

"So, let's cut to the chase and have Lucy read the last passages in both journals, and then we'll head out. It should be plenty dark by then," Saville said.

"Oh, and I have one more thing to share." Earlier, Lucy had set both journals on the coffee table. She pulled a small, yellowed piece of paper from inside one journal. The edges had curled, but the writing was still legible. "I found this telegram in that box of old documents. It stuck to Pearl and Joseph's wedding announcement. Apparently, she accepted Joseph's proposal, and he was that Italian businessman."

"Who sent the telegram?" Saville asked.

"Mae." Lucy pulled her reading glasses from her bag. "I'll read it to you. 'Dear Pearl, I regret to inform you of the death of your parents. The town is overrun with outlaws. Please stay in Boston for your safety. It was your father and mother's dying wish that you remain safe. My sincere condolences, Mae Livingston.'"

"Wow! Short and sweet. Do you think that's what George and Ruth wanted? How is that making things right if they intended for Pearl to have all that gold?" Chelsey asked.

"I think Ruth had internal conflicts. She didn't want Pearl to feel any shame or have her reputation ruined. Let me read you Ruth's final journal entry." Lucy carefully opened the journal and flipped to the last page with writing. "'April 3rd, 1909. Mae's eyes were wild as she came running into the saloon, but it was too late. George wanted me to take the gold and run. He was prepared to face the mob on his own. I could not do that to my beloved husband and refused to leave his side. I will face the same fate as him. He made Mae promise to keep Pearl away from the truth. George trusts Mae, so I must trust her as well. Gold has corrupted the purest soul. I only hope that Pearl will find happiness and continue to live a good life without the burden of truth to weigh her down. We have left her with ample resources to live in luxury.'"

"That double-crossing little turd," Saville interjected. "Mae kept the gold for herself, didn't she?"

"Not exactly. Or at least, an angry ghost intervened," Lucy answered.

"George?"

"No. Actually, I think it was Ruth. She wasn't as trusting as George. Maybe it was both of them, but her diary only refers to one ghost."

"God, Aunt Lucy, you should be a game show host the way you string things out. Just read Mae's last journal entry already." Chelsey drained her margarita.

"Okay. But I need to read the last three entries so you have the full picture. 'April 5th, 1909. I'm getting out of this hellhole. Pearl is at her fancy school and already has a marriage proposal. She doesn't need this gold, but I do. I know I promised George, but they're both dead. What does it matter now? I can start a new life in California. Perhaps when I get to California, I can wire some of it to Pearl. That would be a fair proposition. Surely, I will have made things right by sending a portion to Pearl. I deserve something after ministering to George before she met Ruth. I was the only one who knew her secret and tended to her needs. Throwing me over wasn't right.'"

"Yup, jilted lover. Ruth was right not to trust that harlot," Saville said. "Good on Ruth if she stopped Mae from stealing Pearl's inheritance, even though the gold never quite made it to Boston. Do the final two entries explain what happened?"

"I think so. Here's the first one. 'June 5th, 1909. It's been two months since the hanging, and every time I prepare to leave, the gold is no longer in the hiding place. Even my attempts at sewing the gold into the hem of several dresses have gone awry. I find them shredded to bits, and although I know it is not the work of rats, the alternate explanation is too implausible. Perhaps the talk of ghosts is getting to me. Yet, I wonder if I am going crazy. The box seems to appear and disappear, mocking me. Perhaps I should try to keep the box with me and slip out in the middle of the night. The next time I locate the gold, that is what I shall do. I convinced the new owner to let me stay in Ruth's old sitting room as long as I continue to service his patrons. Three letters have arrived from Pearl. Not knowing where to send the letters, the mail clerk has given them to me, believing I will contact Pearl to inform her of the events surrounding her parents' deaths. I can't risk her coming back and finding the gold. I've sent a telegram to inform her of her parents' deaths.'"

"What a selfish bitch. I hope Ruth or George scared the shit out of her," Fi said.

"Oh, at least one of them did. Final passage, and it's cut off, so I'm not exactly sure of Mae's fate." Lucy began to read the last passage. "'June 7th, 1909. It was her face, but not what I remember. Her menacing grimace hovered not more than three inches above my bed. The distortion in her features caused me to tremble as I slowly took in my surroundings. The gold is no longer in bed with me, and the place is in shambles. The strange happenings in the saloon now make sense. I have seen the ghost they all speak of. The saloon is indeed haunted. All the men responsible for George and Ruth's deaths have left town without warning or notice. Simply vanished into thin air. If I am to believe her, I will not survive the night if I do not leave this...'" Lucy lifted her head and looked at each person in their small group.

"That's it?" Chelsey exclaimed.

"Sorry, that's it. I'm guessing Ruth paid her a visit," Lucy surmised.

"Why do you think that?" Fi asked. "Ruth seems the gentler of the two."

Lucy shrugged. "Just a gut feeling. Ruth has a bit of fire in her. That's clear throughout her journal. I don't think she was ever the shrinking violet type."

"Yeah, but George was the badass sheriff," Saville argued.

"Still waters run deep," Bea added.

Saville leaned back in her chair. "Wow. That was kind of anti-climactic. Do you think a ghost can actually commit murder?"

"The first time we met George, he was pretty scary. If you hadn't been there, I might have broken my neck or something. Do accidents caused by ghosts count?" Fi asked.

"Probably. But I don't suppose you can arrest George or Ruth and hold a trial. They're already dead. Supernatural double jeopardy." Lucy cackled at her joke, then smacked her hands on her thighs. "Right, then. Let's go on a dognapping adventure."

"Does anyone have a dog leash?" Saville asked.

Everyone in the group shook their head.

Chelsey clarified, "Sorry, I only have a cat. He doesn't exactly like taking walks on a leash."

Saville frowned. "I'd rather not lead the poor thing in that horrible chain they have him on. Do you think she would follow us without a leash?"

"Sassy would do almost anything for yogurt. Dogs are even easier than cats. Do we have any ground beef or turkey left? Hold out a little ball of that, and I'm sure the dog will follow." Fi stood and swayed a little. "Ooh, head rush."

Saville smiled. "How many margaritas did you have?"

A sloppy grin appeared on Fi's face. "Two and a few taster sips to make sure I had blended them well enough."

"Did you sip from every drink you made?" Saville asked.

"Maybe."

Saville sidled against Fi, putting her arm around the tipsy woman and giving her a small amount of stability. "Okay, no more tasting sips for you."

Fi pouted. "Aw, you're no fun." Fi brushed her hand down Saville's chest.

"On the contrary, I'm loads of fun. But you're going to thank me tomorrow for cutting you off. I remember how tequila affects you." Saville turned to Bea. "Bea, you're designated driver, right?"

"Yeah, but I still don't think this is a good idea. What if we're caught? I'm too old for prison. And I look horrible in orange."

"Don't worry, honey. I'll be your prison bitch." Lucy stood and held out her hand to her wife. "Come on. I call shotgun."

†

Lucy giggled in the front seat and began a rendition of "On The Road Again". Saville was the first to join her. The rest of the gang soon followed her except for Bea, who wished she'd brought her earplugs.

Bea had tried hard to convince Lucy to stay in the car while the young and foolish women snuck around Saville's backyard, looking for the best place to climb her fence. But Lucy would have none of that, so Bea followed them, hoping to gain a smidgeon of control.

Saville waved the group over and, in a loud whisper, announced, "Here's good. The dog is right on the other side. See, you can put your foot in this little hole here, and then I'll boost you up."

"I'm not going first," Fi said a little too loudly.

"Shh, you'll wake them up," Saville whispered almost as loudly as Fi had declared she wasn't going first.

"I'll go first," Lucy practically shouted, which earned her a round of shushes followed by loud giggling.

"Oh, for fuck's sake. You people are the worst criminals ever. If we all don't land in jail, it will be a bloody miracle," Bea whispered, promptly followed by shushes and more giggling.

"Okay, put your toe in that little hole there and grab the top of the fence. I'll give you a boost," Saville directed.

Lucy grinned as she put her tennis shoe in the hole and reached for the top. She turned her head and asked, "Hey, honey, is it okay if Saville grabs my ass?"

Saville laughed. "I'm not going to grab your ass. Not that it isn't a fine ass, but I'm just going to give you a little push to clear the top of the fence. Big difference." Saville gave Lucy a tiny push. As Lucy cleared the top of the fence, Bea heard a loud rip before her wife tumbled to the other side of the barrier.

"Oomph. Damn. These were my best shorts."

The dog started barking and pandemonium set in.

Saville put her face next to the hole to see what was happening. "Shit, shit. Okay, everyone is on their own. Lucy, can you unchain the dog while we climb the fence? Then we can lead her to the gate."

"There's a gate?" Bea screeched.

"Well, yeah, of course there's a gate," Saville answered.

"Then why didn't we go through the gate?" Bea gritted her teeth.

"It's more stealthy this way." Saville grinned. "No pain, no gain. But I suppose it'd be better to use the gate now, considering the lights just went on. I guess we don't have time to climb the fence anymore."

"Ya think?" Bea growled.

"Why is there a gate to your neighbor's place?" Chelsey asked. "That's kind of odd, isn't it?"

"Not now, Chelsey." Bea just knew they were going to get caught. She felt like she had attached herself to the

Keystone Cops. If they didn't get arrested, it would be a bloody miracle.

"Okay, hurry, follow me." Saville led the group to the gate, and they all stumbled to where Lucy crouched on the ground, accepting doggy kisses from the excited golden retriever. As the rest of the group advanced on Lucy and the dog, she began barking again.

"Shut the fuck up, you stupid dog," a man in boxer shorts yelled from his doorway. The door banged shut, and the light went off.

Saville crab-walked to Lucy, then reached into her pocket and retrieved a ball of ground beef mixed with cheese inside a Ziploc plastic bag. "Don't worry, he's too lazy to come out and see what's going on." She presented her hand with the treat, and the dog slowly approached, cautiously sniffing Saville's hand.

"Yeah, that's it, Sunny. Take the treat and be a good girl," Lucy said.

"Sunny? Is that her name?" Fi asked.

Lucy shrugged. "I don't know. But since she's a golden, I thought of the sun."

"Can you please be a little quieter? And can we hurry this along?" Bea pleaded. "We can chit-chat about gates and names for the dog later," she hissed.

After feeding Sunny another treat, Saville glanced at the rip in Lucy's shorts and grinned. Her white teeth glowed under the light of the moon. "Yeah, very nice ass, Lucy. Nothing like commando, huh?" Saville held up her hand for Lucy to high-five her.

"Really? Not only are we going to be caught, but your ass will hang out in jail for all to see. Forget what our mothers used to say about wearing clean underwear in case we get in an accident and end up in the hospital. This is so much worse," Bea groused.

The group continued to giggle, much to Bea's chagrin. However, Saville coaxed Sunny along as she kept pulling small balls of meat from the baggy. They finally reached the fence, and Sunny decided it must be playtime as she started running in circles, jumping and barking. The light to the neighbor's house went on again, but this time, he moved from his doorway.

"You stupid mutt!" he yelled as he entered the backyard.

"Whoops. Time's up." Saville chased Sunny until she grabbed the playful dog by her fur and dragged her to the open gate. "Shh, please don't bark." She shoved another ball of meat under her nose and kept pulling her along. The group started running toward the open gate as they followed Saville and Sunny.

"Who's out there?" the man yelled. "I've got a shotgun."

Bea had thought about the possibility of getting caught, but she hadn't even considered that someone might shoot at them.

As dog and gang reached Bea's car, it became apparent that not everyone and the dog would fit. It was already tight with five adults. Saville appeared to assess the situation more quickly than Bea thought possible for someone who had consumed several margaritas.

"Go, go, go. I'll sneak into my house without turning on any lights, and if he comes over, I'll act like he woke me up."

"But your Harley is at my place," Fi said.

"We can figure that out tomorrow. Come on, time to go," Bea said.

Lucy and Chelsey lifted Sunny into the car and then climbed in, leaving the front seat for Fi as Bea slammed on the gas pedal, burning rubber as she careened down the driveway and onto the side road. Although she glanced in her rearview mirror, she couldn't see anything. She hoped Saville had made it safely into her home.

†

Before opening her door, Saville counted to twenty, grabbed her shirt, and crumpled it in her hand to create wrinkles. Then, rubbing her eyes, she opened her door and remarked, "What the fuck, Todd. You woke me up. I have to be up early tomorrow for a job."

"Someone stole my fucking dog, and since you've been bitching about me chaining her up, I thought you might know something about this. I heard the car screech out of your driveway," he said accusingly.

Saville shook her head. "Nope. Don't know a thing. Now, if you'll excuse me, I'd like to go back to sleep if you don't mind. Call the cops and leave me alone."

"I'll do that, but if I find out you had something to do with this, I'm gonna fuck you up, you meddling dyke."

"You have a good night, too." Saville slammed her door and breathed a sigh of relief. Then she started laughing uncontrollably. When her phone rang, she was still laughing as she answered.

"Hello."

"Saville, it's Fi. Are you okay?"

"Where are you at?"

"Oh, we're still in Bea's car, heading to my place. Sunny is surprisingly calm. I think she knows we came to rescue her. She's got this raw spot on her neck, but I'm afraid to take her to a vet in case she has a chip or something."

"Bring her to the job site tomorrow, and I'll take a look." Saville walked into her living room and plopped on the couch.

"Um, how were you planning to get there? Remember, your bike is at my place."

"Right, I forgot about that. Do you think you could come to get me?"

"Of course. I'll bring your work clothes. Don't forget that we're supposed to go to Amelia and Darcy's tomorrow. We can knock off early, and you can shower at my place again. And, this time, remember to bring an extra set of clothes."

"Thanks, Fi. For everything. Sunny is going to have a much better life with you and Sassy."

"I sure hope Sunny is housebroken. I don't even have a leash for her."

"We can go shopping for everything tomorrow after work. I'll bet Amelia and Darcy are gonna love her. We can bring her to the farm and let her go wild." Saville smiled at the thought of the sweet dog running free as opposed to chained up all day.

"Do you think that's a good idea? I don't want Sunny running away. It would defeat the purpose of rescuing her," Fi said.

"I say we worry about that tomorrow after determining how well Sunny responds to commands. For a dog who was abused by her owner, she was

186

uncharacteristically friendly. But then again, I think dogs have a good sense about people. She knew we were there to help. I'll see you tomorrow. Give Sunny kisses and hugs for me."

"Goodnight, Saville."

"Goodnight, Fi." Saville sighed as she ended the call. She'd decided to stop messing around and would make her play on Sunday, when it was just the two of them. *What's the worst that can happen? Rejection?* Other women had rejected her in the past, and it wasn't that bad. But this was Fi. If Fi scorned her, that would hurt. A lot. At least they didn't have to contend with an angry mob or jealous prostitute. That would suck. Or be a pain in the neck— literally.

CHAPTER THIRTEEN

Saville pried her eyes open as she heard the three crisp knocks on her door. At first, she thought her neighbor was back because surely it wasn't morning yet, but then she looked through her blinds and could see evidence that the sun had risen.

"Shit, shit. That must be Fi." She grabbed the pair of shorts she'd discarded on the floor and jumped on one foot, trying to put them on, while looking for where she'd tossed the T-shirt. "Just a minute," she called.

Grabbing the T-shirt, she headed for the door and flung it open as she pulled the shirt over her head.

Fi raised an eyebrow. "Did you oversleep?"

Saville attempted to brush down her unruly hair. "Yeah, sorry. You wouldn't happen to have those work clothes I left? Going without a bra is fun and all, but my breasts get especially sensitive right before I get my period, and I have a favorite sports bra that I usually wear to work."

Fi held up a plastic bag. "Right here. I have coffee and bagels in the truck, which I hope won't be destroyed by the time we climb inside. I gave Sunny more of that beef this morning, but I wasn't sure how much. So, if she's still hungry…bye, bye, bagels. I didn't pack a lunch because I'm hoping to knock off around noon. I thought maybe we could go shopping and catch some lunch before showering and heading to Amelia and Darcy's."

Saville couldn't help the smile that blossomed on her face. She took the plastic bag from Fi and answered, "Sounds like a perfect plan. Give me a couple of minutes to brush my teeth, comb this mess"—she pointed to her head—"then I'll be raring to go." Saville glanced at her living room. It wasn't perfect, like Fi's, but it wasn't a complete pigsty either. She opened her door wider and said, "Come on in. I'd offer you coffee while you wait, but you already took care of that."

Saville hurried to her bedroom to change clothes. She thought about giving Fi the borrowed clothes, but that would be rude, so she tossed them into her laundry basket, hoping she had time to do a load before they had dinner together on Sunday. When Saville emerged, Fi stood, and Saville followed her to the truck. Bursting with uncontrollable laughter, she spied Sunny trying to lick off the cream cheese smeared all over her snout.

"Sunny one. Bagels zero," Saville said through her laughter.

Sunny had torn open the bag and left pieces of the brown paper strewn all over the front seat, along with the last bits of cream cheese that she was now attempting to lick off the seats.

Fi sighed and made a half-hearted attempt to scold Sunny. "Bad dog. That's people food. I know it's confusing because we sort of gave you people food last night and this morning, but I'm going to have to teach you the difference."

Saville chuckled. "Yeah, good luck with that. The first rule of dog ownership, never leave food unattended."

Fi pointed at Saville. "You're going to help me train her. I want a dog with perfect manners. I can't have her destroying my house."

"I'd be happy to help. Consider Sunny our dog. I'll pay for half of her upkeep. I'll even buy all the toys and supplies today to get her started out right in her new home."

Fi shook her head at the mess and grabbed for her container of baby wipes, running them over not only the vinyl seats on her old truck but also over Sunny's muzzle. Sunny sneezed in response but remained passive while Fi cleaned her nose and mouth.

"That's a good girl. At least you didn't destroy the coffee." Fi turned to Saville. "Are you okay with fast food? We can hit one of the drive-throughs on our way to the site."

"Sure, I'm not the picky one."

"Just because I try not to put too much crap in my body doesn't mean I'm picky."

"I thought breakfast was exempt. Donuts and those chocolate-filled croissants you love don't seem to rise to the level of crap foods that never pass your lips. But I guess you have exceptions to your rules. We can wait until we reach the saloon and Lucy arrives. She always brings donuts." Saville bit her tongue, so she wouldn't remark about how Fi had also allowed Saville to invade her body, and she was the epitome of a crap person.

"Sometimes it's good to partake in something bad for you, as long as you don't make a habit of it…"

"Hmm. Easier said than done. If it's that good, making a habit of it might be the perfect thing to do. Life's too short to deprive yourself of everything that pleases you." Saville shrugged. "Just saying."

†

Normally, Fi would never have gone out in public without a shower. But she was starving after passing on a fourth day of gooey breakfast foods that would certainly not do her hips any good. The only saving grace was her choice of occupation, which kept her busy and fit. She also convinced herself that she needed to get dog supplies, especially a leash. Sunny was basically a well-behaved dog, but food out in the open proved much too tempting for her. That became apparent as they walked into the pet store, and she made a beeline for the exposed bins.

"Whose brilliant idea was it to allow dogs into a store where the bins with doggy treats are at the perfect sniffing level?" Fi asked.

"Well, all the other dogs are on a leash," Saville answered. "I know you don't want to grab her by the neck to yank her away from temptation, but until we get a chest restraint that won't irritate her raw spot when we give a little tug, you're going to have to hold her a little tighter by her fur."

"Her whimper breaks my heart."

"Do you trust me?"

Fi squinted at Saville and hesitantly answered, "Uh, yeah, I guess."

"Well, don't fall all over yourself to give me a resounding answer. Look, I already offered to buy all the 'welcome to your new home' gifts, so why don't you take Sunny to your truck, and I'll get everything. It'll be a lot quicker, anyway. Then we can grab something to eat. You must be ravenous with hunger."

"I am. So I will take you up on your offer." Fi gently grabbed Sunny's fur and led her outside.

Once they were away from the tempting smells, Sunny obediently walked beside Fi who opened the back of her truck and sat on the tailgate, waiting for Saville to finish shopping.

"Sit," Fi commanded, and Sunny promptly sat on the ground in front of the truck, wagging her tail as Fi absently brushed her hands over Sunny's fur, careful to avoid the raw spot on her neck. "Good girl. You're such a good girl."

Fi smiled as she thought about the previous evening when she'd set a fluffy blanket out for Sunny, who had promptly flopped her body onto it and remained there after Fi had commanded her to get on the makeshift dog bed and stay. The following day, she found Sassy curled next to Sunny with her paw on Sunny's belly. When they'd gotten home, Sassy was nowhere to be found, but apparently, in the middle of the night, she'd taken it upon herself to welcome the new furbaby. Fi had tried to remain somewhat alert in case Sassy wasn't as welcoming as Fi hoped she would be. Her fears were unfounded. They appeared to be best mates right off the bat.

It didn't take Saville long to finish shopping as she nearly bounced out of the store, pushing a large cart filled to the brim. She had a goofy, self-satisfied look on her face.

"Geez, what did you do? Buy out the store?" Fi asked.

Saville reached down and scratched Sunny behind the ears. "After all the years of abuse and neglect, this pretty girl deserves to be treated like royalty. Maybe we should rename her Queenie or Princess."

Fi frowned. "Ew, no. That's like a name you'd force on one of those little yappy dogs. I'd never call her something frou-frou like that."

"And you think Sassy is not a frou-frou name?"

"It's not. What are you, the pet-name police?"

Saville shook her head and laughed. "Okay, I guess we're staying with Sunny."

"We? Sunny is my dog now."

Saville pounded her chest. "Ouch, that hurt. I thought we were going to raise her together. You know pets do so much better with two parents."

"Who says?"

"*Pet Me* magazine," Saville deadpanned.

"You're making that up."

Saville pulled a magazine from one of the bags and held it up. "Am not. At least not about there being a pet magazine. There were actually quite a few to choose from."

Fi began laughing. "Okay, you can be Sunny's other mom because I don't want all the responsibility of raising her alone."

"What about Sassy? Can I be her other mom, too? We can be like a blended family."

Fi grabbed one of the large bags of dog food and tossed it in the back of the truck. "You are so silly."

"All part of my charm, right?" Saville winked.

"Come on, give me a hand. I'm starving."

"Yes, ma'am. Or should I say, yes, my beautiful co-parent?" Saville began helping Fi unload the cart.

†

Saville sat on the sofa in Fi's living room, waiting for her to finish blow-drying her hair. Saville didn't understand why Fi wanted to get dressed up just to go to a barbeque. Sassy had jumped in her lap, and Sunny remained on the floor by her feet, accepting a random scratch to her ears while Saville continued to pet the insistent cat who kept nudging her hand and wrapping her paws around Saville's arm.

"Your momma is primping, even though she looks great finger-combing her hair with no make-up. Don't get me wrong, she's also hot when she dresses up and styles her hair, but I'm just saying she doesn't need it. You don't mind, do you, Sassy? As long as I pet you, she can take three hours to get ready."

Sunny's ears perked up. She stood, nosing Sassy aside to lay her head in Saville's lap. Sassy took a swipe at her nose, then jumped down and sashayed away.

Saville chuckled. "Jealous much? I think you pissed off Sassy. You better do some serious groveling tonight when we get back. That wasn't very nice of you to push Sassy off my lap. She doesn't get to spend all day with us like you. I know you're making up for lost time, but poor Sassy needed some attention from her moms, too."

Fi walked into the room, fluffing her hair. "What's going on?"

"The siblings just had their first tiff."

"Let me guess. Sassy swiped at Sunny."

194

"Yup. Apparently, Sunny felt the need to nose Sassy off my lap because that's where she wanted to lay her head."

"Well, let's just say that Sassy came by her name because she can cop an attitude. I don't think it'll be the only time she bops Sunny in the nose. Hopefully, she retracts her claws, or we'll need to tend to the random scratch here or there. I'm glad to see that Sunny's neck already looks better. That ointment I put on her is helping."

Saville pushed aside Sunny's fur to inspect her neck. "Yeah, it doesn't look as raw and irritated. But I still don't think we should put a collar on her yet. The harness I bought works well."

"Are you sure we should take Sunny with us? I've heard that alpacas don't necessarily mix with dogs."

"Well, they didn't have an article about that in *Pet Me*, but I did an Internet search while you were getting ready, and before our attention-starved kids crawled all over me. They get along fine as long as the dog is well trained and doesn't chase the alpacas. We'll have to introduce Sunny slowly to the herd."

"Our kids?"

"Yeah, didn't we agree to raise them together? If you're worried, I can formally adopt Sassy. We can go see the family judge on Monday to fill out all the necessary paperwork."

Fi laughed. "You do that. Let me know how that goes. Ready?"

"Uh, yeah, I've been ready for"—Saville turned her wrist to glance at her watch—"six hours."

"Hardy, har, har. Exaggerate much?"

"So," Saville hesitantly began, "I thought maybe we could drive together and I could crash at your place tonight.

Then we could spend the whole day together tomorrow instead of just dinner."

"Um…"

"I mean, that's only if you didn't have any plans for earlier in the day. I know Sunday is your day of rest. We could just hang at your place and chill. We don't have to do anything strenuous."

"No, I didn't have any plans. Mostly household chores, like cleaning the house and doing laundry. I really should tend to my overgrown backyard, but that takes a bit more effort than I'm willing to put in on my only day off for the foreseeable future. I suppose if you want to stay that would be okay."

"Well, don't sound so thrilled. I could help with your yard. I find gardening very therapeutic."

"You do?"

"Yeah, don't sound so surprised. I used to have an extensive garden at my old place, but I don't find it very therapeutic working in my backyard while I listen to my neighbor bitch and moan about all kinds of trivial shit. You'd think that with all the sitting and drinking beer in his backyard, he'd let Sunny run free, but no, he is a world-class bastard. Used to let her whimper and periodically tell her to shut the fuck up. I hate that dicknob. Every day I don't have to be home is like a holiday."

Fi's face softened. "Great. I'd love the help."

"Thanks, Fi. So, who gets to be the designated driver tonight?"

"I will. Because I'm not letting you drive my truck."

"Why not? It's a piece of shit. Besides, you could hop on the back of my Harley. I know you want to ride *bitch*."

"Nope. Never going to happen. Besides, where would we put Sunny? And for your information, my truck is a classic. She's not a piece of shit. You better lower your voice before she hears you. She's delicate and doesn't need your aggressive style of driving."

"When you drive a motorcycle, you have to be aggressive because everyone else on the road thinks they own the whole damn thing."

"Exactly. I'm not going to be another statistic. Besides, the helmet will mess up my hair."

Saville laughed. "That's the real reason. Admit it. I'm taking you on a ride tomorrow morning after you've slept all night and have bed head. Then it won't matter if the helmet smashes your precious hair. It will already bc cattywampus."

"I don't have bed head."

"Sorry to burst your bubble, but yes, you do. If it's any consolation, it was adorable." Saville grabbed the harness she'd set on the couch and put the restraint over Sunny's body. Sunny squirmed a little at the unknown restraint, but eventually let Saville secure it around her chest.

"Beautiful. Doesn't she look good in her new harness?"

"Yes, she does. Aren't you a pretty girl?" Fi grabbed the new leash and attached it to the back of the harness. "Come on, girl, we're off to an adventure, but you need to be nice around Amelia and Darcy's alpacas."

CHAPTER FOURTEEN

The barbeque on the farm reminded Lucy of when she first came out as a lesbian, and the primary means of socialization was the women's bar or potlucks at someone's home. Typically, Lucy would have made her way to the kitchen, where most of the action usually occurred. But on arrival, Lucy had made a beeline to the fence where the herd of alpacas had hesitantly approached.

"They're like the punk rock version of sheep. Aren't they adorable, Bea?" Lucy exclaimed. "Do you think I can pet them?"

Bea shrugged. "I know nothing about alpacas. You better ask first."

Darcy approached, smiling at the older couple. "Hi, you must be Bea." She offered her hand. "I'm Darcy, Amelia's wife."

Lucy smiled back at the tall woman with dark hair. "Hey, Darcy. Good to see you again. Thank you so much for inviting us. I've always wanted to visit an alpaca farm. Their little faces are so precious. I just want to kiss and hug them. Can I pet them?"

"Carmen is the bravest. She'll approach, especially if you have a treat for her." Darcy pointed to the fawn-colored alpaca leading the pack.

"I don't suppose cheesecake or wine are the types of treats you're referring to."

Darcy laughed, then glanced to her right. "No, but I think the cavalry just arrived. Amelia always has apple slices in her bag."

"Hello, ladies. I see you met my wife. Did I hear something about apples?" She handed Lucy a plastic bag filled with apple slices. "Carmen will take the treat from your hand. Put a slice in your palm, and she'll come get it from you."

Lucy giggled when the docile animal approached, and her soft muzzle tickled her hand. "I got to bottle feed a baby goat once. Do you bottle feed the babies?" Lucy asked.

"Not usually. A cria, that's a baby alpaca, stays with its mother for five to six months. The only time we had to bottle feed a baby was when we tragically lost the mother. I would not want to repeat that experience. Carmen was that baby. I think that's why she gravitates to people and loves interacting with strangers. From a very young age, she got used to us. She's spoiled rotten," Darcy explained. "When Amelia and I first started dating, I think Amelia fell in love with Carmen before me."

Amelia lightly smacked Darcy's arm. "Now that's a big fat lie. Just look at Darcy. Who could resist that swagger? She was always the hottest butch in the room."

Darcy chuckled. "Lust is not the same thing as love. Besides, Saville and I were always together, and she was the one who attracted all the attention. Not sure how I caught your eye versus Saville."

"Don't sell yourself short. Both of you had women fawning over you. Besides, I met you during the start of Saville's roaching around period. I hope that phase is ending. She needs to pull her head out of her ass and go for it with Fi."

"Roaching around? That's a new one," Lucy said.

"It's a gross term for someone who sleeps around. You know how you might see only one cockroach, but when you turn on the lights, there are a lot more scurrying around. Hidden sexual partners," Amelia added as a clarification.

Lucy nodded. "Clever. Have Saville and Fi always had that chemistry?"

"Saville is my best friend, and believe it or not, she has a heart of gold. But she can also be a total titnob. Amelia wouldn't talk to her for a week after what she did to Fi. There are always two sides, though. From what Saville said, Fi wasn't up for a relationship, either, although you could have fooled me. We see through their bullshit, but I refuse to get involved. They need to work it out on their own. I told Amelia that."

"I wish Lucy subscribed to that philosophy. She had to meddle and brought her niece into the middle of it. Speaking of Chelsey, I think that's her car pulling into your driveway," Bea announced.

"Don't pooh-pooh my methods. If you were paying attention at all to what's been happening, you would have recognized how those two women are circling each other's orbits. It won't be long now. Trust me. Those two are going to knock boobs again. Soon."

Darcy and Amelia burst out in laughter while Bea shook her head. Chelsey had parked and began to make her way to the group.

"Hey. I must have missed something good," Chelsey said.

"Just your aunt being her normal, charming self. You know how she can just blurt something out," Bea said.

"Well, hon, that's the beauty of getting old. We've reached the age where no one expects us to use tact or restraint." Lucy grinned.

"Thank you for inviting us. It's always good to meet other lesbians who live close by, even if you are coupled up. So where's Fi and Saville?" Chelsey asked.

"They aren't here yet. Fi called earlier and said they might be running late. I guess they went shopping for dog supplies. I only heard the Reader's Digest version. I'm waiting for the retelling, but I understand you guys went on a crime spree last night," Amelia joked.

"They're driving together?" Darcy asked.

Amelia smiled. "Yup. And get this. Saville asked to stay the night at Fi's place because they have Sunday dinner plans. She suggested they spend the day together with the new pup. I guess they made arrangements before Saville heard about the barbeque invite. I hope they work things out. I hate having our best friends at war. We all used to have a lot of fun together before Saville fucked that up."

"To be fair, hon, it takes two to tango. Saville didn't exactly force Fi to sleep with her. Fi knew what she was getting into. I'm not defending Saville's asshole move because she had to know that Fi would be way more invested in the possibility of a relationship, but Saville is not a bad person." Darcy leaned against the fence.

"I didn't say she was a bad person. It's just that Fi was so upset, and she's my best friend, so I had to take her side," Amelia clarified. "Besides, you agreed it might be best to keep them apart for a while. Guess that got blown to bits, considering they thankfully agreed to work together on this new project, which I can't wait to hear about. It sounds so intriguing. Ghosts, hangings, lost gold. Nothing that exciting has ever happened to us."

"Shall we head to the patio? Have you had enough petting time with Carmen?" Darcy asked.

Lucy nodded. "Thank you for indulging an old woman. Can we help with dinner?"

"Nope. I don't like anyone messing with my system," Amelia replied. "Timing is everything. I have to make sure the ribs and chicken come off the grill at the same time. Everything else is already prepared and in the refrigerator."

The group walked to the house as Fi's truck barreled up the driveway. Lucy heard the bark before Saville and Fi emerged from the vehicle, holding back an excited golden retriever. She could see Sunny pulling on her harness with her tail wagging furiously with excitement. Amelia was the first to approach, placing her hand under Sunny's nose for her to sniff.

"Aren't you a pretty girl?" Amelia crouched in front of Sunny, who promptly licked her cheek. She pulled back and wiped the wet spot with the sleeve of her T-shirt.

"Mmm, thanks for the doggy kiss. This must be the dog y'all rescued last night. We were just heading to the house. I need to get the meat on the grill."

Fi yanked on the harness. "She's very well behaved, but we haven't quite broken her of that habit. She does love to lick your face. And food seems to be an enormous temptation. I wouldn't put it past her to jump up and steal your ribs while you cook." Fi handed the leash to Saville. "You are on dog-sitting duty. Don't let Sunny nick our food. Amelia's chicken and ribs are way too good for any to end up on the ground or in this one's stomach."

"Don't worry. I have treats in my pocket. Oh, and here's the wine you asked me to bring as an entrance fee to this soiree." Saville handed the bottles to Darcy.

"Thanks. I'll add it to the stash. Two. I'm impressed. And the good stuff, too. Are you housebreaking Saville and teaching her manners along with Sunny?" Darcy joked.

"Sunny has manners," Saville interjected. "I've been working with her, and she's very eager to please. She does well with basic commands. I figure I can train her to leave people food alone. But I'm not going to be cruel and put a piece of meat on her snout and then not let her eat it until I say okay. I always thought that was a really mean trick."

"Yeah, good luck with that. I don't believe Sunny will choose dog biscuits over ribs or chicken," Chelsey said.

Saville frowned and opened her mouth to speak, but Fi grabbed her arm and pulled her away. "Why don't you take Sunny to meet the herd so they won't be afraid. We can help Amelia and Darcy get everything ready."

"I'll go with you, Saville. I wouldn't mind spending more time with those adorable alpacas," Lucy offered.

†

"I know Chelsey is your niece, and I'm sure she's a really nice woman, but damn, she gets under my skin. Sorry, Lucy."

Lucy waved her hand in the air. "She's supposed to get under your skin."

"What?"

"Oh, you know you're jealous. And my lovely niece is just the woman to put the metaphorical boot up your ass to get you to get off your duff and do something about the feelings you have for Fi."

"I'm working on it," Saville grumbled. "I didn't need any assistance from a smart, single lesbian who doesn't have commitment issues."

"Could have fooled me. So what's your plan?"

"I already apologized for being a jerk before, and we sort of cleared the air a little. But I'm not sure Fi will give us another chance at something more than friendship. I was going to have a serious conversation with her tomorrow. I kind of realized how much I care about her. I've always been attracted to Fi, but I'm afraid I can't be the kind of person she wants or needs. I'm not even sure I'll stick around. Work is sporadic at best around here."

Saville tugged on the harness and led Sunny to the fence. She reached into her pocket and held out a dog biscuit. "Sit. Good girl. Come on, Carmen, you know you want to meet Sunny." Saville's smooth voice enticed the alpaca to come to the edge of the fence.

"Why don't the two of you go into business together? We'll sing your praises and tell everyone we know how good you are. Isn't Amelia sending work your way?"

"She is, but construction is full of good old boys."
Saville held onto Sunny, whose tail wagged so vigorously,
Lucy thought it would leave a mark in the grass. "Gentle,"
she commanded, as Carmen and Sunny sniffed one another.
"Good girl."

"Yeah, that's the only thing I don't like about living
in a rural area," Lucy answered.

"People have very particular notions around here
about who should work on their houses. Honestly, this job
we're doing for you was a godsend. It'll keep me here for the
foreseeable future. Then I have to decide whether I need to
move closer to Seattle for more consistent work. If it wasn't
for Darcy, Fi, and Amelia, I would have left months ago."

"Want some advice from an old lady?"

"Sure."

"Just be honest with her. If you're bold and declare
your feelings, do it with genuine emotion, and don't hide
behind your swagger or jokes. I don't think she's going to
give you a third shot, so you better make this one count."

"Way to calm my nerves." Saville grinned. "Like I
wasn't already nervous about my chances with Fi." Saville
kept her focus on Sunny and Carmen as the rest of the herd
drew close. Apparently, Carmen had paved the way for the
curious alpacas.

"We're all rooting for you. Believe it or not, so is
Chelsey. If you weren't in the picture, she would have asked
Fi out, but she figured out pretty quickly what the rest of us
already knew. You two are meant for one another. Even Ruth
and George agree." Lucy reached over and gently ran her
hand over Carmen's nose.

"Seriously? You've had long philosophical
discussions with the ghosts?"

"Not exactly long conversations, but they do talk to me. At first, it was a little creepy how they both looked at me. Can you imagine someone who appears twenty years your junior giving you that look of motherly love? But I understand. They never got to say goodbye to Pearl. Not even in a letter. I think I might be a kind of closure for them. I'm sure they'll continue to pop in, but not to scare anyone. I don't mind. It'll give our retirement community character. Oh, aren't you sweet," Lucy cooed at Carmen. "I should ask Amelia and Darcy about bringing the alpacas to Georgetown Glen after it's finished and we have residents. That would be quite the treat as well."

"They would probably be down for that. They bring them to fairs for the kids sometimes. As for George and Ruth, I don't mind when they pop in, either. They're pretty quiet around us. I get the sense they're curious about the remodel. Thankfully, they've stopped messing with our stuff. I barely even notice them anymore. This morning Fi started explaining her plans for the saloon. I thought it was silly for her to believe she needed their permission as well as yours, but I'm not an expert on ghosts."

"I think that's sweet of her to consider their feelings. Probably prudent, too. Fi is a special person."

"Yeah, she is."

"We hit the jackpot with the two of you. I'm not sure any other contractor would have stuck it out, especially after George tried to rattle you that first day."

†

Amelia leaned back in one of the Adirondack chairs on the patio, sipping from her glass of wine. She was extremely curious about the ghost stories and couldn't wait to get an update. "So, any more sightings of George? There's a local woman who is an amateur historian. She found a photo of the grisly event, but there wasn't a lot of detail in the article."

"Wow! Really? Can we see it? Did you get a copy? I'd love to talk to her," Chelsey said.

"Chelsey is a history buff, too. She teaches history to our future leaders of the world," Lucy said with pride.

"Tess is great. I'm sure she'd love to have a chat with you, especially if you have more information about George. She's also family." Amelia winked. "And single."

"It isn't just George. Ruth pops in, too," Lucy added.

"Ruth? Who is Ruth?" Darcy asked.

"The other ghost. George's wife," Saville answered. "She's a lot nicer than George."

"You're shitting me, right?" Amelia asked.

"Nope. She's more communicative than George, and she left a journal. It's quite enlightening. But we could piece together the rest of the story with Mae's diary. She wasn't a very nice woman. She was a painted lady and in love with George. You know, same old story of a woman scorned. She was the one who revealed that George was a woman," Lucy explained.

"So, you're telling me you've discovered more than the gold and letters? Are Ruth and George still causing trouble?" Amelia asked. "You guys don't look any worse for the wear, so it must be going okay. At least they haven't scared you away."

"Nope, because get this—" Fi's eyes lit up as she shared the big bombshell. "Lucy is Ruth and George's great-great-granddaughter."

"Now you're just yanking my chain," Amelia said.

"No, we're not." Lucy dug into her bag and pulled out a photo, then handed it to Amelia. "That's Pearl, Ruth's daughter. Pretty uncanny how much she looks like me. You should have seen how they reacted to the photo, not to mention how George responded to me the first time I saw him."

Darcy leaned over Amelia's shoulder to look at the picture. "Yeah, I can definitely see the resemblance."

Amelia handed the picture back to Lucy and pulled out her phone. "Here, come look at this. It's a picture of that photo in the newspaper. I snapped this on my phone when Tess showed it to me. It's hard to see their facial features, but I presume the one in pants and vest is George, and the woman in the ruffled dress is Ruth." She gave the phone to Lucy.

Lucy's face went pale. "I can't look at it. Even without seeing their expressions, it's so horrible to see their lifeless bodies. That's the saddest thing I've ever seen."

Amelia took the phone back. "I'm so sorry. I guess I wasn't thinking clearly. I don't know if I could stomach seeing my great-great-grandparents like that either. It's pretty gruesome. Tess was going to do some more research because she vaguely recalls something more about the town and things that happened after the hanging. The town didn't take long to become a ghost town and dry up. Apparently, a ton of strange happenings occurred after the famed hanging. It was rare, almost unheard of, to hang women. So it was a pretty big deal back then."

"I could meet with Tess and help her look through whatever archives she might have back to that time," Chelsey offered. "I can give you my digits if you wouldn't mind sharing them with Tess."

"How are y'all going to deal with Ruth and George if they refuse to leave?" Darcy asked.

"We don't want them to vanish. When they do pop in, it's only for a few minutes. I think it could be a draw. Come on, think about it? There aren't that many retirement communities for lesbians, and this one has its own lesbian ghosts. What more could you ask for? It'll keep us old dykes happy to know that we can remain with our soul mates even after we leave this world." Lucy carefully put the photo of Pearl back into her bag.

"Do you think that after it's finished, people who don't live in the community can visit the place? It would be super cool to have a multigenerational bar for lesbians. Unfortunately, there isn't much around here." Amelia burst with excitement over the prospect of a place to hang that had more character than any bar she'd ever been to. The bar that Saville frequented was definitely not her cup of tea.

"That's the plan," Lucy answered.

"It is?" Bea furrowed her brow.

"Sure. Why not? We can't keep this treasure all to ourselves," Lucy declared.

"But we aren't. I don't want to run a bar in my golden years, especially one we plan to live on top of. I was okay with opening it for a few hours on the weekends, considering women our age go to bed a lot earlier than these young lesbians," Bea whined.

"Oh, don't be a fuddy-duddy. I, for one, would like to keep my youthful attitude. Surrounding myself with young lesbians is one way to do that." Lucy waved her hand in the air. "We can hire a young, cute dyke to run the place. It'll be fine."

"I should have never agreed to this," Bea grumbled.

"We can help," Saville offered. "I wouldn't mind tending bar for a few hours a week. I think it's a great idea. Also, you don't have to keep the bar open until one. You can set whatever hours you want. Having a place that closes early is better than not having anything."

"What about your favorite bar? I thought you liked that place. It's where you are every weekend," Fi noted.

"Too many rednecks. Besides, it isn't a lesbian bar. Just because a few of us hang out there doesn't mean the rednecks are happy about it." Saville tipped the can of beer into her mouth and took a healthy drink.

"Speaking of plans for Georgetown Glen, is there any chance that you could bring a few of the friendlier alpacas to the community? It would be like pet therapy. We could do that once a month, maybe. We'll pay you. It's another way to make our retirement community unique."

"Oh, it'll be unique, all right. Why stop there. Let's bring in Las Vegas-style acts like Cirque du Soleil," Bea grumbled.

Lucy's eyes twinkled. "That's a great idea."

"That was sarcasm," Bea growled. "Unfortunately, I'm never going to get my nice relaxing retirement like I envisioned."

Darcy laughed. "We'd love to bring two or three alpacas over. I'm sure Carmen and a few others would enjoy having women fawn all over them, especially if you have apples on offer."

"Yeah, who doesn't enjoy women fawning over them?" Saville added.

"Oh, if you tend bar, I'm sure you'll have your fair share of old dykes fawning over you," Lucy teased.

"Maybe, I just want one special lesbian to fawn over me." Saville glanced quickly at Fi.

Fi raised her eyebrow. "Since when?"

"Right, then, how about some of that delicious key lime pie that Amelia made for dessert? Who wants a piece?" Darcy asked.

Everyone raised their hands, and Amelia watched Fi as she looked at Saville as if she'd just grown two horns. Yes, everything was coming to a head much sooner than she thought. Amelia would need to corner her best friend to get the scoop. But for now, she believed it was time for another diversion.

"So, tell us all about this dognapping caper." Amelia smiled. "It sounds like it got a little exciting."

"That's an understatement. If we'd known about the gate, we could have avoided almost getting caught," Bea grumbled.

"And my favorite shorts would still be in one piece," Lucy added with a grin.

"But then we wouldn't have had the treat of seeing your very fine assets, Lucy," Saville teased.

Lucy giggled. "Yeah, I've still got it." She raised her fist for a bump with Saville.

Bea rolled her eyes. "Juveniles. I'm hanging with a bunch of juveniles. By the way, you never explained about the gate. Who has a gate leading into their neighbor's yard—especially a neighbor you don't get along with?"

"My landlord wanted easy access to his mother and put in a gate between the two properties. Convenient for him, not so great for me. I almost put a lock on the gate but never quite got around to it. He sold the property next door after his mother passed, then moved to California. Initially, he wanted to sell my place, but he would have had to pay capital gains taxes. So he made his mother's former home a rental," Saville explained.

"I guess that makes sense. So why didn't you use the gate?" Darcy asked.

Saville shrugged. "It seemed more covert to climb the fence. Where we entered the yard was closer to Sunny and farther from my asshole neighbor's back door."

Darcy nodded, as if that made perfect sense. No wonder Darcy and Saville were close. In many ways, they had the same thoughts about how to approach life, except Darcy was definitely not allergic to commitment like Saville. Although Amelia now could see beyond the veneer Saville presented to most everyone, including Fi. Amelia was more convinced than ever that Saville had deep feelings for Fi that went well beyond friendship.

CHAPTER FIFTEEN

When Saville and Fi returned to Fi's historic home, Saville was so nervous. She decided she needed to take a ride on her motorcycle. If she didn't, she might give in to the temptation to kiss Fi and have a repeat of the first night they got together. However, Saville didn't want to make that same mistake. This wasn't about sex anymore, and if she was a weaktit and capitulated to her baser instincts, Fi might misinterpret her intentions.

"Um, I still want to crash at your place and spend the day with you tomorrow, but I have a lot of energy right now and need to blow off some steam. I'm going to take a quick ride on my Harley, and I'll be back within the hour."

The smile slipped from Fi's face. "Right now? Oh, I see. You haven't been able to visit your favorite redneck bar this weekend. I hope I don't need to say this, but you can't bring a woman back to my place."

"What? No. I would never do that. Is that what you think of me?"

"No, I guess not. That would be a bridge too far, even for you."

Saville grabbed Fi's hands and looked into her eyes. "Fi, I promise, going to the bar was the furthest thing from my mind. I have a lot to mull over in this stupid brain of mine, and I needed to get a little clarity. A long ride always does that for me. I'm not going out for anything other than that."

"You don't need to justify your actions to me. It's not like we're a couple," Fi answered.

"I know. You've made that abundantly clear." Saville turned away. "I won't be long."

"You're okay to drive now?"

"Yeah, I only had two beers, and we were there a long time."

"Okay, be safe. I'll leave the door open. Look, Saville, we're friends now, right? If something is bothering you, no matter what it is, I'm here for you. I can be a good listener, you know."

"I know. I'll talk with you about what's been going on in my head tomorrow. I promise. That was my original plan. So I'll stick with that."

"Wear your helmet."

"I always do!"

Fi stood in the doorway and gave a little wave as Saville eased out of the driveway. Maybe this was a ridiculous thing to do, but Saville knew precisely where she would go to get a little clarity.

†

"Hey, George, show your ugly mug. Casper, you are not, but I need to ask you something." Saville swiveled her head, looking for the errant ghost.

"Ah, the pompatic one. Where are your companions? What is a Casper?"

"Pompatic? I hope you are not calling me pompous. You know, Casper, the friendly ghost, of which you are the exact opposite. But I want to know how you managed to get Ruth to marry you. No offense, but you didn't have money, and she seems to have done fine running the saloon by herself. It didn't seem like she wanted to be tied down after her first husband passed. Why you?"

George hovered in the corner, and if Saville wasn't desperate to understand why Ruth would take such a chance on George, she would have laughed when she saw George fold her legs like a pretzel and sit.

"Mae did us one favor when she brought Ruth over. Had Ruth not learned of my secret, she never would have come to know the real me. Vulnerability is not a weakness when shown to those you love and who love you back."

"Wow, that's sort of profound. It also tracks with what Lucy told me. So you think she won't run if I share how terrified I am of letting her get to know me? Insecurities and all?"

"You don't need my advice. You know what you need to do. Tell this beautiful woman how you feel. It will all work out. It is a glorious feeling to have a woman look at you the way she does. I should know. I still have that with Ruth, but there are limitations. I can't touch her as I used to. We had nearly twenty years together. Don't waste the time you have left on this earth. You will regret it. I must go now." George disappeared, and that left Saville with her thoughts.

How was she going to convince Fi to give her another shot? If she were in Fi's place, she certainly wouldn't take a chance on someone like herself. But, at least they'd managed to re-establish a friendship. Maybe that would be enough for Saville. She didn't think so, but she might have to settle for whatever Fi willingly gave her.

Using her phone as a flashlight, she carefully navigated her way down the stairs. Roaring into the murky black night, the only sound, the rumble of her motor, Saville missed the glow of the deer's eyes as he crossed her path. With a hard jerk to the right, Saville barely avoided the young buck but lost control as the bike spun out onto the shoulder and laid her flat. The last thought before total darkness was that Fi would be pissed she'd stayed out so late.

†

Fi had considered remaining awake until Saville returned, but her body had a different notion. Finally, she allowed her lids to close and settled on the couch, pulling a light blanket over her body. A ringing next to Fi's ear woke her from the pleasant dream she was having. Dreams were the one place she allowed herself to envision a life with Saville. At first, she was a little disoriented, but then she remembered curling on her couch after her eyes became too heavy to keep open.

She grabbed the phone from the coffee table and groggily answered, "Hello."

216

"Fi, sorry if I woke you. Look, the hospital called. Darcy is Saville's medical power of attorney, so they called here…" Amelia began to explain.

As the words registered, Fi sat up, now wide awake. "Oh, my God. I told her to be safe. Was Saville in an accident? What hospital? Where is she?"

"Whoa, calm down. Saville is pretty banged up, but the trauma team expects she'll make a full recovery. They took her into surgery a few minutes ago. Darcy and I are heading to the hospital right now. The doctor mentioned that Saville had mumbled your name, so we thought you ought to know in case you want to meet us there."

"Of course. Did they take Saville to Harborview?" Fi knew that if they had transported her to Harborview, the premier trauma center in Seattle, it was a lot worse than Amelia let on.

"No, they transported her to Issaquah. Do you want us to swing by and pick you up?"

"You don't mind? I know that's a little out of your way."

"Of course not. We don't mind at all," Amelia answered.

"Yeah. I think that would be good. I'm a little frazzled right now." Fi had almost forgotten about Sunny. Sassy could come and go as she pleased through the cat door, but it wasn't big enough for Sunny to fit through. "I hate to put Sunny in the backyard chained up."

"Bring her with. Maybe they have a program that allows pets to visit. If not, we can always drop her off at the farm. Plenty of room for her to run."

"Thanks, Amelia."

"Darcy is jingling the keys in front of my face. We'll be there soon, okay?"

"Yeah, I'll be ready."

After Fi ended the call, she hurried to her bathroom to brush her hair and teeth. She knew she wouldn't have time for a shower, but at least she could remove that icky taste from her mouth. Although, the toothpaste would not remove the bile that threatened to erupt as she thought of Saville in pain, lying in a hospital bed.

CHAPTER SIXTEEN

Saville felt like someone had glued her eyes shut, but then she felt something else a lot more pleasant. Someone held Saville's hand and murmured words she didn't quite understand yet in her altered state. She smacked her lips and realized how dry her mouth felt. The previous evening came back to her in flashes. Had she swallowed the dirt on the shoulder of the road? Was that why her mouth felt like the Sahara desert?

"Water," Saville croaked.

"I can only give you ice chips," the voice answered.

Saville knew that voice. "Fi?" Saville worked at prying open her eyes, but when she turned her head, another sensation threatened to take over, causing Saville to groan and spit out one word.

"Nauseous."

Saville felt the bed move, and she repeated her cry for help. "I'm gonna be sick."

"Here." Fi put a small yellow basin under her chin. "It's the anesthesia. It does that to some people even after they give you medicine to stem the nausea."

She used all her energy to make sure the vomit landed in the basin. Letting her head rest back on the pillow, she turned to get a better look at Fi. She was always beautiful to Saville, but the dark circles under her eyes told the real story. Fi must have been sitting by her side for hours. *Why would she do that?* Maybe Saville would have a second shot to make things right if Fi cared enough to be by her side at her worst. What could be more vulnerable than puking in front of the woman you lust after?

"Sorry. That's gross," Saville managed to say.

"It's okay." Fi brushed back her sweat-soaked hair and kept her hand on Saville's forehead, continuing to stroke it. "You had us worried. You had a bad break to your femur that required surgery. The road rash is pretty gnarly, too." Fi set aside the basin on the roll-away table.

"At least I didn't hit the deer."

Fi gently tapped her forehead with her index finger. "That's what you're worried about? You could have died. Do you still want some ice to suck on?"

Saville nodded, and Fi held a cup of ice to her lips.

With every second, Saville became more coherent. "What's the damage? Is my bike totaled?"

"Again, not the right thing to be concerned about. No, it survived better than your body. A few scratches. That's all. Lucy offered to ride it back to my place." Fi smiled.

"You didn't let her, did you?"

"No, I called Chelsey, and she took care of it."

Saville could tell Fi had tried desperately not to laugh.

"That's not funny."

"It wasn't actually a joke."

"Then why are you trying not to laugh."

"I held back my laughter because of your face. You are so transparent sometimes. Darcy and Amelia brought me here. So, we didn't have a lot of options if you wanted someone to retrieve your bike from the side of the road. Let's get something straight right now."

"Straight? Please, not that," Saville joked.

"I'm serious. I want to settle something once and for all. Chelsey and I are friends. So if a certain someone ever wanted to say, ask me out, that person does not have to be jealous of someone I am not at all interested in romantically."

"You mean me?"

"Yes, don't be obtuse. It doesn't fit your personality. Are you still nauseous?"

"A little."

"Okay, I'll press the button for the nurse, and hopefully, she can give you something. Let me wash the basin while we wait for her to answer the call button." Fi stood and grabbed the yellow basin.

"You don't have to do that."

"It's fine. I have a strong stomach."

When Fi returned, Saville decided it was now or never. "I *do* want to go out with you. On a proper date, not a hook-up," she blurted. "I lied. It was never a mistake. I shouldn't have said that. I wanted you then, and I still want you, but for a lot more than a quick fuck. I'm not saying this right. I don't want to waste time beating around the bush or leaving obscure hints about how I feel. I'm kind of crazy about you, Fi. I always have been. George told me vulnerability is not a weakness."

"George?"

"Yeah, that's where I went. I wanted to ask George how he had talked Ruth into marrying him. I figured he had some secret mojo I could duplicate."

"You're not asking me to marry you, are you?" Fi sputtered.

"No, no, I figured I'd be doing good to get you to give me a second chance. How bad are my injuries?" Saville lifted the covers and saw the large splint on her right leg. "I think dancing is out of the question for now."

Fi frowned. "They're kind of bad. You have a long recovery ahead. You can stay at my place while you get back on your feet."

An internal debate had already started forming in Saville's head. Spending a lot of time with Fi over the next few weeks was definitely tempting; however, she wasn't sure this level of vulnerability was copasetic for a fledgling relationship. She hated depending on anyone. Then there was Georgetown Glen to consider. How the hell was she going to run cable with a bum leg and whatever else was wrong with her?

"I can't be out of work for a long time. What about Georgetown Glen?"

"We can figure that out later. I've already talked to Lucy and Bea, and they understand the situation. It might take us a little longer, and you'll have to rely on someone else to do the more physical tasks while you direct them, but we've had offers from everyone to be your apprentice, including Chelsey. I think Lucy wants you to pick her, but

Bea's worried about her crawling around in areas she has no business being in."

Saville banged her head against the pillow and then regretted doing that almost immediately as her nausea resurfaced. Taking in deep breaths, she successfully quelled the urge to hurl. "Fuck."

An older woman bustled into the room. "How's the patient doing? I see you're fully awake."

"She's nauseous. I emptied the basin, but she got sick earlier. Do you have anything you can give her to help settle her stomach?"

"Of course. Let me double-check with the doctor, and I'll be right back," the nurse said.

"I don't want to be a burden on you. I'm sure I can handle things on my own." Saville attempted to shift her body, but a twinge of pain caused her to stop.

"Don't be stubborn. Either you stay at my place or no date for you," Fi deadpanned.

Saville sighed. "Fine, but I'm buying all the groceries for both of us. And paying all the utilities while I stay there," she added. "Now, if only the acrobats in my stomach would stop practicing their routines, I'll be good as gold."

"Do you want any more ice to suck on?"

Saville grinned. "Anything else on offer to suck on?"

Fi chuckled. "Wow, you must be feeling more alert. I think active bedroom calisthenics are out for at least twelve weeks."

"Please tell me you're kidding. No sex for twelve weeks!" Saville exclaimed. "I just got you to agree to go out with me, and now we have to wait three months."

Fi laid her hand over her forehead and dramatically replied, "Oh, the tragedy. This accident was not a good thing to happen to you, but maybe the gift is the ability to reacquaint ourselves with one another without the complication that sex adds to the mix. So it's not all bad."

"I vehemently disagree, but I suppose I don't have a choice in the matter."

"You'll survive. And just think what the anticipation will do for us."

"Be ready for the explosion in twelve weeks. I'm going to buy a calendar just so I can mark off the days."

The nurse bustled into the room and fiddled with the IV, injecting something into the port. "This should help with the nausea. Keep feeding her ice, and a little water is okay, but don't gulp it down. You have control over the pain medication. Just push this button on the pump whenever you feel pain." The nurse lifted the line leading to the pump to show Saville which button to press. "Will you be staying with her?"

"Yeah, if that's okay," Fi answered.

"I'll have maintenance bring in a recliner for you."

"No, go home. You've undoubtedly been here all night. I'll probably fall back to sleep soon. I don't want you seeing the unattractive drool that will undoubtedly sneak out of my mouth."

"If you're tired, just let your eyes close. I'll go home a little later and take a shower, then I can come back. If you're feeling up to it, I could bring something for you to eat besides hospital food."

"Thanks." Saville was so overcome with emotions that it was difficult to stop the tear from slipping from her eye.

Fi kissed her forehead. "Always. Now close your eyes and get some sleep."

That sounded almost too good to be true. *Always.* No one except Darcy had ever been there for Saville before and definitely not always. Saville let her droopy lids close and was fast asleep almost immediately.

CHAPTER SEVENTEEN

Although tempted to push the button for Saville when she saw her grimace, Fi didn't want to take Saville's control away. She already sensed Saville wasn't too happy about relying on others. She hoped the warring emotions that had so clearly shown on Saville's face meant Fi's offer had pleased her. Fi celebrated the chance to spend a lot of time together over the next twelve weeks.

When Fi heard the light knock on the door, she lifted her head. Darcy cautiously opened the door and whispered, "How's she doing?" Amelia followed Darcy into the room.

"She's sleeping now. The anesthesia made her sick, so the nurse put something in the IV." Fi pointed to the door. "We should probably talk outside. I don't want us to disturb her sleep."

"Good idea," Darcy answered.

Both Amelia and Darcy followed Fi to just outside the room.

Fi leaned on the wall. "I was pretty insistent that she stay at my house while she recovers. She agreed to that plan. Reluctantly, I might add. Her primary concern was being out of work for that long. I told her that everyone offered to be her apprentice, including Chelsey."

Darcy laughed. "Oh, I bet that went over really well."

"Yeah, no. But honestly, Chelsey is the best person to help her. I know Lucy is champing at the bit to be her sidekick, but I don't think that's the best plan. You and Amelia will be too busy with the farm and Amelia's real estate stuff for either of you to be a good choice. And Bea is probably less physically able to crawl in tight spaces than Lucy," Fi explained.

Amelia shook her head. "Yeah, that makes perfect logical sense, but Saville isn't Chelsey's biggest fan."

"I know. Saville is still jealous of Chelsey. But I think I laid that gooey mess to rest for now. We sort of agreed to start dating. Or at least I think we did. Apparently, Saville's little excursion last night included a chat with our resident ghost, George."

"Seriously?" Darcy asked.

"Uh-huh. She rambled on about something that George said about vulnerability."

"Yeah, Saville's not big on that. The one time she let herself be vulnerable with someone, it ended badly. She's been a she-whore ever since," Darcy shared.

"She-whore. That's a new one." Fi chuckled.

"It rolls off the tongue better than woman-whore. You know, the female equivalent of man-whore," Darcy explained. "Good for you two, though. Amelia and I always thought you'd eventually get there. The chemistry between you two is off the chart, even when you're both trying to needle each other. Hey, you look wrecked. Do you want Amelia to run you home? I'll stay with Saville. Lucy, Bea, and Chelsey are planning on coming by later. Between the four of us, I'm sure we can keep her adequately entertained and in good spirits."

"Yeah, I'd be happy to drive you home," Amelia offered.

"I do feel kind of grungy. I wish this hospital wasn't so far from home. Unfortunately, it's not like I can run home for a shower and be back within the hour. I should probably check on Sunny, too. Hopefully, she is behaving herself and not chasing your alpacas."

"Carmen is not shy. She'll spit at her as a warning. That usually works. I'm not worried," Darcy said.

"Amelia can drop me off at my house, and I'll swing by the farm to feed Sunny and check on her after I've taken a shower."

"You should get some sleep, too. I know you're worried, but Saville will not take a turn for the worst in a few hours. The surgery went well. She just needs to heal right now." Amelia patted Fi's arm in reassurance.

"The nurse was going to have maintenance bring in a recliner. I'll catch some sleep in that when Saville is resting."

"Man, you have it just as bad as Saville. You're in love with her, aren't you?" Darcy asked.

"What? No, well, maybe. What do you mean by as bad as Saville? Did she tell you she was in love with me?"

"Not in so many words, but I've known Saville a long time. I can tell when she's head over heels for someone."

Darcy smiled. "I'm happy for her. It's been a rough road for her since she moved back here."

"She did say she was crazy about me." Fi wrinkled her nose. "I wasn't sure how to interpret that. I just assumed she felt fragile after her accident. Or maybe she was under the influence of too many pain meds."

"Wow! Really? She admitted that to you? That's the equivalent of an 'I love you' from Saville. Trust me. She needs to work on being more communicative and sharing her feelings with others. You both do."

"Message received. I told Saville I wasn't interested in Chelsey and would go out with her if she asked."

Amelia held her hand over her mouth, but a snort sneaked out. "Oh my God, Fi. That's your idea of a declaration of love? You two are meant for one another."

"We can't all be the perfect, married lesbian couple. Some of us need to make sure before we run headlong into a relationship for life."

"Yup, a match made in heaven. The only difference between the two of you is that you've been willing to admit out loud that you want a partner." Amelia looped her arm inside Fi's. "Come on, let's get you home for that rejuvenating shower. I won't even try to talk you into staying home and getting some decent sleep."

"Thanks, Amelia. Darcy, will you call if things change with Saville? And, please tell her I'll be back as soon as I take care of things."

Darcy saluted Fi and then, before she pushed open the door and went back into the room, answered, "Will do."

†

Saville opened her eyes and tried to tamp down her disappointment as she looked around the room, and the only person sitting in the chair next to her bed was her best friend, Darcy. She wondered where Fi had gone. She was probably tired of sitting next to a lump of clay. It wasn't like Saville was an expert conversationalist even without a ton of pain meds overtaking her brain. Fi was most likely bored out of her skull.

Saville decided to mask her disappointment. "Hopefully, Fi went home to get some rest."

Darcy lifted her head. "Yeah, she did. Don't worry, she'll be back soon. Amelia took her home. She only went back to her house for a shower and to check on Sunny. You know, she stayed by your side all night long while Amelia and I took over the family lounge. Fortunately, we could stretch out and catch a little sleep. By the way, I'm proud of you."

"For what? Managing not to kill myself last night?"

"No, asshole, for telling Fi how you felt about her, finally."

"Wipe that smug look off your face," Saville playfully growled. "What did she say about us?"

"Oh, no. I'm not getting in the middle of your dyke drama. If you want to know if she looooves you too, you'll have to ask her."

"Aw, come on. I know Fi talked to you. Did she agree to go out with me because she felt sorry for me? It's not going to be some pity date, is it?"

"God, you can be so dense. No, you titnob, she cares about you. Um, didn't you hear me say she sat in this chair all night long? And let me tell you, it isn't at all comfortable. No way she got any sleep last night."

"I vaguely recall telling her I was crazy about her." Saville groaned. "How lame is that? I could always claim I was under the influence of massive drugs."

"I thought someone had finally gotten through that thick skull of yours. Letting Fi know how you feel is a good thing. I don't think she would have agreed to give your lame ass another chance had you not confessed your feelings."

"Well, for your information, smarty-pants, I was already going to talk to her. I had it all planned for Sunday. I wasn't exactly sure what to say. The accident wasn't in my original strategy, nor was it my intention to blurt everything out like I did. Just tell me what she said, please?" Saville pleaded.

"Fine, but I'm not being your go-between. You two are adults, for fuck's sake, not two adolescents passing notes through your best friends. Does she like me, like me?" Darcy mocked in a high-toned impression of a teenager. "She didn't exactly say she was in love with you, but she didn't deny her feelings, either. She thinks she might be. Happy now?"

Saville grinned. "Yes, I am."

Two crisp knocks preceded Lucy, who barged inside the room, followed by Chelsey and Bea.

"Yoo-hoo. Oh, good, you're awake. We were so worried about you. When Fi called this morning to tell us what happened, I knew we had to see for ourselves that you were okay. We already talked about helping with whatever is needed." Lucy laid the flowers she carried in her hands on the side table.

Saville forced herself to smile. "Thank you for the flowers. Yeah, I heard. I suppose I'm about to take on an apprentice."

"I know it seems incongruous for a history teacher to want to learn how to do electrical work, but I get bored during the summer." Chelsey lifted her shoulders and offered a tiny smile.

Lucy bounced on the tips of her toes. "You can have both of us at your beck and call to perform the tasks that are difficult with your bum leg. But don't think we're rushing you back to work. We'll set you up in a comfy wheelchair after your doctor clears you, and you can order us around. I've been watching YouTube videos on how to rewire a house."

Saville laughed. "Perfect. Ordering beautiful women around is my specialty."

Suddenly, Saville choked up with all the love that poured so freely out of relative strangers. Darcy had always been there for her, but now she had other people not about to let her down. Even Chelsey had made a sincere offer. Ever since Fi had explained that she wasn't interested in dating Chelsey, Saville had reformed her opinion of the cheerful woman who had been nothing but gracious toward Saville, even after she'd been so rude. Saville awkwardly moved her hand to her face to brush away the tears.

"Thanks. I'm not worth all this fuss, but I'm not too proud to take it," Saville said.

"Nonsense. I always say that anyone kind to animals is a good person. Since you masterminded the dognapping caper, you're good people. Don't I always say that, Bea?" Lucy turned to her wife.

Bea half-smiled. "Yes, you do. While I won't be taking the chance of touching any live wires, I can carry supplies for you."

"With me sort of out of commission, Fi will have a lot on her plate without me helping her. Maybe the two of you should assist Fi," Saville gently suggested. "I'm sure with Chelsey's assistance, we can remain on schedule."

"We're not worried about the delay. Are we, Bea?"

A genuine smile formed on Bea's face, and it transformed her beauty. Saville could now see how Lucy and Bea fit together. Of course, Saville would never say it aloud, but she thought Bea should definitely smile more.

Lucy grabbed Bea and kissed her fully on the lips. "Doesn't Bea have a beautiful smile? That's all it took for me to fall madly in love with her."

"She does," Saville agreed. "Listen, Chelsey, I need to apologize for the way I've been acting around you. It's not an excuse, but…"

Chelsey flicked her hand. "No need. I'm guessing you and Fi are working things out. I want you to know that I would never get between the two of you. It wasn't hard to see that I didn't have a chance with you in the picture. I'm happy to just have more lesbian friends. My person will come along. Probably when I least expect it. Without the interference of my meddling aunt, I might add."

"I hate to ask this, but would one of you lovely ladies like to round up some toothpaste and a toothbrush. It feels like something crawled into my mouth and took a dump."

All three women screwed their faces and said, "Ew."

"Yeah, well, a poet I am not," Saville defended. "But can you get another spit bucket for me? Um, that one, had, uh…"

"Anesthesia's a bitch. I remember after my surgery," Chelsey said. "I'll look in the bathroom to see if there's another one."

A new nurse came into the room and frowned. "There should really only be two visitors at a time."

"I could slip you a fiver, if it helps you to look the other way," Lucy said.

"What?" The nurse looked at Lucy, who grinned back at her.

"Unfortunately, my wife is serious," Bea added.

"Are you trying to bribe me?" The nurse chuckled.

"Bribe is such an ugly word. Entice? Reward? Show our sincerest gratitude for taking care of our friend, who, I might add, seems much better with all of us visiting and cheering her up. By the way, two more friends plan to show up a little later. You can join our party if you want. Are you single? My niece here is single." Lucy pointed to Chelsey. "She's a cutie, right? Also, smart as a whip, and her kids love her. Not like her own kids. I mean the kids she teaches history to."

"Aunt Lucy. Stop, just stop." Chelsey turned toward the nurse. "I'm so sorry. She means well."

The nurse grinned. "I can tell I'm going to have my hands full with you lot. Don't worry. I have an aunt just like her. I think they reach a certain age, and all social filters fly out the window." She walked to the IV line and hung a fresh bag. "Good morning, Saville. I'm Emily. We had to rearrange assignments today, so I'll be your day nurse until seven tonight." Emily walked to the whiteboard and erased the name at the top, replacing it with her name. "Can you tell me your pain level right now?"

Usually, Saville would have noted how attractive the nurse was with her short spiky hair styled in a trendy hairdo, accentuating the delicate features of her face, including a pair of piercing blue eyes. But she was still reeling from her conversation with Fi that morning. She had a second chance with Fi, and she wasn't about to blow it.

"I'm okay. The in-room entertainment has kept me occupied enough to not think about my discomfort," Saville answered.

"Use the pump before your pain skyrockets. Healing occurs much faster when pain is under control. The physical therapist will be by after lunch to get you up and moving. That usually stirs things enough that you'll want to press your pump afterward. But it's important to get you moving as quickly as possible. Are you still nauseous?"

"Thankfully, no. I'm starting to get hungry. So that's a good sign, right?"

"Yes, I'll make a call to the dietary department for them to deliver some clear liquids to start with. How about we wait on solid foods until we see how you do with a liquid diet. The anesthesia can do a number on your digestive system, but we'll get that working again. And as soon as you have a proper bowel movement, the closer you'll be to discharge. I understand you won't be going to a rehab facility. Your other friend is going to have you stay with her, right?"

Saville smiled. "Yeah. So if I get this right, pooping is a prerequisite to escaping this joint?"

"Yes, that and your ability to move around on crutches."

"Fair enough. Bring on the physical therapy and coffee. That's how I get moving in the morning. In more ways than one." Saville winked at the nurse.

The nurse smiled at Saville. "Oh, and in answer to the earlier question, yes, I'm single." She shot Saville a meaningful look.

"Nope, that one is taken. Remember that friend Saville is staying with? I don't believe she's going to be just a friend for very long," Chelsey added.

Saville smiled. "I certainly hope that's the case."

CHAPTER EIGHTEEN

Saville could tell that she was definitely on the mend. On the way home after her discharge from the hospital, all she could think about was when she might be able to kiss Fi. She wondered if she would have to wait for when they could go on a proper date.

"I have the guest bedroom all set up. I'll make a trip to your house later today, and you can tell me what to pick up for you." Fi put the truck in park and ran around to the passenger door to assist Saville. She reached behind the seat to grab the crutches. "Lucy said the wheelchair is coming later today. You can use that when the doc releases you for light duty."

"What if I need something in the middle of the night? I think it would be better if I stayed in your bedroom with you." Saville grinned.

"Oh, um, I thought it would be easier if you didn't have to use the stairs. The guest bedroom is on the main floor. No stairs. But, I suppose I could stay with you."

Saville pivoted in the passenger seat and grabbed the crutches from Fi, who stood so close, all Saville needed to do was balance herself on the crutches and lean forward a few inches. It would not be the best kiss she'd ever given to a woman, but she couldn't wait one second longer. She'd been dreaming about those lips for months.

Unfortunately, this first kiss didn't go as planned. When Saville leaned on her left side, using the one crutch, and tried to use her right hand to bring Fi's head close, she lost her balance and toppled onto Fi.

"Shit, shit. I'm so sorry. Are you okay?" Saville asked as she indelicately rolled off of Fi.

"Yeah, I'm fine. I'm more worried about you. Did you tweak your leg?"

"No, the only thing I tweaked was my nonexistent pride. I've been thinking about kissing you for days. Months, if I were completely honest. What an epic fail."

"Maybe not. Will you settle for me kissing you?" Fi asked before turning toward Saville and closing the distance between the two.

Saville wasn't positive who moaned first or if they expressed their delight at the same time. The kiss was more undemanding than when they'd hurriedly removed their clothes the night they'd gotten together. However, there was a simmering passion beneath the kiss that made it ten times more satisfying. Fi had sucked on Saville's lower lip before languidly pushing her tongue inside, stroking in a way that caused Saville to want to reach out and pull Fi closer. The pulsing pain in her leg no longer mattered, as every nerve ending in her body felt this kiss.

Saville sighed. "That was incredible," she declared after Fi ended the kiss.

The right corner of Fi's lip turned up as she blushed. "So, not an epic fail after all."

Saville flipped on her back and looked at the sky. "Not even a tiny bit, despite the hard ground we're both lying on. Any chance I can get a hand? I don't think I can get up without help. But I would like to continue this on something softer."

Fi scrambled to her feet. "Oh, God, I probably shouldn't have done that. I almost forgot about the other parts of your body that you scraped up. This can't be a lot of fun for you. Are you in a lot of pain right now?" She held out her hand for Saville.

Saville grabbed onto Fi's hand, and Fi's strength surprised her. Saville was not a very petite woman, yet Fi did almost all the work to help her to her feet as Saville wobbled on her good leg. She still felt frail after the accident as her body started the healing process.

"Just keep kissing me like that and trust me, I feel no pain. In fact, if the kissing graduates to more, I am sure my body will be singing, not stinging." Saville accepted the crutches that Fi had collected from the ground where they'd fallen tangled together. The crutches had almost mimicked Saville and Fi with one on top of the other.

"Saville," Fi warned. "I don't think it's a very good idea for us to have sex while you're still recovering."

Saville groaned. "I'm finally honest with you. Get you to agree to go out with me, and this is my reward? How about we get naked and see where it goes?" Saville gave Fi her best puppy dog eyes.

"Don't look at me like that. You know I can't resist when you do that."

"You can't? Why did I not know this?" Saville secured the crutches under her arms and began walking toward the front door. Fi moved her hand to Saville's back and lightly touched her. Saville appreciated the small amount of stability provided as she hobbled along the walkway.

"I would have thought you knew. Why else would I be so upset after you said it was a mistake? Obviously, your charms are no match for my stubbornness to avoid coming into contact with you at all costs. I didn't want to admit it, but I was glad you signed on for the Georgetown Glen project. It's been more fun, despite the minor mishaps, than I ever thought possible. We make a pretty good team." Fi let go long enough to unlock her door and lead Saville to her couch, where she'd already laid out pillows and a blanket.

"That we do. Perhaps the universe wasn't done with our deceptive asses. I'm so sorry I lied to you. I wasn't ready to admit how much I cared. I thought you might be like Katrina. Now I know you're nothing like her. There isn't a pretentious bone in your body. Plus, you like beer and cider, none of those sissy-ass drinks Katrina used to order when we were out with her friends." With Fi's assistance, Saville settled onto the couch, as Fi helped her prop her legs on top of one of the down pillows. She set the crutches to the side but within reach.

"You don't talk about Katrina much. Did it end that badly?" Fi fluffed another pillow, placing it behind Saville's back.

"Depends on your definition of badly. Did I feel this small?" Saville held her thumb and index finger up to indicate a minuscule amount. "Yup. She said our worlds were too different. Translation: I embarrassed her. I didn't quite fit in with her friends. I was only arm candy until that wasn't quite enough for her."

"I'm sorry. I can understand the arm candy, but you are so much more than a hot little butch. Even though you try to hide that part of yourself. Don't think I miss the thoughtful things you do, like remembering my favorite food and drink. I knew you had to go out of your way sometimes to bring me those treats. And don't let this go to your head, but I even appreciate your more obnoxious side. This will be the one and only time I admit that to you."

Saville smirked as she held her head.

"Does your head hurt?" A concerned look crossed Fi's face.

"Nope, just attempting to stop my head from swelling. You might have to bring me a baseball cap to keep that from happening."

Fi shook her head, then leaned in and placed a chaste kiss on her lips. "Can I get you something to drink? Tea, coffee, juice?"

"What kind of juice?" Saville asked.

"Grapefruit or apple."

"Aw, you got my favorites. Apple, please. Don't let me forget to give you some money. That was the deal. I'm sure you went out and filled this place with groceries, probably with all the foods I like."

"Don't worry about that now. We can figure that all out later. Apple it is, coming right up." Fi went into the kitchen to fetch the juice.

Saville watched as she poured the juice into a glass and then added ice, just like Saville liked it. She always wanted her drinks ice cold, except for coffee in the morning. She hated that trend of iced coffee. That was just wrong, in her opinion. But to each their own, she always said. Fi handed Saville the glass of juice and then began digging in her bag. Pulling out the small amber container of pain medication, she struggled with the cap, finally retrieving one pill from the bottle.

"Here. I know you're in pain, especially after that fall. I want to make sure to keep ahead of your pain."

"Like I said, kisses everywhere, and I'm all good." Saville waggled her eyebrows.

"One-track mind. I'm not much of a television person, but I got Netflix and a few other premium channels so that you have something to watch."

"You didn't have to do that."

"I didn't want you getting too bored while I'm at the worksite." Fi held up her hand. "And before you whine about work and the need to get back on the job, the doctor is not releasing you for at least three weeks, and then there is a long list of restrictions that I will be sure to monitor. You'll be following the doctor's order even if it ends up killing both of us."

"So, you trust me to my own devices all day long?"

"Not exactly. There will be rotating visitors."

"Rotating visitors?" Saville rolled her eyes. "You mean babysitters. What fools signed up for that duty?"

"Everyone, including Chelsey. You're not going to be rude to her anymore, are you? Oh, and I'll come home for lunch every day."

"No, I'll be perfectly charming with Chelsey," Saville grumbled. "But, I don't like the idea of everyone waiting on me hand and foot."

"We already settled it. To make up for lost time, I'll work a full day on Saturday and Sunday."

"Not a ten or twelve-hour day, I hope." Saville did not like the sound of that. It was bad enough that the doctor hadn't released Saville to work light duty for another three weeks at a minimum, but knowing Fi would bust her ass while Saville sat on hers did not sit well with Saville's deeply ingrained work ethic.

"No, I'll only be working eight hours a day. Plenty of time to fix you dinner each night."

"I'm going to have to think up some way to repay the favors. It feels uncomfortable letting people care for me. I'm drawing the line at anyone helping me pee. Although, I would let you give me a bed bath or join me in the shower. You know, just to make sure I don't fall." Saville grinned.

"Oh, I bought one of those orthopedic chairs for the shower. No need."

"God, you aren't any fun at all."

"On the contrary, I'll be a lot of fun, but only after you heal." Fi winked.

"Promise?"

Fi nodded. "How about a sandwich and chips before I leave for the worksite?"

"Only if you let me slice the tomatoes or help in some small way. I don't do invalid very well."

"God, you are so stubborn. Do you ever let anyone help you without raising a ruckus?"

"I agreed to stay here and convalesce at your place. I didn't break my arms, you know. I can still help. I'm not ready for you to put me out to pasture yet. And, if you would just let me show you how uninjured my hands are, I'm sure you would agree."

"Impossible," Fi said, but she smiled as she pulled a tomato from the refrigerator, setting it on a cutting board and retrieving a knife before she brought them over to Saville.

Saville started to shift, but Fi laid a hand on her and set everything on Saville's lap. "You need to keep that leg elevated. And be careful with that knife. I wouldn't want you to carve off one of those talented fingers of yours."

Fi made quick work of putting together two sandwiches while Saville awkwardly sliced the tomato. Exchanging the cutting board for one of the plates, Fi added the tomato slices, cut the sandwich in half, then placed the plate on Saville's lap.

"Do you want more juice or some water?"

"Water, please. Then come sit and have a leisurely lunch with me. The work can wait a few minutes longer."

"Okay. Chelsey should be here any minute. I told her to swing by shortly after noon." Fi grabbed a bottle of water from the refrigerator and handed it to Saville, who balanced her plate and the bottle in her lap.

"Super," Saville said with little excitement.

Fi narrowed her eyes. "You promised."

"I did, and I won't break that promise. Just yanking your chain. You are so easy." Saville grinned. "I might have to check out that show, *Gentleman Jack,* that every lesbian seems to think is the bomb. Chelsey should appreciate it. A little piece of lesbian history for her to ooh and ahh over. We can bond over that show."

Fi sat in the chair across from Saville and took a large bite of her sandwich. "Mmm, I was starved."

Saville followed suit and also bit into her sandwich, moaning with pleasure. "Wow, this is fantastic. What's the secret?" She mumbled around a mouthful of food. "This is like the best turkey sandwich I've ever had."

"It just tastes good compared to hospital food. I put arugula on it instead of lettuce and then sprinkled a little old bay on top."

"I never want to eat another turkey sandwich any other way," Saville declared as she took another bite.

"Maybe you won't be that hard to care for if you're so easily pleased by a simple turkey sandwich."

As Saville finished her sandwich, Fi's doorbell rang. "That must be Chelsey. I'll be right back."

"Hey, Hop-a-long," Chelsey greeted.

Saville scowled. But she'd promised Fi she would be nice, so she forced a smile on her face. "Have you seen *Gentleman Jack* yet?"

"Of course. Hasn't every lesbian?"

"Nope. Neither one of us has seen it." Saville pointed between Fi and herself. "We aren't huge television people. Unfortunately, I'll probably be able to catch up on every lesbian series available on cable TV now that I'm relegated to the couch for a few weeks. So, you get to pick what we watch because I haven't seen any."

"I could watch *Gentleman Jack* again," Chelsey said.

"Right, then, I'll leave you two to enjoy your afternoon with Anne Lister. I'll pick up Sunny from the farm on my way home. Although it sounds like she gets along with the alpacas, I miss her." Fi gave a tiny wave before leaving.

Saville had forgotten all about Sunny. She looked forward to spending time with the dog. Chelsey, not so much.

†

Fi heard a strange thing when she entered her house. A totally bizarre thing. Laughter. She would have bet her entire house that Chelsey and Saville would figuratively dance around one another like two boxers in a ring. However, the giggling in the other room told a different story.

Sunny bounded into the room while Fi carried the takeout bags into the kitchen. She stepped into the living room and raised her eyebrow. "I'm glad to see you two haven't killed each other."

Sunny wagged her tail, laying her head on Saville's lap. "How's my pretty girl? Did you miss me?" Saville asked.

Chelsey quickly grabbed the remote and hit the pause button. Fi glanced at the television to see two naked women clearly in the midst of making love. "Um, we decided to save *Gentleman Jack* for later."

"I can see. That doesn't look like a period movie," Fi answered.

"Uh, no. We were kind of ripping the movie apart because of the lesbian porn angle. I didn't even have to look it up to know the director is a man," Saville said as she continued to pet Sunny. Sassy had apparently settled on top of the couch next to Saville's head. When Saville began giving Sunny attention, Sassy made her presence known and stretched her paw to touch Saville's shoulder.

"Saville is hysterical. We've been bonding over our mutual obsession over how Hollywood portrays lesbian relationships. Oh, and our need to keep rewinding the sex scenes. Clearly, I need to learn a lot more about the different ways to get a woman off." Chelsey laughed.

"Really? Well, I'd love to hear more about that." Fi smiled. "I hope it's okay that I brought home food from that hole-in-the-wall Mexican restaurant you like. I was too lazy to make dinner tonight. Chelsey, would you like to stay for dinner? There's plenty of food."

"Nah, I promised Aunt Lucy I would drop by their place and give a status report. They're looking forward to visiting with Saville tomorrow. You should play a few of these movies for them. Aunt Bea will grumble, but secretly, she'll love watching some of these shows. Aunt Lucy will definitely want to see *Blue is the Warmest Color*, no matter how pornographic it gets. In fact, I wouldn't be surprised if Aunt Lucy has some old lesbian porn on VHS hidden away somewhere in that jam-packed storage unit. Saville, you should ask her about them."

"Oh, I will. I definitely will. Damn, I love that woman. I hope to have half the spunk she has when I finally retire. Maybe this babysitting gig you've arranged won't be so bad. This has certainly been an entertaining afternoon."

"Right back atcha, buddy." Chelsey lifted her fist, and Saville bumped it. "See you in a few days. We can watch *Lip Service* next. The lead has the sexiest gray eyes I think I've ever seen."

"It's a date. Even better if you sneak in some beer for us."

"No beer. Not while you're on pain meds." Fi put her hands on her hips and glared.

"Oh, right. I almost forgot about them. I didn't even take anymore after you left. Maybe I can wean myself off of the meds. Laughter seems to be a more natural way to control pain. That or sex. I'll bet that would sufficiently distract me from the pain." Saville grinned.

Chelsey waved. "On that note, I'm leaving you two to work that out." She winked before exiting.

"I'm surprised but thrilled that you and Chelsey are getting along."

"Yeah, she's a lot cooler than I thought. It was a little rough at first, but then we cleared the air. I even apologized for my boorish behavior."

"You did?"

"Yes. And don't act so stunned. I've been known to recognize the error of my ways on occasion." Saville shifted on the couch, then grimaced.

"Either I have to make you laugh again, or it looks like you are way past due for more pain medication."

"There's always sex," Saville offered with an expression of hope on her face.

Fi carefully sat on the edge of the couch and leaned in to kiss Saville. She began a slow exploration of Saville's lips by placing her hands on the sides of Saville's face. As Saville's breathing rapidly increased, Fi pulled away, not wanting to get Saville too worked up.

"Why did you stop? It was just getting good."

"That will have to be enough."

"My clit is blue now."

"It is not. Quit exaggerating."

"I am not. Look it up. Women get blue bean or blue vulva, just like men. You're lucky that you've never felt it."

"When we make love again, I want you to be healthy enough to enjoy it. If I think I'm causing you any pain at all, I won't be able to get out of my head."

Saville waggled her eyebrows. "Some people like to combine pain and pleasure."

Fi wrinkled her brow. "Are you into that?"

"No, but I'm desperate for your touch. A little pain is an acceptable price to pay."

Fi stroked Saville's face. "Patience. We'll get there."

"Here's a little confession for you. Ever since we got together that one night, I've been dreaming about touching you again. It's an obsession that I haven't been able to set aside. I tried so hard to forget that night. Granted, whoring around was not the right path to take, but I didn't think you'd ever talk to me again. After that, I knew I'd blown my only chance."

"But you didn't. And we're good now. Aren't we?" Fi asked with a small amount of trepidation.

"Yeah, we're perfect. You're flawless. The waiting is going to kill me, but I'll deal."

CHAPTER NINETEEN

Fi lay next to Saville, her e-reader in her hands, while Saville watched a show on her tablet. She paused, then turned to Saville. "I can't wait for you to see the place. You aren't going to believe it. It's mind-boggling that three weeks have gone by since your accident." The edges of Fi's voice lifted in excitement, a lot like when the corners of her mouth lifted when she was happy.

"Maybe for you, the time has flown. For me, not so much. Although I am enjoying all these lesbian movies and series. I feel all caught up now. What I'm excited about is for the doctor to release me to go back to work and her approval for other activity." Saville waggled her eyebrows, then continued, "Chelsey and I have already mapped out a plan of action. She's not so bad, you know."

"I know that. I wish Chelsey would find someone, though. I think she's a little lonely."

"She has a crush on Tess," Saville answered.

"Tess?"

"Yeah, the friend of Amelia's who is the amateur historian that found that picture of Ruth and George after the hanging."

Fi shuddered. "So, are they dating?"

"Not exactly. I guess Tess is like twelve years older, and she has quite a bit of hesitancy about the age gap."

"Bummer."

"Yeah, it is, because Tess is a really cool person. Chelsey doesn't want her Aunt Lucy to know anything because then she'll overstep and get involved. And that's the last thing she needs."

"Why do you say that?"

"I think it's better for the people involved to work things out like we did. I'm not saying I didn't appreciate George and Lucy's advice because I did."

"You asked Lucy for advice?"

"She offered, and I didn't discourage her from giving it to me. I might have also asked Chelsey about something, too. I haven't been the greatest in the relationship department, so I need all the help I can get, but I draw the line at matchmaking."

"You better draw the line at matchmaking. Unless…" Fi's face crinkled as she wondered if she had made assumptions. They hadn't gone on an official date but had easily melted into domesticity. They acted like a proper couple—without the sex. But maybe Saville was only interested in dating Fi and not being exclusive.

"Unless what?" Saville turned her body and stroked Fi's cheek. "What's going on in that beautiful head of yours?

251

I can almost see the wheels turning. And I fear those wheels are heading in the wrong direction."

"Um, we've never talked about whether or not we're exclusive."

"Of course, we're exclusive. I'm living in your house. I sleep with you every night. I told you I'm crazy about you. What's confusing about that?"

"We haven't even had sex yet. And you're only living here because of your accident. After you're all healed, this little bubble of domesticity is going to pop and probably leave a colossal mess behind."

"We have, too, had sex. Not enough, I would add, but I hope that all changes tomorrow after the doctor says I can resume normal activities with a few minor adjustments. Besides, if you asked me to move in tomorrow, I wouldn't turn you down. And that's not because I have a shitty neighbor and love this house. It's because I'm crazy in love with you. I thought you knew that."

Fi blinked rapidly. "You said you love me?"

Saville's eyes went wide. "Um, yeah. I guess I did. And I'm not taking that back," she said defiantly.

Fi smiled. "I love you too." Fi brought their faces together and put everything she had into the kiss that followed. She hadn't admitted to anyone but Amelia how hard it had been to not give in to Saville, who had not wanted to wait the three weeks for the doctor to give the okay to make love. As their kiss intensified, Fi wondered if it would be so bad to let nature take its course.

When they broke apart, Saville was nearly panting. "Can I please touch you? Honestly, I'm not feeling any pain right now. I'll be careful with my leg."

All of Fi's hesitancy flew right out the window. First, she lifted her T-shirt over her head, exposing her breasts. Then, she tugged on the bottom of Saville's nightshirt and had removed that so quickly that the look on Saville's face was almost comical—a cross between surprise and absolute bliss.

Reaching out to splay her fingers over Saville's breasts, she answered, "You first." She moved her mouth to Saville's right breast and made small circles with her tongue. Saville writhed underneath her touch, moaning in pleasure.

"Oh, that is so not fair. I've been dreaming about your breasts for weeks. Months, actually. But, Goddess, this feels so divine I would be crazy to not let you finish."

After Fi had thoroughly sucked on the nipple, she let her warm breath flow over Saville's perfect breasts. They weren't enormous, but they fit Saville's physique. Saville was almost lanky. She had just enough curves to ensure no one mistook her for anything but a beautiful woman, but without an ounce of fat. Unlike Fi, who always thought her breasts were too large, and Fi believed she had too much padding around her hips. Having an active job kept Fi fit, but she supposed her love of carbohydrates didn't help keep her slim. By the look Saville was giving her right now, she instinctively knew that her hang-ups about her body were unfounded in Saville's eyes.

Fi carefully navigated to a position that would not put undue pressure on any part of Saville's body that was still healing from her accident. She brushed the tips of her fingers over Saville's muscled stomach as Saville reached up to touch Fi's sensitive breasts.

The first touch sent shivers down Fi's body and activated the center of her arousal as she felt herself react to the touch. As much as she needed to experience those long fingers expertly playing Fi's body like that song about the fiddle player in Georgia, Fi wanted to make Saville cry out first. She readjusted to begin her descent, kissing, licking, and caressing her way down.

Fi's mouth hovered just above Saville's center for a few seconds as she let her warm breath barely reach Saville's pretty pink pussy. Opting for a long teasing approach that she remembered had driven Saville wild on the night that seemed almost a distant memory, she gently kissed the inside of her thigh. Her mouth made its way to the other thigh, not wanting there to be an asymmetry in her approach. Just like the attention she had paid to both breasts, she tried to pay equal attention to the sensitive place on the inside of Saville's thighs.

In response, Saville placed her hands on Fi's head, trying desperately to get Fi to move to her center. But Fi was having none of that. She was going to take her time. Saville opened her legs wider, giving Fi perfect access to her clit.

Saville groaned in frustration. "You are going to kill me. Haven't I been patient long enough?"

Fi chuckled. "You'll live. And if you keep trying to rush me, I'm going to stop and wait for the doc to give you the official go-ahead."

Saville mimicked turning a key on her mouth and locking in any future comments. "Shutting up now."

When Fi finally used the tip of her tongue to stimulate Saville's clit while she stroked Saville's opening with her fingers, Saville used her hips to signal she was ready. But Fi would not rush this. Her overwhelming feelings of love dictated Fi's need to take her time to make sure that Saville received the message loud and clear. She was not having sex with Saville; Fi was making love to her. She wanted the physical intimacy to represent all those bottled-up feelings she'd tried so hard to keep in check.

"Yes," Saville hissed as she bucked. "Please go inside."

Fi worried Saville might move around too much and would cause further harm to her injuries. "Patience. I thought you were shutting up."

"Don't be mean."

Fi laughed again. "Oh, I could be really mean and stop right now."

"Noooo. Please don't. I promise I'll be quiet."

"Oh, I don't want you to be quiet. I want to hear you shout my name so loud that you wake the neighbors."

Fi returned her attention to Saville's clit, and when she sensed Saville couldn't take any more teasing, she pushed one, then two fingers inside and slowly pulled them out, only to plunge them back inside. Saville rocked her hips as the two women found the perfect rhythm, causing Saville to moan loudly before she tumbled over the edge and cried out.

Feeling pleased with herself, Fi teased, "I'd give that shout out a seven out of ten. I think you can do a whole lot better." Ignoring Saville's weak protest, Fi found her way back to Saville's center and began teasing her clit until Saville's arousal returned. A second orgasm quickly followed.

"That's never happened before. There's usually a period where I can't come again for a little while," Saville said with a fair amount of awe in her voice. "Just give me a few minutes, and then I'll do what I've been dreaming about for months."

Fi returned to her side to face Saville while continuing to stroke her stomach and collarbone. A goofy smile remained on Saville's face.

"You know, I meant every word I said. I do love you, and not because you just gave me two of the best orgasms I've ever had in my life."

"I know." Fi pushed a sweaty lock of Saville's hair aside and noticed the sheen of perspiration on her upper lip. "Hey, are you okay? And don't lie to me. I know when you aren't telling the truth because you won't look me in the eye."

"I might have moved my leg a little and tweaked it. I just need a minute for it to settle."

"Dammit. I knew this was too soon."

"No, it wasn't. It's already subsiding. Maybe it was a temporary cramp. Please don't deny my overwhelming need to show you how much I love you. Sometimes I feel like my only language of love is to touch you in ways I hope no one has ever affected you before. I'm not great at relationships or expressing my feelings, but I am good at sex."

"You sell yourself short. Even when I didn't want to receive your subtle messages, I did. I'm starting to think I know you better than yourself. I don't think you recognize when you're attentive and loving. But I do."

Saville shifted and offered that smile that consistently reduced Fi to a pile of mush. "Let me be attentive and loving right now. I need this." She began her exploration of Fi's body, and Fi was too far gone to resist. Lying down, she melted into Saville's expert hands. It didn't take long for Fi to writhe in pleasure. She was sure that when she shouted Saville's name, she had been loud enough to wake the neighbors.

†

Saville slowly opened her eyes and stretched. When she turned her head, she found Fi's side of the bed empty and then registered the sound of the shower in the master bathroom. She almost joined Fi, but it was such a production to cover her splint and protect her leg that she tossed out that idea. Saville wanted to surprise Fi, but that was not possible with her stupid broken leg. She couldn't wait for the doc to tell her she didn't need the splint anymore, but that would not happen anytime soon. Saville still had several months of recovery ahead of her. At least she had the first appointment with the doc this morning, and if all went well, she'd be at the worksite by ten. Sure, that was an optimistic view, but Saville was going crazy sitting on her ass all day, watching every lesbian series imaginable. It was fun for the first few days, especially with Chelsey, who had proved to be an entertaining companion. They'd developed an unlikely friendship. Now the tables had turned, and Chelsey sought advice from Saville on her crush on an older woman.

When she heard the shower turn off, Saville used her arms to pull her body into a sitting position on the bed. A twinge of pain traveled along her body, but she ignored it, determined to present a false front that she was completely pain-free and ready to tackle the day. Saville felt a twinge in her pussy from all the activity. After a dry spell, she relished this feeling. With so much inaction lately, she had worried her lady parts would wither and die. Saville definitely wanted more of that almost raw feeling. A lot more.

Saville was still naked, and the bedsheet pooled around her waist, leaving her breasts completely exposed.

She grinned when Fi exited the bathroom and gave her an appreciative look.

"That is so not fair. You, looking all sexy in bed. If we didn't have to be at the clinic in less than an hour…"

"We have time for a quickie," Saville suggested.

"No, no quickies. It's bad enough that I gave in to my dishonorable side last night before we got the official go-ahead. So I'm not even going to help you in the shower. Far too tempting."

Last night, Fi had lost all her modesty, but it still surprised Saville when Fi dropped the towel from her body while pulling her work clothes from her drawers.

Saville pouted, but the sooner she got released for light-duty, the quicker she could return to regular activity. She craved being a part of the world again. Tossing the covers aside, Saville swiveled her body and then reached for her crutches. She'd gotten pretty good at navigating the bathroom and taking her morning shower.

"I'll make us some breakfast and coffee, and we can take it in the car. I hate being late for anything, but being on time for your appointment is critical. I want to make sure we haven't, uh, messed things up because I was too weak to resist you last night." Fi picked up the towel she had dropped on the floor and tossed it into the hamper. Then, after finger-combing her hair, she left the bedroom.

Saville crutched into the master bath and went through the laborious process of showering. She smiled when she saw Fi had already set the chair in the shower. She glanced at Fi's claw-foot tub and sighed. For now, the tub was impossible to navigate with her splint. She hoped, sometime down the road, she could convince Fi to take a bath with her. She would have to buy some candles and sweet-smelling bath oils to set the stage. Lavender. That was Fi's favorite. Lost in thought, she didn't notice Fi sneaking into the bathroom and placing a cup of coffee on the antique bath vanity.

After drying off, she smelled the coffee. When she noticed her work clothes sitting on the toilet seat, she smiled at Fi's optimism. Saville was sure the doc would give her positive news today, but that Fi also expected her release to work felt exceptionally good. Although Saville enjoyed when Fi helped her dress because her touch was always welcome, she also loved that Fi respected her need for some independence. Leaning on one crutch, Saville finished brushing her teeth and combing her hair. She lifted the cup and took another large swig, almost finishing the coffee. Hobbling to the kitchen, Saville watched as Fi packed their lunches and placed two bagels with cream cheese onto paper towels.

Fi pointed to the two travel cups. "More coffee. Let me take this to the truck, then I'll collect our breakfast." Fi grabbed the travel cups and mini-cooler. "You ready?"

"Definitely."

†

Chelsey, Lucy, and Bea were already at the saloon when Fi and Saville arrived. Fi was happy to find that the three women had already brought in the tools and supplies Saville would need to complete the rewiring. Lucy lifted the box of donuts, offering it to both women.

Fi shook her head. "We had a bagel on the way to the clinic this morning, but thanks. Maybe I'll have one later as a mid-morning snack."

Saville grabbed one. "I'll never turn down donuts."

"I am so jealous that you've kept your slim build no matter what you eat," Chelsey said. "I've gained ten pounds hanging out with you these last couple of weeks. How is it fair that even without working out or doing anything remotely physical, you still have that six-pack?"

Fi raised her brow. "You've seen Saville's flat stomach?"

"The house was sweltering one day. Damn global warming. And you know how Saville doesn't have a modest bone in her body. So she stripped down to shorts and her sports bra," Chelsey explained.

"Yeah. I know all about Saville's immodesty. Shameless hussy," Fi joked.

Saville shrugged. "If the Goddess didn't want us to be naked, we wouldn't be born without clothes."

Fi laughed. "That is the most ridiculous excuse for your propensity to strip in front of others that I've ever heard."

"You can strip in front of me anytime you want," Lucy added, before turning her head and saying, "Oh, hello George. Look who is back."

"Hiya, George. Did you miss me?" Saville asked.

George scoffed. "I have survived."

"Wow! George, you've developed a sense of humor. Lucy, did you teach your great-great-grandfather humor while I was convalescing?" Saville chuckled.

Even through the translucent outlines of George's face, she could see the confusion on the ghost.

"You are aware of my history. Why do you call me Lucy's grandfather?" George asked.

"I assume since you dressed as a man and passed yourself off as a man, you identify as a man. Would you prefer different pronouns? Or shall I be more generic and say great-great-grandparent?"

"This is a choice now?" George appeared even more confused.

"Well, yeah. We've come a long way. Some people don't identify as male or female. And some that are born women identify as men. There are even some women who identify as men who have surgery to change their physical appearance in a way that matches how they feel," Saville explained.

Ruth shimmered into the room and made her presence known. "It is too bad we were not born of this time. While I knew George's secret, it was easy for me to think of him as a man." She looked at George with such love and admiration. "And yet, I appreciated the intimate times we had together and his softer side. Helping George remove his bindings was always a special time. I do not find it confusing that these women see you in the same way."

"Will the others who come to live here have the same perspective?" George asked.

Saville looked around the room from one person to the other and then focused on George and Ruth. "George, you're as chatty as your wife now. What's up with that? Plus, you aren't disappearing after spending a few moments either causing trouble or berating me."

"We are evolving and gaining strength," Ruth answered.

"Does that mean you can party with us once the saloon is open?"

George scowled again. "I will always be the sheriff. I am still capable of keeping the peace."

"Thank you, George, but I don't think a bunch of old ladies will cause much trouble," Bea said.

Lucy grinned. "Speak for yourself. Besides, it won't just be old ladies. I suspect this will be a gathering place for any lesbian within driving distance."

"Does that mean bisexuals or pansexuals aren't welcome in Georgetown Glen?" Chelsey asked. "Tess doesn't identify as a lesbian, but she's had relationships with women before."

"Oh, no. Of course Tess is welcome," Lucy amended.

"Not to be a killjoy because I do love our daily chats, George and Ruth, but we're already starting late today, and I'd like to finish the saloon before I retire and come to live at Georgetown Glen. I need to show Saville how far we've gotten. Are you going to be okay climbing the stairs on your crutches?" Fi suddenly realized what a challenge it was going to be for Saville to return to work. She brushed her hand down Saville's arm as she rested on her crutches.

Saville glanced at the long, curving staircase. "Yeah, I'll manage. Good thing we don't need to make the upstairs handicapped accessible. That would ruin the feel of the restoration. Everything down here looks so good. I can't believe how much you've accomplished."

"Wait until you see upstairs. We were just waiting on you to finish rewiring the loft, and then we'll bring in the appliances, finish the plumbing, paint the walls, and add the molding."

"I've been reading up on do-it-yourself wiring. I'm ready," Chelsey added cheerfully.

A rare smile appeared on George's face. "Something has changed between you two."

Fi blushed when George pointed between herself and Saville.

Lucy clapped her hands and bounced on her feet. "You two finally did it!" She gyrated her hips suggestively.

Bea lightly smacked her wife on the arm. "Lucy! That is none of our business."

"Oh, yes, it is. We are all family here. I want details later. What do you want us to work on now?" Lucy asked.

Fi scrunched her face. She needed to give them a task that would keep them busy. "Would you mind terribly working on sanding and refinishing the wood at the hotel?"

"Not at all. We're quite good at that now," Lucy answered. "Shall we meet back here at noon? Then we can hear all about you and Saville. I just love to listen to someone else's love story."

"Only if we hear yours, too. And I want all the details." Saville winked.

Bea groaned. "Lucy doesn't have any filters."

"That's what I'm counting on," Saville answered.

CHAPTER TWENTY

"We should talk about it," Fi said as they relaxed in bed.

Saville knew this conversation was overdue. She was about to lose her splint and didn't need to stay at Fi's house anymore. The sadness she felt at returning to her place nearly overwhelmed her, but she couldn't very well ask Fi if she could move in with her. That was way too presumptuous.

"I know. You're getting ready to give me the boot."

"What? No. I was kind of hoping you might move in with me. You hate your neighbors. This place has plenty of room for both of us and then some. I've gotten used to having you around all the time. It will be a big adjustment if we have to navigate new dating rules."

"Really? You want me to move in with you? I haven't overstayed my welcome?" Saville pivoted her body to look Fi in the eyes. She had to make sure Fi was serious and not just offering out of obligation.

"No. I think we've already established I'm in love with you. I know the circumstances kind of moved us closer to this place in our relationship, and maybe it's too soon for you." Fi's brow furrowed in that adorable way when she was unsure of herself.

"No, no, it isn't. I'd love to live with you, but I don't want to mooch off of you. I insist on paying my share of the mortgage and everything else. I have another two months on my lease, but I can afford to pay both, especially with the bonus we're getting from Lucy and Bea."

Fi let out a breath. "We can figure out the finances later. God, I was so scared you wouldn't be at the same place that I am. I've known that I wanted you to stay for weeks now."

"Why would you even question that? Have I not done enough to show you how I feel about you? I see us growing old together. I want us to be like Lucy and Bea. Well, not exactly like Lucy and Bea. I know Bea loves Lucy to pieces, but she's a little too practical."

"I'm practical."

"I suppose. But I don't see you being as serious as Bea. Some people give in to aging, like Bea. Lucy doesn't. I love that about her."

"Did you ever think that maybe they complement one another? Bea keeps Lucy from completely going off the rails. I'll probably be like Bea when I get to be her age. Are you going to be able to handle that?"

"Of course. You can keep me from going off the rails anytime you want. All you gotta do is shoot me those bedroom eyes." Saville waggled her brows and leaned in to kiss Fi.

"I'm serious here. Do we really want the same things? Like, I want to get married someday and maybe even have kids. We haven't talked about the important things for our future. Are we too opposite from one another?"

"You want kids?"

"Maybe," Fi answered hesitantly. "Have you ever thought about having kids?"

"Not really, but that doesn't mean I'm opposed to the idea. Well, at least I'm not opposed to the idea of you having kids. I don't think I've ever wanted to be pregnant. That was certainly a bonus of being a lesbian. I could have all the sex I wanted without having to worry about getting pregnant. You would make a beautiful mother. I can see it now. You, looking all angelic with that pregnancy glow. Plus, I heard pregnant women get really horny. So yeah, I'd be down for you popping out a few little ones."

Fi frowned. "Is that all that's important to you? Sex?"

"No. But I won't apologize for thinking that sexual intimacy is just as important as emotional intimacy. Nor will I apologize for being wildly attracted to you. I guarantee I will never lose my lust for you. Honestly, just because I've never considered kids before doesn't mean I'm not warming to the idea. The more I think about it, the more it appeals to me. I could be the fun mother," Saville joked.

"Oh, no, you don't. You will not relegate me to the role of disciplinarian."

"Are we having our first argument? Because if we are, this is a piece of cake. I still love you."

Fi smiled. "I love you, too. And my offer to have you move in with me is still on the table."

Saville grabbed Fi and gave her a passionate kiss. "I'll let the real estate office know that I won't be renewing my lease."

†

Lucy plucked the T-shirt from the floor and pulled it over her head before shuffling into the kitchen to start the coffee. Tess had called last night with some news, and everyone was meeting at the saloon after Saville's doctor's appointment. Tess had sounded so excited. Lucy couldn't wait to learn what she'd discovered in her research on Pearl. That was a missing piece that both George and Ruth had desperately wanted to learn about.

The women had almost completed the saloon remodel and would turn their focus on the hotel next. The other houses and additional tiny homes they had planned for phase two would need to wait until the crew finished with the older buildings.

Bea rubbed her eyes, stretching her back as she ambled into the kitchen and accepted the cup of coffee Lucy held out for her. "I thought we had a late start today with Saville having her doctor's appointment this morning."

"We do, but I couldn't sleep. I was so excited about what Tess found out about Pearl. George and Ruth will be over the moon. At least, I hope they will." Lucy frowned. "What if Tess discovered Pearl had a rough time of it after learning her parents died? Or even worse, she discovered how they died."

"She's been dead for years. So what does it matter?" Bea sipped her coffee.

267

"That's terrible of you to say that," Lucy chastised. "All Ruth and George ever wanted was to make sure their daughter had a good life. It's why they hid the gold and sent her to Boston for a proper education. They need that measure of reassurance to get some peace, finally. Wouldn't you want that for your only child?"

"They're dead, too. It should be enough that George and Ruth met you," Bea grumbled. "I doubt I'll haunt this place after my death or particularly care what happens to any of my nieces and nephews."

"Well, I can tell you right now that if I die before you, expect me to haunt you until your last breath, you old curmudgeon. Every year you get grumpier. We should fill our golden years with love and adventure. I can't wait to embark on this new chapter in our lives. Isn't it exciting? Fi says the saloon will be ready to move into soon, but I don't want to open it until everything else is ready. That should give us plenty of time to find the perfect tables and chairs for the place. Fi said she would put the word out to her connections."

"We're not moving our furniture ourselves. I'm too old for that."

"The girls offered to help, but I think it would be best to hire a moving company and be done with it. I feel like we're already taking advantage of Fi and Saville's good nature by how little they quoted for the project."

"I wouldn't worry about that. Remember what that guy said about how much he would give us for the gold. Their cut will more than compensate them for their work. Don't forget, we're meeting with him later this week."

"Oh, goody." Lucy clapped her hands together. "I can't wait to see the look on their faces when we present them with their bonus check. We can do that soon, right?"

"Don't you think we should wait until they finish the project?" Bea asked. "Everything is likely to take at least another year to complete."

"Exactly, which is why I'd like to give them the money now. Maybe Saville and Fi will use it for their wedding."

"I think you're getting way ahead of yourself. I haven't heard anything about the two of them getting married. They aren't even living together yet. Saville is only staying with Fi until she recovers. She'll probably go back to her place after she loses her splint today."

"I wouldn't be too sure of that. They're obviously in love. Fi told me she wants to ask Saville to move in, but she's afraid that will send Saville running again. I told her to go for it because I was sure Saville didn't want to leave. She planned on talking about it with her before they went to the doctor's office."

"Why can't you keep your nose out of things? Leave those young people alone. Saville and Fi are entirely capable of figuring things out without you butting in. That includes whatever you're doing with Tess and Chelsey."

"What?" Lucy batted her eyes. "All I've done is make sure Tess feels welcome in our inner circle. She's just as invested in learning the history of Georgetown Glen as we are, including finding out what happened to Pearl. Whatever they discover, we can add to the promotional materials."

Bea rolled her eyes. "You don't fool me. Not one bit, Lucy. I see all your scheming. You go out of your way to bring those two together. And maybe some of that is personal. I don't think George or Ruth will be very excited about you exploiting their tragedy for personal gain. Those are your ancestors. Have a little respect."

"I think it would be more disrespectful not to share their story. So often, history gets distorted. But history is there to teach us all valuable lessons. Through tragedy, we learn what not to repeat. Just because history is cruel and unforgiving doesn't mean we should shove it under a rug and never evaluate our mistakes. It's all part of our shared lesbian history or herstory, I should say. I'm going to jump in the shower. Want to join me?" Lucy grinned and winked.

†

Although Saville knew she would probably still have to use her crutches for a while longer, she was disappointed to hear she might not fully recover for another five to six months. Using her crutches, she hobbled into the saloon. Fi offered her arm to help Saville lower herself into the chair. She was grateful to not have the splint anymore, but her leg was nowhere near recovered enough to navigate certain activities without a bit of assistance. She was still unstable on her own but working hard every day on her physical therapy to get back to normal as soon as possible.

The rest of the gang had already made themselves comfortable on the camping chairs and sipped on coffee while eating scones Lucy had brought. Tess was a beautiful woman, with her tousled reddish-brown hair that had a few strands of gray, barely noticeable to most. Her expressive brown eyes demonstrated both warmth and wisdom. But it was Tess's smile that transformed her face into something extraordinary. Saville could understand why Chelsey wanted more than friendship with her. Saville had rooted for her new friend.

"So, what's this exciting news you have to share?" Saville asked.

"I was curious about Pearl's friend, Clara. So, I tugged on that thread. After contacting a friend of mine who lives in Boston, I found pay dirt. Clara's ancestors were very particular about preserving everything related to this amazing woman. Apparently, she was a force of her time, and, wait for it…" Tess paused for effect. "Although both Clara and Pearl married, they maintained their friendship, which was a lot more than friends. They were most definitely lovers, and after both their husbands passed, they indeed had a Boston marriage."

"How do you know that?" Lucy asked.

"After I explained about Georgetown Glen, the family showed me letters written between the two women shortly after both had married. Pretty steamy for the time," Tess explained. "Get this. Clara's ancestors live in Seattle now. They're interested in visiting Georgetown Glen after the remodel is complete. And, they want to meet Lucy."

"Ooh, did you make copies of the letters?" Saville asked.

Tess nodded. "I scanned the documents. Clara also kept a journal. She was there for Pearl when Pearl received the telegram from Mae. Apparently, Clara made a trip to the West to learn more. She struggled all her life with keeping the secret of Pearl's parents' demise, not believing Pearl was strong enough to learn the truth. Obviously, she didn't judge George and Ruth, but she thought the gruesome hangings were not something she wanted Pearl to remember about her beloved parents. Clara had wanted to confess to Pearl what she had learned, but that meant revealing the nature of their death."

"Can we read the letters and journal?" Lucy asked.

Tess grinned and glanced at Chelsey. "I already sent the scans to Chelsey."

"I haven't printed everything out, but I will," Chelsey added. "It's like a whole other story. I think we should share it with George and Ruth. They'll want to know Pearl and Clara stayed together and made things work despite the times and both women marrying for optics. Pearl was well loved."

Saville jumped in her chair, tweaking her newly liberated leg when George popped in, followed by Ruth.

"Share what?" George asked.

The first time Tess met George and Ruth, her mouth had hung open, and she could barely get out a word, much less converse with them. But now they were like old friends.

"Oh, hello, George and Ruth. I found out more information about Pearl and Clara. They were each other's one great love. They might not have married like you two, but they spent a decent portion of their lives together. From what I read in Clara's journal, and the letters they sent to one another, they were happy. There were struggles, of course, but what relationship is free from challenges."

"I'm not sure if you want to read the letters or the journal," Chelsey said. "That might be a little weird for you. I don't believe I'd choose to read my daughter's love letters—especially one's as, uh, detailed as these are. But I could make a copy for you and leave it on the bar. Or you could take our word on this and know that Pearl did fine after your death."

Ruth swiped at a tear and said, "Thank you."

Saville didn't even know ghosts could cry. George remained stoic, but Saville could tell now that she'd spent so much time in his presence that the news equally affected him.

Chelsey pulled out her phone and read a few of the more ambiguous passages that revealed Clara's affection for Pearl, without too much specificity for a parent to listen to. Saville wanted to read the steamier parts but knew it was probably better not to do that in front of George and Ruth. That got her thinking about having kids. She was definitely warming to the idea. She wondered if she would be a good mother. That, more than anything else, worried her. Regardless, she understood why Chelsey picked the passages she read aloud. Listening to graphic details of your daughter's love life was a lot like imagining your parents having sex. That was a big hell no.

Fi stood. "I hate to break this up, but I want to start on the finish carpentry. I'd rather not have Lucy and Bea move into the loft before we complete the upstairs."

"And the taskmaster has spoken," Saville joked. "Just kidding, honey. I'm ready." Saville grimaced as she attempted to stand.

Fi was quick to lend her a hand, narrowing her eyes at Saville. "No overdoing it today. Remember what the doc said."

"Yeah, yeah." Saville pecked Fi on the cheek. "I know I need to save my strength for later tonight. We have to celebrate the evolution of our relationship."

"What evolution?" Lucy asked.

"Fi has generously invited me to move in with her," Saville answered.

Lucy smirked and turned to her wife. "Told you so."

Epilogue

"Who ordered the U-Haul?" Tess asked. "I thought you two moved in together a long time ago," she joked.

"Shh, it's a surprise." Fi put her finger to her lips. "I finally found the perfect tables and chairs for the saloon. Before the grand opening, Saville and I worked hard to refinish them and repair a few legs. Chelsey gave us the name of the company that was supposed to deliver the rented chairs and tables, and we canceled the order. I can't believe we're going to pull this off. Lucy put on a brave face, but I could tell how disappointed she was when I told her I hadn't found the right furniture for the saloon yet. I convinced her to wait before purchasing something temporary for the grand opening because I wasn't giving up just yet."

"They're at the store right now, but should be back any minute," Chelsey said.

"Right, then could you please distract them while we unload the truck? Take them to the hotel. Okay?" Saville directed.

Chelsey saluted. "Will do."

Saville tugged on Sunny's leash when she whined and tried to greet Chelsey. "Sorry, girl, your buddy can't play right now."

After patting Sunny on the head, Chelsey leaned in to whisper into Saville's ear and then headed off to greet her aunt. Fi wondered what that was all about. You never knew with Saville. She was up to something, but what was anyone's guess.

"What was that about? What are you two up to?" Fi asked. It amazed her how close Chelsey and Saville had become over the past year after their rocky start.

Saville attempted her most innocent look, one that she thought fooled Fi but never did. "Nothing. Just some bestie stuff." She led Sunny over to her blanket and commanded her to stay after undoing her leash. She'd worked hard on training Sunny, and it had paid off because Sunny was the most well-mannered dog that Fi had ever known. Sunny had already endeared herself to the new residents of Georgetown Glen and reveled in the attention they lavished on her.

"I thought Darcy was your best friend," Fi challenged.

"I can have two best friends. It's not like I have to be exclusive with friends. In fact, I also consider Lucy and George close friends."

"George?"

"Yeah, we've worked through our initial animosity, just like I did with Chelsey. George gives excellent advice sometimes. So do Chelsey and Lucy."

"What do you need advice on?"

"Relationships. Remember, I kind of suck at those."

"You seem to do just fine. We're good, right?" Fi frowned.

"We're better than good. We're perfect." Saville grabbed Fi in her arms and showed her just how good they were.

Tess cleared her throat. "Um, still here. I'd say get a room, but Georgetown Glen hasn't had their official grand opening ceremony yet. Besides, I think they're all full up already. Who knew there were that many lesbians in retirement?"

"I had hoped that Amelia and Darcy would be here already. I need their muscle. It's going to take us forever to unload the truck."

"We're here. Don't get your panties in a bunch," Darcy said as she pushed open the ornately carved swinging doors to the saloon.

"What do you need help with?" Amelia asked.

"We need to get that truck unloaded before Lucy and Bea catch on that Chelsey is distracting them. Wait until you see the tables and chairs I found. They're perfect. I was sweating it for a while there. It's like some divine intervention happened when my friend called and said she'd found them." Fi smiled with pride.

"Not divine intervention, hon. Remember, I was there when you made all those phone calls and roped me into making a shit-ton more. You did good."

276

Saville looked at her with such love. Fi couldn't believe how much Saville had opened up over the past year. She'd been the perfect girlfriend, and Fi was tempted to pop the question because she thought Saville was now ready for the ultimate commitment.

"*We* did good." Fi beamed. "Okay, chop, chop. That truck will not unload itself. I'd like to run it back before they close today. I should have plenty of time before the festivities begin."

Fi caught a strange look shared between Saville and Amelia right before she offered to follow her to the rental place. Yup, Saville was definitely up to something, and everyone seemed to be in on whatever she had planned.

✝

Saville's stomach roiled as her nerves got the best of her. She absently touched the bulge in the side pocket of her cargo shorts.

"Hey, don't worry." Chelsey placed her hand on Saville's shoulder and gave it a quick squeeze. "We have plenty of time to set everything up. I love how this saloon combines the old and the new. It was absolutely brilliant to add that state-of-the-art sound system."

"I think I bought enough lilies for two to go in each vase. They're Fi's favorite flower because they smell so divine." Saville ran her hand nervously through her hair before reaching into her pocket to retrieve the key to Lucy and Bea's loft above the saloon. "I'll go get them and the table cloths. I stored the lights behind the bar."

"Is there a ladder I can use? That should make it easier to hang the lights," Darcy chimed in before turning her attention to the apparition that appeared a few feet away from Saville. She lifted her hand to wave. "Oh, hey, George. No funny business with the ladder." Darcy grinned. "Where's Ruth? Are you both coming today while my friend here jumps into the deep end of the pool?"

George tilted her head. "Pool? Is today not opening day?"

"It's just an expression, George. But I suppose you're right. It's really the pre-plunge day. Saville has to get Fi to say yes before Saville takes the plunge," Darcy explained.

Saville's stomach performed more gymnastics, and she almost puked on the refurbished wood floor. "Do you think Fi will turn me down? I suppose I wouldn't blame her if she did. Why did I listen to you guys? It's too soon, and I'm not exactly a great catch."

Darcy sidled next to Saville and lightly punched her shoulder. "You got this."

"Of course, she'll say yes," Chelsey added. "You brought the ring, right? She's going to pee her pants when she sees it. You totally outdid yourself, Saville."

After the small team had decorated the saloon, Saville lifted her T-shirt to wipe the sweat from her face. She wasn't sure if the excess perspiration was because of her runaway nerves or the exertion of creating the ambiance for what she was about to do.

"Goddess, I'm glad that Lucy and Bea offered their loft, so we didn't have to drive back home to get ready. I'm going to run upstairs and take a shower. I feel grungy, and I don't think Fi will appreciate the way I smell right now. Good thing I brought a change of clothes."

Saville mentally prepared for the afternoon while washing her hair. She needed to remember to transfer the ring to her nice slacks. She'd briefly entertained the idea of tying the ring to Sunny's collar but didn't trust that Fi would find it before she was ready to propose. Plus, Saville hadn't wanted to let the diamond out of her reach, even though Saville knew she would take a shower and change after setting up. Her question would be an epic fail without the princess-cut diamond ring she'd bought, using a good chunk of the bonus that Bea and Lucy had given them upon completion of the job.

Saville dried her face, and when she saw George in the bathroom, staring at her, she growled, "Dammit, George, you startled me. I'm naked here."

George smirked. "You do not care that people see you naked. Your Fi has come back. I thought I should tell you she is on her way upstairs."

"Okay, thanks."

George disappeared as quickly as he had appeared. Saville rushed to the bedroom to grab the ring. While she transferred the small box to her black pants, Saville heard Fi approach.

"What are you doing?" Fi asked.

"Oh, uh, we were done setting up, so I decided to take my shower and get ready before everyone else arrives," Saville answered.

"Darn, I was hoping you'd wait until I got back. You better have left me some hot water," Fi joked. "By the way, y'all outdid yourselves. It looks fabulous downstairs, and it smells heavenly with all the lilies on the tables. You missed Bea and Lucy's reactions. I even saw Bea wipe a tear from her eyes. I don't ever think I've seen Lucy speechless before. She was so overcome with emotion."

"Um, I felt pretty gross and stinky," Saville offered as an excuse. Then, after pulling her sports bra over her head, she reached for her button-down shirt, quickly fastening the buttons.

Fi leaned in to kiss Saville. "Well, you smell divine right now. I better jump in the shower before the rest of them catch onto grabbing a shower before the water turns cold."

Fi stripped in front of Saville as Saville watched. She felt like she was the luckiest woman in the world. By nearly anyone's objective standards, Fi was a stunning woman. Those emerald eyes of hers had enchanted Saville the very first time she'd laid eyes on them. Fi mostly favored her handsome Irish father, but the delicate contours of her perfectly shaped face were an exact replica of her mother.

"You are so beautiful," Saville whispered as she pulled the pants over her hips. She reached into her pocket to feel the assurance of the ring but realized how snug her pants fit and panicked that Fi would see the bulge in her pocket.

Fi smiled. "And you are so sexy in those fitted slacks and your royal blue shirt that I love. I'll try to be quick and not take up too much of the hot water. See you downstairs in a few."

Saville breathed a sigh of relief that Fi had not noticed the ring in her pocket. After she dressed, Saville ran down the stairs, looking for Chelsey or Darcy. She trusted either of them to hold the ring until she needed it.

†

Fi was happy their small group had a little time with what Saville referred to as their inner circle. The residents of Georgetown Glen would arrive in another hour. The town's owners had hand-selected the fifteen couples after an almost obscene number of applicants who wanted to move to Georgetown Glen. Word had gotten out quickly, and Lucy and Bea had been invited to one of Ellen DeGeneres's last shows where Ellen had featured the feisty couple and their vision for a lesbian retirement community. Lucy had charmed the pants off of Ellen, suggesting that Portia and Ellen might want to consider living there themselves. Ellen had graciously declined but promised to visit and have a drink with the couple at their saloon.

Of course, they had consulted with Ruth and George, wanting them to be intricately involved in the final selection. Having friendly lesbian ghosts was a must, lest George misbehaved again and caused trouble for the new residents.

Lucy and Bea had bought several bottles of champagne for the event but had saved two special bottles for their gang. Fi only wished that George and Ruth could partake in the toast, but unfortunately, ghosts couldn't eat or drink anything. Pity. They both felt like family to Fi.

Saville looked a little green, and Fi wondered if she'd caught a stomach bug. Saville nodded at Darcy, who went behind the bar and turned on the sound system. Brandi Carlile's voice filled the room with her latest song, the one Fi loved so much. One night she had listened closely to the lyrics and told Saville it could be their love song because it sounded so much like them. *We had a rocky start, but it wasn't too late for us, either. Maybe it was right on time, and the fates gave us a second chance when we started on Georgetown Glen.* Fi smiled at Saville, knowing she was the one responsible for this song playing.

After "Right On Time" finished, Saville cleared her throat. Fi's face crinkled in confusion because Saville was not the type of person to give speeches. Besides, this was Lucy and Bea's big day, not Saville's.

"Um, before everyone else arrives, I have something I'd like to say. Well, I'd like you, my inner circle, to be a part of this. Thanks for helping me set this up." Saville extended her hand and gestured to Chelsey, who handed her a small box.

All the blood drained from Fi's face as realization set in. Was she ready for this? Yeah, she was. She'd already thought about having a preliminary discussion with Saville to feel her out, but never in a million years did she believe Saville would go there after only a year together.

"Fi, I fell in love with you the first time I laid eyes on you. Okay, maybe it was lust, but friendship wasn't enough when I came to know you. Then I made that epic blunder, but you gave me a second chance. Which I'm eternally grateful for. This past year, I've been so deliriously happy with you. Happier than I deserve. I can't imagine my life without you." Saville dropped to one knee and opened the box. "Will you please put me out of my misery and say you'll be my wife?"

Dumbfounded, Fi nodded.

"Use your words, dear," Lucy joked.

"Yes, of course, yes," Fi said as she wiped a tear from the corner of her eye.

"Yes? You said yes," Saville said with a fair amount of awe in her voice.

"Of course I said yes," Fi answered. "God, this ring is gorgeous."

Saville smiled as she pushed the ring onto Fi's finger, and everyone crowded around to check it out. Sunny was not about to be left out of this momentous occasion and whined loudly while remaining on her blanket.

Saville patted her thigh and called to their beloved dog, "Sunny, come."

Sunny promptly bounded over, and with her tail wagging furiously, she accepted scratches to her ears from both of her mamas.

Lucy grabbed one of the champagne bottles from atop the bar and popped the cork. "Woo-hoo. Let's party!"

Bea grabbed the champagne glasses, and Lucy filled each one, handing them to everyone who had gigantic smiles on their faces. Fi glanced to her right and caught Ruth and George arm in arm, smiling and nodding.

The color had returned to Saville's face, and a broad smile blossomed. Saville was downright irresistible to Fi when she smiled.

Fi leaned in and whispered in Saville's ear. "You've made me happier than I thought possible. I love you."

"I love you, too. So much. You have no idea."

"Oh, I think I have a pretty good idea. I can't wait to get you home tonight to show you how much."

Saville grinned. "I think we should stay the requisite hour, then make an excuse to leave early. Somehow, I think our friends will understand."

"I can't believe no one spilled the beans," Fi said.

"I told them I would sic George on them if they did."

"It's sad to think that when we're ready to move to Georgetown Glen, Lucy and Bea will probably have passed. I hope they leave the place to Chelsey. But at least we'll always have George and Ruth." Fi leaned on Saville, who slung her arm around Fi's shoulder.

"Yeah, I love those two, even Bea and her curmudgeonly ways. Maybe they'll join the haunt. That would totally be something Lucy would do."

"What are you two whispering about?" Lucy asked.

"Nothing," Saville answered as she sipped her champagne. "Tasty. I hope to have half your class when I mature."

"You Neanderthal," Chelsey teased. "You drank before the toast." Chelsey held up her glass. "To Fi and Saville, a match that all of us saw before the two of them stopped being so stubborn. To think it took a ghost to get through to you. Finally."

George tipped his hat and nodded. Sunny added her own approval with an excited bark.

About the Author
Annette Mori

Annette is an award-winning author, published by Affinity Rainbow Publications, who lives in the beautiful Pacific Northwest with her wife and their four furry kids. With twenty-six published novels, three Lesfic Bard Awards, and one Goldie Award for her fourth novel, *Locked Inside*, she finally feels like a real author. Annette is as much a reader as a writer and is always looking for the next sapphic novel to queue up. She came up with the One Fan at a Time tagline, because it rolled off the tongue much better than One Reader at a Time. After pondering who she was at her core, she feels it was all about connecting to each reader on a personal level. Annette would be the first to admit she doesn't do well with the masses. If someone picks up her book and it touches them, she believes she has achieved what she wants with her writing by reaching each reader. It is who she is at her core. Drop her a line. She loves to hear from readers.

Email: annettemori0859@gmail.com.

Sign up for her mailing list: http://eepurl.com/cS7nr9

Check out her blog: Everyday Occurrences:
https://annettemori0859.wordpress.com/

Visit the Affinity Rainbow Publications website for her books and many other outstanding authors:
www.affinityebooks.com

OTHER AFFINITY BOOKS

<u>Serenity</u> by K Belmar
After Kirby MacLennan had lost her partner and her only sibling in a horrific accident, all she wanted to do was move from the city and live the rest of her life alone in a small mountain village. When she meets Samantha Parker, the village sheriff, they soon become friends. Samantha's cousin Jackie, and her wife Beth, along with their children, moved into the old farmhouse next door to Kirby. Something makes Kirby uneasy about the couple's relationship and she finds herself drawn to Beth, and her silent plea for help.
Can Kirby overcome her own trauma of the past to help a neighbor in need? Will she finally accept love back into her life, enough to move out of the shadows and into the light?

<u>Along Came Sally</u> by JM Dragon
Angela Barossa is content with her life as the local realtor in the small town of Whistler. Until a request to see a property that can only be sold to a local or ex-local disturbs her.
The name of the potential client...Sally Maguire. Why on earth would her childhood nemesis want to return to

Whistler? Angela needs to be dispassionate in her dealings
with Sally, but can she?
Simply a timeless romance.

Artist Free Zone by Annette Mori
Melissa just moved to a conservative part of Washington
State. A move designed to set her and her longtime partner
up for early retirement. But best laid plans go awry when her
partner, Colette decides, out of the blue, their relationship
isn't working for her. The only thing left to do is sob all over
her beloved kitties. Vowing never to get involved, ever
again, with another artist.
Colette is torn up about hurting Melissa. She hasn't been
entirely honest about her reasons for leaving and that tears
her up even further. She keeps calling to make sure Melissa
is okay. Life is exciting and wonderful for her because she's
met her soulmate and plans on moving to Alaska. But will
Karma exact its revenge?
This is a raw and honest portrayal of love lost and love found
again.
Not to mention the soothing influence of a beloved feline.

Finding her Heart by Samantha Hicks
Ellis Davis's self-imposed isolation is blown apart when a
new neighbour moves in next door. Having spent the last five
years working from home, shutting herself away from the
world she once knew. The last thing Ellis wants, or needs, is
the woman next door challenging her beliefs about herself
and bringing out feelings Ellis has never experienced before.
Melissa Cole moves into her new home as a recently
divorced woman, raising her young son as a single parent

with the help of her parents. Melissa is instantly intrigued by her mysterious neighbour next door.

Forever Home by Ali Spooner
Nat, Marissa and Maggie survived their first winter by the ocean. Spring brings new growth, friends, and unwelcome visitors to the homestead. Find out how Nat and Marissa's tiny community deal with the hazards and rewards before them, as their homestead continues to grow and prosper. Expect romance, adventure, danger, good fortune, and the odd meal or two, in this sequel to The Bee Charmer.

Disconnected by Annette Mori
Vanna has always felt like something was off with her parents, leaving her feeling oddly disconnected. She decides to move across the country and establish a new and independent life after college. On the way to her new position in Flagstaff, Arizona, Vanna meets out and proud Trey, who loves to flirt.
Trey has never forgotten the beautiful young woman she met briefly and is determined to ensure their paths cross again. Thousands of miles from home, Vanna finds out more about herself, but not her feeling of being disconnected from her parents. Will Vanna ever form the connection she desperately seeks? Does Trey's determination work out?

Darcy Comes Home by Jen Silver
After twenty-five years Darcy and Angie meet again and from the faintly flickering embers of their forbidden teenage love, a flame erupts. Family complications arise including a reluctant engagement, secret surrogacy, and a persistent ex-

wife.

Villagers in Professor Darcy Belsfield's childhood home of Sycamore Haven remember her being sent away to a Christian conversion camp in Canada when her father discovered her making love to her school friend, Angie. Angie has never married but she does have a past and some unenthusiastic plans for the future. Will the differences in their lives doom the chance of Darcy and Angie discovering if they can build a future together?

Hat Trick by Ali Spooner and K.L. Gallagher
Alexandra "Alex" Hawthorne is on the fast track to the top of one of the most formidable, white-collar, criminal defense law firms in New York. She can ill afford any distractions, especially those with dark-brown eyes, who can rock a power suit while coaching professional hockey players. Not now. Not when Alex is so close to making senior partner. Not after all she has sacrificed.

After a devastating end to her playing career, Janelle Leblanc channeled her passion into coaching and reached the pinnacle of success as the first female head coach in NHL history. Despite her accomplishments, she hears whispers that she was hired as nothing more than a publicity stunt. Janelle's focus needs to remain on the ice if she is to prove them wrong, not on a certain curly haired attorney with the most arresting emerald-green eyes she has ever seen.

Once the spark is lit, their chemistry is impossible to ignore. Can Janelle break down Alex's walls to give them a real chance? Or will Alex's past heartache be too much for them to overcome?

<u>The Lone Star Collection *II*</u> by Various Authors
Saddle up for a wild ride! *The Lone Star Collection II* has something for everyone! If you enjoy romance, Kris Bryant and Dena Blake have penned hot contemporary stories in *Heat* and *Horseplay*, while *Pins and Needles*, by Julie Cannon, is a historical adventure. Annette Mori also contributes to the romance fare with a beautiful, enduring love story in *Rainstorm*. If you want sizzling erotica check out *50 by 50*, from Renee Mackenzie. What would a collection be without fantasy, paranormal and swashbuckling adventures? *Lured to the Rocks*, a unique work of fantasy by Barbara Ann Wright. In *The Devil's Backbone*, Lacey L. Schmidt spins a thriller about overcoming evil and personal loss. MJ Williamz explores dark passion in *Take Me All the Way*. Del Robertson offers *Return to Me* a classic pirate story, and Yvette Murray tosses in the *Ghostly Galleons*.

<u>Footprints</u> by Ali Spooner
Sandy, the youngest sibling of Gator Girlz, Inc., has worshipped her older sister Cam all her life and wanted nothing more than to be just like her hero. *Footprints* provides readers with Sandy's story of growing up in the Bayous of Louisiana. When the devastating floods of 2016 impact the Baton Rouge area, Cam and Sandy join the Cajun Navy to help rescue families trapped in the rampant

floodwaters. The story also revisits Sandy's victory over Bubba Gump and how Sandy's injuries started her down the path to find the love of her life. Food, adventures, and great family relationships fill the pages of *Footprints*.

Love at Leighton Lake by Samantha Hicks

Tallulah 'Tally' Roberts decides that a few weeks staying in a cabin at Leighton Lake will help mend her shattered pelvis and broken heart.

Caitlyn Matthews works at the lake resort her mother owns, loving nothing better than spending her morning swimming in the lake. That is until she meets Tally. Their attraction is instant, but both are wary of these new feelings with their history of previous relationships.

As they get to know each other, secrets from Caitlyn's past come to light. Caitlyn fears her mother has been lying to her and together they search for the truth.

Love at Leighton Lake is packed full of love, drama, and a cow called Houdini who likes to roam the cabins, much to Caitlyn's delight.

Affinity
Rainbow Publications

eBooks, Print, Free eBooks

Visit our website for more publications available online.

www.affinityrainbowpublications.com

Published by Affinity Rainbow Publications
A Division of Affinity eBook Press NZ LTD
Canterbury, New Zealand

Registered Company 2517228

www.ingramcontent.com/pod-product-compliance
Lightning Source LLC
Chambersburg PA
CBHW051522260626
47170CB00003B/749